Paper Spurs

Olga Merino was born in Barcelona in 1965. Having graduated in media studies, she studied Latin American history and literature at the University of London. Between 1993 and 1998 she worked as a foreign correspondent for *El Periódico de Catalunya* in Moscow, where she lived through the transition of the Soviet regime to a market economy. Based on her experiences there she wrote her first novel, *Cenizas Rojas* (*Red Ashes*), which describes the collapse of the Soviet Union. Her short story 'Las Normas Son Las Normas' ('Rules Are Rules'), about a Welsh nurse in the Crimean War, won the NH Mario Vargas Llosa Prize. *Paper Spurs* is her second novel.

Aneurin Gareth Thomas was born in 1963 and brought up in Gorseinon, Swansea, and later in Brecon. He studied philosophy in London and spent many years in Madrid working as an English teacher, journalist and translator. He currently lives in Brecon. *Luggage from Elsewhere* was his first novel. Its sequel is *Excess Baggage*. He is currently working on a novel set in present day Madrid; a tragic love story, provisionally titled *Foreign Languages*.

Paper Spurs

Olga Merino

PARTHIAN

Parthian
The Old Surgery
Napier Street
Cardigan
SA43 1ED
www.parthianbooks.co.uk

ISBN 978-1-905762-30-9

Cover image © Ferdinando Scianna at Magnum
Cover design & typesetting by Lucy Llewellyn

Printed and bound by Dinefwr Press, Llandybïe

Published with the financial support of the Welsh Books Council

First published in Spanish in 2004 as Espuelas de papel by
Santillana Ediciones Generales, S.L.
First published in Great Britain in 2010 by Parthian.

The publication of this work has been made possible through a
subsidy received from the Directorate General for Books, Archives
and Libraries of the Spanish Ministry of Culture.

British Library Cataloguing in Publication Data

A cataloguing record for this book is available from the British
Library

To my grandfather, who taught me
to distinguish flamenco styles.

To all those who had to leave
the sun of their childhood.

The Andalusians

They say: 'Jesus, how cold';
not 'how dreadfully, tremendously,
unjustly, inhumanly cold'.
Resigned, they say: 'Jesus,
how cold...' The Andalusians...

Where they had left
their ponies; where they had
left their sun, their wine,
their olive trees, their salt marshes.
Where they had left
their hate... They seemed made
of indifference, poverty,
whiplash... 'Jesus, how cold'.

These who are waiting,
from Huelva to Jaen,
from Jaen to Almería,
beside village squares of lime
and night, they must be
their children. They wait
for someone to come and put them
behind bars. Like those ones,
they won't ask why.

They won't complain about anything.
Not one will rebel.
'Things are as they are,
as they've always been, as
they should be tomorrow... Jesus,
how cold...' The Andalusians...

JOSÉ HIERRO, Libro de las alucinaciones

Part One

1

The young woman walking to while away the time on the irregular cobbles of Carmen Street is called Juana. Her eyes are almond-shaped, coffee-coloured and slightly puffy like those of a croaking frog. She is beautiful but does not yet know it. Chachachica used to say she was just tuppence short of having a body to bow down to. Juana drags a bulky cardboard suitcase with cinnamon-coloured edgings; holding two pairs of knickers, a chequered housecoat, a nightie, several white rags and a bottle of olive oil. She is ashamed to show her hands, clumsily bandaged in strips of cotton. She walks with her shoulders hunched because each step of the way the looks she gets shout: peasant. She would love to be invisible, to go unnoticed in the big city that smells of silence and thyme soup. Her wool skirt scorches her thighs; it is hot. She thought she would be more presentable to the lady if she wore stockings and her white, kitten-heeled shoes, the ones with a sticking plaster hiding a hole in the toe. Juana checks the time by the watches on display in the corner jeweller's showcases and sits down on a bench on the Rambla to wait for the Belén church clock to strike seven. Her skinless hands sting; softened and covered in strips of torn bed sheet. The lady made an appointment with her at seven o'clock in the evening. Señora Monterde gabbled out her words.

'My daughters and I work at night and we get up after midday. Don't come early; better in the evening, round about seven, it'll give me time to explain your duties to you.'

They have a telephone at home.

The spring evening in May bursts with the dense odour of lilies and rotten fruit; and with the squawking of swallows threshing the plum-coloured sky. Carmen Street on the corner of San Lázaro. The female concierge lets her through without asking where she is going. Juana takes a deep breath, filling her lungs with air, brushes the imaginary dust off her pencil skirt with her bandaged hands and rings the doorbell. She hears footsteps approach and a brisk opening of locks and bolts. The door opens on a pair of small green, almost cruel, eyes, trapped in purple bags. On the phone the lady sounded younger; she must be over fifty.

'Señora Salud Monterde?'

'Come in, girl. I've been waiting for you.'

A discoloured silk dressing gown, with Chinese dragons and cherry trees faded by the rain, covers the woman's flabby nakedness. Her open neckline reveals gold chains, a key and a handful of moles scattered over sagging breasts. Black dyed hair, taut over her temples and tightly collected in a ponytail over the back of her head. Salud Monterde and Juana make their way in the half-light down the corridor crammed full of furniture. The flat smells of vinegar, late nights and rancid tobacco smoke.

'Sit down. What did you say your name was?'

'Juana, señora. Juana Merchán.'

The dining room, spacious despite the chaos of furniture, overlooks Carmen Street. On the wall, next to the mirror and the crockery display cabinet, hangs an embossed silver Last Supper and an urn containing a fan. A yellowing blond-lace tablecloth covers the chest of drawers. There is a smell of vinegar for shining wood. On the half-opened balcony a withered geranium, covered in dust, leaves Juana seized with a pang of nostalgia.

'Are you alone in Barcelona?'

'No, señora. I came with my sister Isabel, born next after me, and with my father. The rest have stayed in the village.'

Salud Monterde drags an ashtray full of cigarette butts across the table and takes a packet of Chesterfield and a box of matches from her dressing gown. Salud Monterde bites her nails down to the quick. Traces of insanity shake in the thick hands that strike the match, perverse hands, with both husband and wife rings digging into the flesh of her ring finger. Instinctively, Juana clenches her bandaged fists inside her raincoat pockets.

'By your accent, I'd say you're Andalusian, aren't you?' Salud Monterde spews out a snake of smoke through her cracked lips. From the other end of the corridor female voices can be heard.

'From Puebla del Acebuche, señora, in the province of Seville.' Juana notices the silver framed photographs displayed on top of the tablecloth that covers the chest of drawers; not a single man can be seen in the portraits. Her hands burn in her pockets.

'Your father and sister, where are they staying?'

'In a sublet room on Conde de Asalto, but my sister has been promised work in a house.' Juana's own voice sounds strange to her.

'Girl, take your coat off, you're going to roast...'

Scorpions are the Devil's vermin. Chachachica used to say, who handled herself so well when there was shady business. It was she who caught Juana one summer afternoon, with her sister Isabel and Andrea, the carpenter's daughter from next door, on the patio setting alight a crown of kindling in the centre of which a scorpion lay dying. The girls had heard it from the school teacher, Doña Amalia: the scorpion sticks its curved sting into its shell and injects itself with its own poison when cornered by flames. Doña Amalia shaved on Sundays to go to mass, and her breath stank of paprika-seasoned lard.

'Girls, don't ever forget; knight, knot and knee are spelt with a K.'

Juana is now a scorpion trapped in a siege of words.

'Girl, take your coat off.'

Juana gives in to the inevitable. This is her new home. She will live here every day, except Sundays and for a few hours on Thursday afternoons. There is no alternative. She carefully takes her raincoat off, revealing her bandaged hands.

'Well, I never! What's happened to you?' Salud Monterde's tiny eyes spark with an ephemeral shine.

'It's nothing, señora. I'm better now. I had an accident at the house where I served before. They didn't kick me out; it was me who left, señora.' Juana lowers her eyes and fixes them on the blue mosaic floor tiles.

'And can you tell me how you expect to work without hands?'

4

'But now I'm almost better, señora. Give me a week's trial, I beg you on my knees. If I return to Conde del Asalto without a weekly wage, my father will kill me. He doesn't know nothing, he hasn't seen my hands, he doesn't know nothing. By all that's sacred, señora, only a week, you won't regret it...'

Salud Monterde goes toward the light, dragging her feet, and pulls the balcony doors wide open. The sickly-sweet aroma of lilies floods the dining room. The woman's eyes are fixed on Juana's throat.

'Have you seen a doctor?'

'There's no need, señora. I healed myself with olive oil.'

At nightfall the flat on Carmen Street becomes immersed in the silence of a cloister. Salud Monterde and her daughters, Montserrat and Mercedes, have just gone out. They left separately, very smartly dressed, each with a shoulder bag worn across her chest. Montse, with her rosy, peachy complexion, squeezed into a waisted polka-dot dress, making her seem fatter. Mercedes, thin, tall, bony, a plunging black neckline, elastic calves on stiletto heels. Doña Salud said goodbye at the door with her shoulder bag squeezed against her stomach.

'Don't open to anyone, Juana, do you hear me? Not to anyone. We've each got a set of keys so you don't have to wait up for us. Go to bed once you've tidied up in the kitchen. And listen to me: don't open to anyone, even if they say I or Merche sent them. Don't take any notice of them. You can answer the phone, but don't let on that we've gone out. You simply have to say: Señora Monterde can't come to the phone right now, can I help you? Do you understand me, girl?'

'Yes, señora. Don't worry.'

'And don't even think of nosing around in the boxroom, I've

5

already told you. Besides, it's no use: I've always got the keys and the keyhole is sealed with soaked bread. You've been warned, so watch out. Just think, not even my daughters go in there. Good night, girl. When you go to bed, turn the gas off.'

Juana is alone in the house. The room the lady has given her is a narrow hole. The teardrop-lamp, hanging unreachable from the ceiling, casts a lazy yellow light over the crocheted bedspread. The room is ventilated by a small open window adjoining the kitchen. The metallic bed bars have been repainted white, leaving messy spilt drops. With bandaged hands Juana clumsily opens her cardboard suitcase. She takes out a tangle of rags and the bottle of olive oil and places them on the marble-topped bedside table; drapes her nightie on one side of the bed and takes out the photograph, kept in the pocket of her chequered housecoat.

In the portrait appear seven women and only one man, her father. Manuel Merchán poses at one end, away from the bunch of females, his face gloomy, his receding hairline disguised by frying pan grime. Matías Iruela, the carpenter from their tenement house, doesn't appear in the photograph; he had already died because Manuel Merchán is wearing his shoes. They shrouded the carpenter barefoot. That was in May, when Puebla del Acebuche had its village fête. The seven women are dressed in short sleeves, and the white stain one can make out behind her mother's back is a night jasmine in flower. Chachachica is in the middle, sitting on the bulrush chair; she hides her naked feet behind the legs of it because she said her skin made her toe joints ugly. Chachachica has her eyes closed: expressionless, her white hair gathered in a ponytail, tiny in a black percale housecoat, jet earrings hang from elephantine ears, her hands rest on her belly, a wide nose and a very fine curve

6

suggesting a mouth. Juana, next to her, looks absent, staring off into space beyond the patio and the rooftops, one hand resting on the back of the chair, the other inside her housecoat pocket. Juana is thirteen years old. To her right, her sister Isabel smiles with a mischievous face and a flirtatious pose: one hand on her hip, the other covers the flat of her stomach. To Chachachica's left, a little in front of the chair, is Elvira, the third of the Merchán daughters, with her skinned knees and a thick plait of hair falling over her shoulder. The photographer has cut off her feet, and those of the carpenter's daughter, Andrea Iruela, and her mother, Dolores, with her premature widow's blouse and deep bags under her eyes. At the other end of the photograph, next to Isabel, the figure of Juana's mother stands out in profile, the bitter groove of her mouth, her hair held by two clips behind her ears. Her belly makes the drill apron bulge: she is pregnant. Pregnant with Consuelo, or Luz, or Cecilia perhaps? Her mother always pregnant and her father wearing a dead man's clothes. The portrait is six years old, Juana left school soon after. It was the village fête and Manuel Merchán sent word for the photographer to come to the tenement house on Alpechín Street with his tripod and black camera hood. It says on the back: 'Serafín Peinado, photographer, Puebla de Acebuche (Seville), 1949.' The photographer grumbled under the hood.

'Let's see, girls, keep still, you'll ruin my plate. One, two, three.'

A flash of white light and, suddenly, a cloud of smoke and a pungent stink among the patio flowerpots. Chachachica crossed herself with closed eyes.

'Almighty Jesus.'

Juana still has to treat her wounds and she steels herself in anticipation of the pain. Her hands ruined forever. Hands

7

that were once lovely, out of a fairytale, a princess's hands.

'You've got a rich girl's hands; soon enough they'll age.'

Juana lost her fingernails two months ago, when she began working in the Amat household, her first job in Barcelona. She burnt them on purpose with nitric acid. She was alone, like now, in the house on Muntaner Street, and the couple returned from the theatre earlier than expected.

'You're going to scrub the bath right now, you dirty pig.'

Juana became paralysed with fright in the middle of the corridor, the towel embroidered with the Amats' initials hardly covered her body. She felt ashamed to justify herself, to admit that she had never seen a bath before, nor perfumed towels, nor jars of bath salts, nor rose-scented soap. She bit her lip so as to not to cry in pain, so as not to cry at the prospect of a succession of stingy meals – quince jelly and cottage cheese – served on china plates on linen tablecloths. On her knees, barefoot, with the towel fastened under her arms, her skin still wet, she got ready to clean the bath. The bottle contained nitric acid. Juana knew it; she herself had bought it at the household goods store, and she poured it on purpose over her hands and the scouring pad. She scrubbed away in rage at the tide mark left on the bath enamel until she skinned her hands. But she did not cry. Her flayed skin stung. Two fingernails came off like shelled almonds and got stuck in the plughole grating. The lady screamed behind her back. Clean, clean, clean!

The treatment hurts. It will not be long now. Juana unties her hands wrapped in oil-soaked bandages. She bites on a piece of bed sheet to help stand the pain of peeling off the cotton stuck to her skin. One pull, for the Virgin of the Abandoned; another, for Chachachica; one more, for her mother's resting soul. She grinds her teeth. Another tug, for her grandfather Curro, disembowelled with a pair of sheep shears. Her thumbnail is already growing back. Another pull for her five sisters and for little José. Water, water, water. Her hands will be marked for life. The last yank, for her father. For her father?

Andrea, the carpenter's daughter from next door, next to the cemetery wall, pointed out the bullet holes. Her mouth was full of mallow buds.

'*My father says Merchán is a coward.*'

2

The staircase that led up to the pigeon loft was narrow and steep, and had to be climbed with one hand against the side wall to avoid losing your balance. The pronounced list of the girders meant you had to lower your head to open the tiny window to air out the room, or to wash the wooden floor with a scrubbing brush and sandstone. In spring, swallows nested in holes in the roof, and dirt, black feathers and pieces of straw fell onto the bed sheets made of clam sacks sewn together. Frail female bodies covered the sacking, which was stamped with red lettering: TRINITARIO FLORES, FRESH FISH AND SEAFOOD, PUNTA UMBRÍA, HUELVA. The sack sheets scratched their skin. Chachachica's feet were rough, hardened from walking barefoot around the patio and the stubble fields. Juana slept with Chachachica on a straw mattress on the floor of the room that used to be the pigeon loft, next to the bed Isabel and Elvira shared. Isabel, weak and rachitic, struggled to breathe with her mouth open; Elvira, on the edge of the flock mattress: her unplaited black hair, her legs tucked in against her and covered in sores. On the ground floor, in the only room apart from the kitchen, Consuelo and Luz slept imprisoned head to foot in a barred cot. Cecilia, in a cradle infested with bedbugs beside the Mercháns' bed, next to the cupboard where pots and pans cohabited with patched-up clothes and the paprika pot. Nothing in the house had a proper place.

Chachachica did not sleep much. Four hours' rest was enough for her to regain her strength and resume the spiral of domestic drudgery in a house crammed full of children and flowerpots. She slept little and with starts. Some nights Juana had to put up with her suffocated kicks and heard barely intelligible mutterings among which she sometimes seemed to distinguish a named spoken with anguish: Captain Díaz Criado.

'For God's sake I beg you, Captain. Have mercy, he isn't even eighteen yet!'

Chachachica looked after Manuel Merchán when he became an orphan; his mother, Josefina Vázquez, died in the devastating flu epidemic of 1919, when the boy was two years old. Some time later, his father, Curro Merchán, was murdered after a binge paid for by the young masters. Although Chachachica had no kinship ties with the Merchán family, Juana and her sisters considered her a great-aunt. No one in Puebla del Acebuche knew her real name. Anxious, superstitious, standing by her quiet dignity, Chachachica had confessed to the Merchán girls that she was the daughter of a *payo*, a non-gypsy man, and a quarter-gypsy girl and they abandoned her on being born two months premature at a foundling hospital in a village in Cadiz, where the colour of the bay stained her eyes sky-blue. She did not know the date and did not have a birth certificate. Truth and lie combined in her deep voice.

'Chacha, what's the sea like?'

'Salty and never ending. It's like the sky, but it's below.'

Although they slept breath to breath, Juana only saw her naked once, one Sunday searching for the calmness of Chachachica, whose body had left a warm hollow in the straw mattress. Juana went out to the patio and heard a sound behind the shed door, as if someone were pouring water from the well. She placed her nose to the planks and looked through a crack. Chachachica, with a hand resting on the well's rim, was pouring water over her flaky skin; her feet were in a zinc washing bowl in which mint leaves floated. Her empty and withered breasts, crowned with blackened nipples like fig skin. The sight of her first naked adult body: the skinny and water-shiny flesh, stalks for legs, the pubic hair sparse and grey. Her straight long hair in two white partings went down to her waist. Her deep voice repeated the same phrase in the lonely darkness of the shed.

'Captain Díaz Criado: the evil you long for will lead you to the grave. The evil you long for will lead you to the grave. The evil you long for will lead you to the grave.'

The sight of a naked body and, suddenly, an instinctive pounding on the two buttons – rosy, alien, painful to touch – which had begun to bud on Juana's bust. The light fuzz, almost invisible, hurt her pubis. Chachachica's profile framed in the crack of the door, her head down, her blue eyes immobile on the water's surface. Her rough voice emerged from the depths of the well.

'Girl, what you're looking at is the shell of an empty nut. Go back to bed, the sun isn't even up yet.'

Juana was convinced. The number of times Chachachica talked to herself; in reality she was conversing with the dead, mainly with grandfather Curro who, at dusk, when the sultry heat eased off, howled in pity of having been disembowelled with a pair of sheep shears before he was thirty. On All Souls' Day Chachachica lit tea lights, chain prayed and consoled them in their wandering desperation. Chachachica must have had her soul and her bones full of easterly wind and glass. When she stared into the eyes of who was in front of her she could draw out even their most hidden passions. Women who had lost their minds would travel from distant farms to the tenement house on Alpechín Street and sleep in the open air waiting for her to calm them. They would ask her to foretell the whereabouts of a loved one, and although they scratched at her fists to place money into them, she did not usually give in to their pleas because it upset her, then she would lose her senses and each time it was harder to recover. When she agreed they would give her a glass of brandy to drink and carefully sit her in a corner where she could not hurt herself. The adults locked the girls in the pigeon loft room.

'What shall we play?'

'What do you want us to play? Nothing. Just listen to what they're saying below.'

'We can't hear anything from here... Go on, open the chest of drawers and get the tin.'

Inside the tin box Juana's father kept a bullet, various pages torn out of the Old Testament, a watch with its face crushed and a military campaign record with an eagle on the cover.

'Go on, you read, Juana, you stumble less with words.'

'Date and aim of the armed actions in which the person

concerned took part. 26th of March 1939: breaking the Red front at Sierra Mesegara, continuing the clean-up operation across the fields and village of Belalcázar until Almadén.'

Chachachica got up first. Among bluish shadows she enjoyed alone the fullness of the day to come. Before the sun rose she buttoned up her black percale housecoat and went barefoot down to the patio with her hair loose and her jet earrings swinging from the flesh of her ear. As she combed her white hair into a bun she talked in an undertone to the potted jasmine and to the night jasmine and woke up the aspidistras, the bed of hydrangeas and the houseleeks, planted in rust-eaten buckets.

'What a delightful patio you've got for us, Chacha.'

'Flowers keep me alive.'

Chachachica mixed mud and vinegar to ease wasp stings. She used to say that tomato skin dried pus. Larkspur lotion killed lice. Together, lime and mint leaves and orange flower pacified distress. Corn-ear tea drained the kidneys. The patio plants fell ill as she fell ill. Meticulously and in silence, before the heat and the bustle of the tenement house got worse, Chachachica selected the best jasmine flowers, carefully wrapping them in old newspapers that the club saved for her, and stored them under the jug frame, next to the shed, the coolest place in the house. After the slow drowsiness of the siesta, Chachachica strung the jasmine stems together into slender hairpins so that Juana and Isabel could adorn their hair or the buttonholes of their dresses when, at dusk, they went out walking around Nueva Square and sat under the lime trees in front of the club doors or when they went to the nine-day long festival of Saint Nicolás de Bari. The most fragrant bunch was for Juana, her favourite. And the saddest.

'Daft Juana thinks she's the daughter of a rich landlord. Look at her, how she walks, how she moves... Little missy, little miss lordy.'

It was a July Sunday, before attending twelve o'clock mass, when Juana dared to ask. Under the patio vine Chachachica was washing her hair with a piece of homemade soap, which she herself had made from caustic soda and oil used for refrying potatoes. The piece of soap slipped through her red fingers and fell into the tub water with the happy splash of a fish.

'Poor but clean, little one, always clean.'

Chachachica rinsed her hair one last time with vinegar so that it would shine like a filly's mane. With her eyes closed Juana listened to the buzz of the wasps drinking the sour juice of the grapes. Arrows of light pierced the vine leaves, tingeing the skin of her eyelids a mandarin colour. Juicy and perfumed mandarins that made her think of her father. One day on returning from the market Manuel Merchán brought two mandarins wrapped in a handkerchief.

'Let's see who can guess in which hand the present is. You've got to concentrate on the tattoos on my forearms, both of them: the Moor in a turban here on my left, and the Moor with a beard on the other. The one that winks his eye is the one hiding the present.'

'But just looking at them doesn't make them move!'

'Because you're not paying attention, Isabel.'

'What did the Moor who made the tattoos say? Come on Dad, tell us again. Come on, make us laugh. That's it, limping the way the Moor did... What was his name?'

'He was called Hamito, and he sucked threads of cheap

15

tobacco with his palate. He'd say: "Cold cedar, silly water, girlfriend writing paper. Cold cedar, silly water, girlfriend writing paper." He was like me, but even darker. He'd always say the same thing.'

The two mandarins were tiny and hard to peel. Splinters of skin got stuck under their fingernails. Segments piled up on the kitchen table. There is always somebody faster, always, Isabel.

'You eel, long fingers, green cigar, spider legs.'

'Angel of God, she's almost dying of pleurisy; let her eat.'

The burning July heat sealed her mandarin eyelids. Chachachica's hardened hands untangled Juana's mop of hair with a gap-toothed comb. Each tug hurt. But only a little. Juana then dared to ask.

'Chacha...'

'What?'

'Nothing.'

'What is it? Out with it, I know you as if I'd given birth to you myself.'

'Why are there so many of us at home?'

'You're still too young to understand. Life is as it is, and you have to play along with it as it comes.'

'Andrea only has one brother, and we are six.'

A cricket sang monotonously among the basil leaves.

'Chacha...'

'What do you want, you pest?'

'Tell me, why doesn't father go work in the fields?'

'Don't be daft, Juana... Your father is your father. Don't disrespect him.'

Life on the patio slowly stretched awake. The windows and door looking out onto the upper balcony opened little by little, and bed sheets covered the handrails to air the perspiration of night. Antonio Maldonado, the cobbler, was the first of the men to get up. In Puebla de Acebuche he was known by the nickname 'Setefo'. Robust, wide shouldered, short, crew cut grey haired, his fingers stained with shoe polish, Setefo would go down to the patio and open the workshop shutters with the calmness of his prominent paunch. Setefo and his wife, Felisa, never had children; they lived at the first door, turning right on crossing the hallway. During the long summer Setefo's hammering on half soles pierced the density of the heat and imposed a lethargic rhythm onto the suffocating stillness of the patio.

The family of barbers lived next door to the cobbler's room. The father, Nicolás Falcón, already retired, had taught the trade to his sons, the three men: Rafael, Paco and Juan de Dios. After Setefo opened his workshop the three *falcons* left with briefcases under their armpits containing shaving equipment and went their separate ways as journeymen at the two barber shops in the village. Some Sundays, or when Puebla de Acebuche's village fête was close, Rafael, the eldest brother, shaved the neighbours for free. Juana was terrified of his extreme thinness, his high laugh, the saliva shine of his teeth, the sadistic elasticity of his fingers – fast, the nails of his little fingers long, like those of a rich old woman – that moved the razor with delectation along the leather strop smeared in oil to smooth the shave. Juana could not look him in the eye; she was terrified of the idea that hunger and heat, tapping away at his skull, would drive him crazy and, with a cutthroat razor in his hand, he would slit Setefo's bovine throat and dye the white corollas of the geranium with splashes of blood. The *falcons'* mother,

Balbina, prepared stews in the open air on a coal stove taken out to the patio to free space inside her home; at night she covered it with an esparto mat.

The Merchán family shared noise and a thin partition wall with the Iruelas and their two children, José María, the eldest, and Andrea. Juana was silently jealous of Andrea for the tooth-decayed smile of her mother, always cheerful, for the present of that clean laugh that broke the sky, the walls, the roof eaves and the harshness of misery. Dolores's soft hug smelt of laurel. Juana's mother was called Carmen and she never gave hugs.

Next to the trained vine, beside the carpentry workshop entrance, Andrea's father, Matías Iruela, hung a cage from a meat hook holding a yellow winged goldfinch with a white feathered collar that tuned its voice. Matías dragged his feet on walking and coughed spasms of sawdust. In the light and shadow of the workshop the carpenter worked slowly on the pine shaving covered floor, with an earthenware drinking jug of fresh water next to him. On the back wall, between differently shaded planks, Matías hung photographs of bullfighters cut out of newspapers that the club kept for Chachachica; in one, the only one framed, Pepe Luis Vázquez was carried out of the Maestranza Bullring on the shoulders of the crowd. Eventually the carpenter's hands stiffened from jack planing wood. The gouge chisel seemed big in his waxy fingers and jobs became few and far between.

'What can I do for you, Marcela?'

'A washboard, Matías. When will it be ready?'

'Come by in a week.'

A washboard. A plate rack. Correcting a wonky chair. A dirty blood and sawdust cough.

Matías and Juana's father killed time by saying everything indirectly. The image of her father forced to be idle, in the shade of the vine, his torso naked while his shirt dried on the wire. Her father leaning against the whitewashed wall, under the goldfinch cage, his black eyes used to the workshop's semi-darkness.

'You're not going to the market today?'

'The fish haven't arrived.'

'Damn it, man. So what are you going to do, Merchán? Patience and card shuffling? Listen, listen... Have you heard what a darling little bird it is? It even seems to sing Andalusian songs for me!'

Shrouded in an orange-coloured haze, patio life – the goldfinch song, the hammering and swearing of Setefo with nails between his teeth and tongue, the stink of heated glue, Matías's melancholic cough, the nothing stews that Balbina seasoned with garlic and cumin, Dolores's hands sprinkling water from an earthenware bowl to ease the scorching red floor – all existence in the tenement house seemed impregnated with a cheerful façade that did not manage to completely stifle the silent sadness, the narrow-mindedness, the promiscuity and the foul-smelling sticky breath of poverty.

The adults were deaf and dumb. That day when Juana dared ask, the vermilion sun melted into the line of the horizon. Sitting on an empty box of fresh anchovies Juana watched the passing of a file of ants; the women had not noticed her presence. Dolores Iruela was hanging out the last of the clothes. Chachachica was watering the hydrangeas in the evening cool.

'Chacha, where's Carmen? I haven't seen her all day.'

'Lying down.'

'Still in bed! Is she ill?'

There was a liquid crystal pause between the two women.

'She's not pregnant again, is she?'

'I can see where others can't, Dolores.'

'For Christ's sake! Are you sure, Chacha?'

'As sure as I'm to die.'

Sitting on the fish box, Juana bit her bare thigh. The pressure of her teeth left a cracked blue crown on her flesh. Another sister. Inés? Aurora? There were not any saint names left. Cecilia's crying, in the cradle infested with bedbugs, fell wearily over the flowerpots.

The adults believed that the children were also deaf and dumb. Twenty days later Juana heard another women's conversation in the kitchen. Chachachica was cooking; Juana's mother, Carmen, touched at her belly with fear.

'Chacha... My period's late.'

'How late?'

'On Tuesday it'll be a month and a half.'

'Did you do the chickpea thing?'

Juana did not need to hear more. Chickpeas: the cutting certainty of words. Chachachica had an answer for almost everything: soak a handful of chickpeas overnight, the next morning Carmen should drink up to the last dregs of that water tasting of damp earth, worms and roots. If Juana's mother did not menstruate within two moons there was no hope. Juana swallowed the steamy bowl full of stew and fished girl names from the skins of the pulse that had announced the coming of another sister. Inés? Aurora?

3

In the dining room three bowls of noodle soup are steaming on the daisy patterned oilcloth. Salud Monterde and her daughters, Mercedes and Montserrat, have early hot dinners to go to work later with settled stomachs. Recurring phrases at the table:

'To work safe and sound, the belly hard and round. Champagne goes straight to one's head on an empty stomach. And I want you awake, girls, like two hares.'

The cheerful bubbling of lemonade in wine soothes the silence. The chest of drawers under the photographs shines brightly with the sour gloss of vinegar. Salud Monterde taps persistently at the oilcloth petals eaten away by bleach with the filter of a Chesterfield; she lights it. The cigarette trembles between her meaty feverish fingers. She usually crumbles bread into her soup and smokes between courses. The crumbs tickle her elbows. A hangnail, red from blood, stings her ring finger, where the flesh strangled by her wedding rings turns blue. To her regret she is wearing no other rings. Jewellery fascinates her. Her eyes – tiny, absorbing, of a brown-green colour – twinkle when she contemplates a gem. Over the years she has learnt how to distinguish jewels, to rate the patience invested by a goldsmith in engraving, to reserve quality pieces for expert customers who know how to appreciate them and to pass beryl off as emerald to the tight-lapelled naive and to the occasional American marine. Over time Salud Monterde has also understood that danger and money give off the same stench as sulphur. Through the half-opened balcony over-looking the lilacs of Carmen Street rises the asthmatic wheeze of an engine and the rattle from the shops as shutters are being pulled down.

From the kitchen Juana catches threads of conversation and the syncopated clink of three spoons against the bowls. In the frying pan she is preparing the last pieces of meat which she went to buy in the morning from the Boquería market.

Juana went out with the purse clutched against her chequered housecoat, at the level of the pit of her stomach. The butcher smiled on seeing her arrive and drew a semicircle in the air with his index finger for her to go round the stall and enter through the back. The passageways of the market covered in puddles, the noises absorbed by pyramids of fruit and the familiar pestilence of fish dragged the echo of a paternal voice from far away.

'Whiting, girls, whiting, they're silver! The pomfrets, fresh anchovies and plaice they bring me all the way from Sanlúcar and still wriggling!'

Inside the purse Juana carried a golden bracelet wrapped in tissue paper.

'Señora Monterde says you're to give me four and a half kilos of loin and make up the bill of what's owed.'

The butcher did not ask any questions and put the bracelet into his trouser back pocket. He did not unwrap it.

'See you later, love.'

The two corridor clocks, suffocated by useless furniture – drawers full of photographs, reels of sewing thread, leaking bottles of syrup – strike eight o'clock in the evening in unison with an antiquarian melancholy. Juana places the platter of loin fried in breadcrumbs onto the oilcloth and takes the soup bowls away with white cotton glove-covered hands; she washes them up every night in the sink when they go out. Señora Monterde is used to squashing her cigarette butts into her leftovers; the noodles sizzled by the cigarette suggest a bitter outpour of desolation and loneliness. Señorita Mercedes has hardly touched her soup. The sharpness of her scorn hurts. Juana does not take the bowl away and runs her black eyes over the burnt noodles, ashamed of her own beauty. Señorita Mercedes – her harsh stare, her mannish gestures – makes her feel uncomfortable. She usually leaves Juana to do her sex-stained lace knickers soaking in the washbasin, and she does it to humiliate her. Señorita Montserrat, on the other hand, washes her own underwear, sometimes smiles, calls Juana 'queen' and has two peaches on her cheeks. Juana uses the Monterdes' make-up behind their backs when she prepares to go out for a walk on Thursdays. Señorita Mercedes knows how to make her harsh face up and she smokes with style, throwing back her long hair like María Félix at the cinema in Puebla de Acebuche.

'It works out as one cent a head, and the carpenter's Dolores should go too, she's got a very good memory.'

23

The patio women analysed the same film over and over again, reconstructing it, reinventing it. A circle of women on the patio. The floor covered in lupin shells. The dreamlike fragrance of jasmine.

'How are we going to organise the night, girls? I don't know whether to go to the Boadas bar or to the Liceo at eleven when the show is over.' Salud Monterde speaks while chewing on a mouthful of meat.

'I've arranged to meet Feliu at nine-thirty at the Brindis in Real Square... He wants to see me before the bar gets crowded. He says he's agreed a price for the ring with an American,' Mercedes replies.

'The emerald?'

'Yes.'

'Juana, bring me a little more bread,' Salud Monterde's voice falls onto the frying pan oil. 'Keep an eye out Merche, Feliu knows all the tricks.'

'Why do you say that? We've always trusted him.' Montserrat joins in the conversation with a weak tone of voice. Her voice is always muted.

'I know what I'm saying, girl. Let it be Feliu who sets his percentage, and bring what he says down to half. If he turns up his nose to it, increase it a bit, but only a little. And take your sister with you. I don't want you to go alone, Merche.'

'I don't know what all this is in aid of, mother. I'm used to clinching deals with that greasy pianist. Anyway, he says the American is a lieutenant and is the serious type, and white.'

Juana brings bread and a fruit bowl of pears to the table.

'He makes me suspicious, don't ask why. I don't trust him. Take care, Merche.' Salud Monterde pours herself another glass of wine and lemonade. 'Salvador Feliu, with that fat priest's double chin of his, he's a fine one. If I told you all that these eyes have seen!'

'Well, well... Saint Teresa of Jesus has spoken!' Mercedes extends an arm and takes a pear with a theatrical gesture. Montserrat shrinks in her chair. Wooden hair curlers, covered in a rose coloured hairnet, pull on her hair roots, thin, straight and dyed platinum blonde.

Salud Monterde observes her daughter Mercedes with an expression halfway between anger and tiredness. She places her elbows onto the oilcloth and begins to bite on her hangnail. She says:

'Can you tell me what's up with the lady marchioness today?'

'Merche, you haven't touched your meat,' Montserrat intervenes clumsily with the intention of dispelling the electricity that knifes the dining room.

'I'm not hungry.'

Juana has returned to the kitchen. She is standing, leaning against the marble worktop, trying to cut a mouthful of loin with gloved hands. The fingernails that the nitric acid removed have begun to grow back with a slight wavering off their course. The treatment does not hurt now, but the skin between her princess's fingers will be scarred, forever. Burnt skin for life. Señora Monterde and her daughters usually argue over dinner. Mercedes uses gross words and her sister Montse cries. Señora Monterde does not shout; except maybe to order a brandy from the bottle covered in a mesh. Señora Monterde never slams the door.

'The fears and scruples of certain people make me throw up.' Mercedes talks without looking at her mother; she plays with the pear peel floating in her cold soup with the point of a knife. 'Salvador Feliu is a poor devil, as honest and as rotten as the next. Why should Feliu be any worse than us? Because he's a friend to all the whores in the neighbourhood? Because he finds girls for anyone who pays him well? Before, the slags gave him cuddles and caresses when he opened the piano lid and took out perfume and his box of silk stockings. But that was before, mother. You should see him now, poor Feliu. Now nobody invites him to smoke smuggled Virginian tobacco, nor buys him a drink; they don't even look at him and, if they do, it's with pity. His hands shake when he bangs away at the piano. And he sweats in his velvet suit. He sweats like a pig and his teeth are rotten from plaque. Your disgusting partner, mother.'

'Merche, please, don't talk like that. Feliu isn't our partner. We don't have any partners.' Montserrat is scared.

'Please what... Now we're whimpering? It seems incredible you don't grow up. You don't like hearing unpleasant things, I know, but you've got to get used to it, true, mother? Your mother knows so much about life! You've still got a lot to learn from her.'

'Merche... why do you treat me so?'

'So that you wake up, dear. You're living in the clouds; you don't think, that's certain. You expect the rest of us to think for you; it's easier.' Mercedes' upper lip, thin and fleshless, quivers.

'Juana! Juana!' Salud Monterde's booming voice bounces off the ceiling beams. 'Bring me a brandy and soda, hurry up. From the yellow mesh-covered bottle.'

The trident of a pause is thrust into the dining room air. Salud Monterde's eyes glare, trapped in bags of jelly.

26

'Listen well to what I've got to say, Mercedes: I should have shoved a knitting needle up myself the day I became pregnant with you. The door is open; if it doesn't suit you being here, clear off. But while you still live under this roof you've got to respect me and back off. Do you know the effort it took to bring up two children alone? Alone... All that you eat, the skirts you wear, the cigarettes you smoke, your whims, all of it you owe to me...'

'Thank you, mother. I'd expect no less from you.'

'Don't interrupt me! No, no I'm not going to take part in your game; at least not tonight. I'm tired and I don't want to argue. Today is Wednesday and we have to work hard. So, come on dimwits, get moving, that means now: get dressed in the clothes you buy with my money, put mascara on your eyelashes and go out and earn your daily bread.'

Salud Monterde takes a long swig of brandy. The brown liquid scratches at her oesophagus.

'And you, what are you doing there listening, blockhead? Not only slow but an eavesdropper. Haven't you got anything to do in the kitchen? I must have lost my head! You don't even know how to fry an egg, nor starch, nor even handle an iron... Didn't your mother teach you to be a housewife? Go on, back to the kitchen; I don't want to even see you.'

Through the small window that opens onto the inner patio a hopeless beating of eggs can be heard. It smells of old sorrow. Juana washes up with a pita scouring pad under the running water, her chequered housecoat absorbing soap splashes. Señora Monterde's microscopic eyes impose; there was no need to raise her voice.

'Didn't your mother teach you to be a housewife?'

27

An August siesta submerged in the slime of memory. The rattle of cicadas bursts into the kitchen through the mosquito net and the half-closed shutters, filtering the orange fury of the sun's glare. Juana and her mother are folding patched up bed sheets, the only set of sheets in the house. Juana's mother tugs on the cloth and draws it to her bulging belly in whose lukewarm darkness floats the embryo of a sister. Juana's small body resists the vigorous shaking from the other end of the sheet. Mother and daughter do not look each other in the eye. They fold the washing and pile it onto the table in silence. What is Juana's mother thinking in this instant of memory? Words never spoken, dead caresses in her hands.

Tiredness dulls the possibility of crying. Bloated noodles sail adrift in the sink. Juana bites her lip and thinks about her father and Isabel, sitting on the two identical beds in the sublet room on Conde de Asalto, face to face without knowing what to talk about.

'*The end of the war caught me in Almadén, in the province of Ciudad Real.*'

Her father and Isabel would have gone down to the bar to eat a sandwich of leftover meat livened up by a plate of dressed olives. Tomorrow is Thursday. Juana and Isabel will go out for a walk in the late afternoon. It will be at four o'clock when Isabel rings the doorbell on Carmen Street, on the corner of San Lázaro.

'*Isabel, lanky, long fingers, eel, spider legs.*'

Isabel arrives late everywhere raised in her high heels, the only pair she has got; Juana imagines her on her way, entranced by the shop windows of the Sepu department store. The girls will pick up their father from the underground entrance in Urquinaona Square, as every Thursday, when Manuel Merchán returns from the building site with his shoes splashed with plaster. Juana will hand over the envelope with her wages to him. The money – worn, crumpled, dirty from recounting it every night – now rests inside a crocheted bag, provisionally in her cardboard suitcase, lying on the floor of her room. Manuel Merchán sends a postal order every month to Puebla de Acebuche for Chachachica, alone in the village with a bunch of kids. Save, save, save, the drug-like obsession of saving to bring them to Barcelona.

Night falls across the walls of the building's light shaft. Water softens the skin of her damaged hands. Juana hears the voice of Señora Monterde behind her.

'Girl, we're leaving now. Remember to turn the gas off before going to bed. Call me in the morning when you wake up; I'll get up with you. You've got to go on an errand for me in the morning, nice and early. Don't open the door to anyone, you hear me? See you later.'

The silence of the flat when she is alone. Señor Feliu, the pianist whom they argued about over dinner, comes round to the Monterdes' flat some Sundays to eat paella. Juana has never seen him but has heard the lady mention his name.

'One cup of rice to two cups of water, and prepare the fried onion, garlic and tomato base before going. Feliu is coming to eat today.'

The flat sour without men, the rice on Sundays for Señor Feliu, the nights out, the keyhole sealed with soaked bread and the errands for Señora Monterde.

'Call me in the morning when you wake up; I'll get up with you. You've got to go on an errand for me nice and early.'

Juana senses where the lady wants to send her. She has

already been there before, only once, and on imagining the reunion she feels a burning in her stomach, between anxiety and fascination. Señor Pech lives in the Gothic quarter, on Baños Nuevos Street, behind the cathedral, on the second floor of a staircase with wooden treads that lament being stepped upon. Juana does not know his first name. Señora Monterde and her daughters refer to him as Pech, just Pech; the name is difficult to pronounce. Señora Monterde sometimes talks about him at the table, with a certain respect or perhaps fear, although she only used señor before his name when she asked Juana to go to Baños Nuevos Street to take him a packet.

The first time, the weight of defeat had shrunken those eyes of his, impeccably blue, almost grey. Screwed into the wooden door, an enamelled sign, indigo background and white lettering: WATCHMAKER – REPAIRS. Señor Pech came to open the door with his shirt tails unbuttoned over his trousers, from whose bottom right side stuck out a wooden leg. Juana did not want to make him feel uncomfortable, but her eyes insisted on piercing the rubber tip of the false leg prudently dancing on the loose floor tiles of the hall.

'Good morning, Señor Pech... Señora Monterde has sent me.'

He invited her to come in and offered her a seat. The flat smelt stuffy. Señor Pech rolled up the Persian blinds and tied the rope to the balcony rail with agile hands. The harsh light of the Gothic quarter slowly penetrated the room. The watchmaker sat down with difficulty at a small round table, and placed his crutches up against it. There were books upon the shelves, on top of the unmatching chairs, on the floor; and years of dust. In one corner of the room a large table stood out, longer than wide, covered in shiny aligned objects

30

like a surgeon's instruments: an office lamp, a chamois leather, tweezers, weighing scales, a lathe, an eyeshade, an eyepiece, a blowlamp, mounting chisels and various amber coloured jars; the label on one of them read: 'Copper Chloride Solution'. The cleanliness of the worktable contrasted with the opaqueness of the rest of the living room. Señor Pech is tall and extremely thin, and two stony vertical wrinkles frame his meaty-lipped mouth. In his look there is sarcasm, profound sadness and circumspection. Señor Pech lives with a cat.

'I've brought you this packet on behalf of Señora Monterde.'

The two blue jewels did not respond. They looked at her, they dissected her silhouette, her eyes, her gloved hands, and split the soft tissue of her recently pronounced words. Still looking at her, Señor Pech untied the knots in the cord wrapping the packet with sure hands, his flesh sculptured, his fingertips stained with nicotine. He took out two shiny bars of an intense yellow colour and somewhat smaller than sponge fingers. It seemed to be gold but Juana dared not ask. She had wanted to run down the stairs of the flat on Baños Nuevos Street, but she could not get up from her chair. Señor Pech rewrapped the ingots in brown paper and took the packet through the shadows of the corridor with unequal and laborious steps. Tack, tack, tack.

'Well, see you again. You said you were called Juana, is that right? Tell Señora Monterde that I need copper; she'll know what it's for. Listen, does that bitch make you wear gloves?'

'No, señor; I burnt myself with nitric acid at the house where I served before; that's why I wear cotton gloves... Sorry, what did you say you needed?'

'Copper. It's for melting with gold to make it more flexible.'

Salvador Feliu is already waiting when Mercedes and Montserrat Monterde walk through the door of the Brindis bar well dressed and arm in arm to avoid confusion. When Mercedes puts on make-up to go out at night she exaggerates the contours of her mouth with a brown coloured pencil and, if her hand is shaking and the profile line zigzags, her mouth, thin and fleshless, looks like an old doll. The Brindis does not usually fill until after dinner, but tonight, when it is not even nine o'clock, there is already a customer sitting at the bar. The red velvet of the bar smells of flat beer and cheap cologne. A black saxophonist, with a slender young body and huge eyes, practises the first bars of *Paper Moon,* while his fellow band member uncases his double bass. In a corner, blurred in the mist of the bar, a marine chats to a blond woman, the voracious vulva of her lips is red and expectant.

'Good evening, Ángelo, how's it going?' Mercedes greets the waiter drying glasses behind the bar.

'The Monterde sisters in person! What an honour. I haven't seen you for days. Your pianist is having dinner in the storeroom. Poor Feliu is on tenterhooks. What shady deals are you mixed up in?'

'Nothing that concerns you.'

'What character, girl, what character...'

'If you weren't such a gossip and so queer, I'd marry you, in white and covered in a mantilla.'

'You've got a sugar candy mouth, Merche. And, tell me, your pussy, is it the same?'

Salvador Feliu is standing in the Brindis storeroom, leaning against a pile of wooden crates holding empty bottles. Under the crude light of the bulb and the flytrap tape he is trying to clean an oily grease spot that has just fallen onto his tie with the soaked tip of a serviette. He has stained it having dinner:

a tuna and sweet red pepper sandwich. Impatience makes him sweat in his velvet waistcoat.

'Don't come so late, I've work to do. The musicians are already here and I can't be detained any longer. They pay me for playing there outside and not for waiting for you two, damn it.' Salvador Feliu, a restrained and cultured man, only swears when he is nervous.

'Well, let's get to the point.'

Mercedes gestures to her sister to put her fingers into her bra cup and take out the ring covered in black felt. Mercedes is too thin to hide merchandise between her breasts; she moves under the light bulb and shows the jewel to Feliu.

'It's a filigree: eighteen-carat gold. And look at the shine on that emerald. Here, under the light, come closer. Look, what facets. The emerald doesn't have a single fault. A marvel. How much are you going to get from the American?'

Salvador Feliu looks at the dry woman watching him through half-closed eyes; he moves his tortoise-like neck and rests his gaze with tenderness on Montserrat, who has not opened her mouth since entering the bar. He has a soft spot for Montse because he knows she is his daughter. A secret daughter. Feliu wipes the sweat off his brow with the back of his broad hand.

'The guy wants to see you before fixing a price. He's coming tonight, later, and with a bit of luck he'll get drunk. I don't know if we'll get as much out of him as your mother says.'

'Feliu, don't try to be so clever, this is above board, as always. We don't owe you any favours, understand? If you can place the ring with the American, perfect, you'll get your ten percent and that's that. And if you cause any problems or have ideas of taking a bigger cut, we'll end the matter right here and now. Do you think we're not going to be able to sell it? We're up to here with customers, serious people with money, you already know that. Orders have to wait because we can't meet them. This is a family business, Feliu. You know that better than I do. In the Boadas, in the Brindis, in the Ópera bar, people at the Liceo... ask anywhere. They know us; we're the neighbourhood jewellers. You know that. Everything is above board and crystal clear, as always.'

'You're the same as your mother, Merche, not someone to mess around with. It depends on you two, on knowing how to coax the American. I've already done what I had to do... Sit down and have a drink, you're invited. Tell Ángelo to put two glasses of champagne on my tab. Come on, let's go. Don't get nervous. And for me, it's down to work until the American comes. I'm going to dedicate a piece to you, Merche, one you like, so that you know I like you.'

Mercedes and Montserrat Monterde sit down at the most discreet table in the Brindis, next to Ángelo's bar, shielded away from the rest of the customers.

'What are you having, loves?'

'A glass of champagne on Feliu's tab.'

'And for you, Montse?'

'A lemonade, with only a little peppermint liqueur, it goes straight to my head.'

The customer at the bar, thin and small, observes them at intervals in front of a cup of cold white coffee which he clutches in both hands because he fears the waiter will take it away and force him to order another one or else leave. But Ángelo is completely indifferent to his presence, and one could even say he enjoys watching the man in the narrow tie, who visits the Brindis every Wednesday and Friday, slowly drink his coffee, making it last until the early hours. Ángelo, used to scrutinising life from the parapet of the bar, would swear the man with the white coffee is a musician because he follows the rhythm with his feet and, when marine jazz groups play, he takes notes on a paper serviette he keeps in his shirt pocket; he has been in the trade many years. The red-mouthed scrubber, the one talking to the marine, is called Esperanza, but in the neighbourhood she is known as Espé, like that, with an accent. She laughs with noisy and vulgar guffaws that bother the waiter; the American soldier paying for her glasses of coloured water enjoys himself popping chickpeas and toasted broad beans down his throat. The street door opens and a gust of clean air comes in followed by a gypsy woman with a string of lottery tickets and two robust men, broad backed, with their black hair still wet. They seem to be brothers. They sit at the bar and order two beers in a Portuguese accent. Ángelo fixes his eyes on the slightly taller of the two. They must work on one of the merchant ships anchored in the port. He has seen them before, he is sure. The tattoo on a right forearm convinces him: *Pas de chance*.

There is no luck, there is no way out, there is no escape, there is no oxygen in the city smelling of silence and damp ash.

The Brindis fills and it begins to get hot. Salvador Feliu perspires stiffly in his pianist's waistcoat. The public applaud reluctantly. Feliu speaks quietly to the saxophonist and the double bass player half in English, half with gestures. The saxophone is positioned behind the pianist to follow the score; Feliu snaps his fingers and draws rhythmic crosses in the air; the double bass player nods in approval, without words. The spotlights illuminate Feliu's sweaty socks in blue, he turns to face Mercedes and suggests a hint of a smile. Mercedes raises her glass of champagne. The American lieutenant is about to arrive.

4

There was no room for boys in her womb; Juana's mother expelled them from her uterus, puny, palpitating and half-cooked, like runny boiled eggs. The first Manuel – Merchán had insisted on baptising him with his own name – was conceived forty days after Juana was born and opened his eyes onto the world with fate tangled up in his eyelashes. The tender corpse was kept for three days covered in a sack, inside a box of horse mackerel and embraced by a block of ice, in a corner of the upper balcony overlooking the patio so that the persistent heat would not ravage his flesh until Matías, the carpenter, finished his coffin; meanwhile Chachachica had taken the fragrant flowerpot of basil up to the balcony. The second Manuel saw the light of day after the third girl, Elvira. The second Manuel was buried in a crossless white box, with brandy and adult mourning.

Juana's father wanted a boy.

'What, Merchán, yet another pussy? Let's see if you can hit the mark next time.'

Setefo's words, the cobbler – his greying crew cut hair, his sarcastic belly – nightfall in June when Cecilia was born, the sixth girl. Setefo had been a Carlist militiaman and kept his red beret in the wardrobe.

Juana's coffee-coloured eyes learnt in silence about the confined world of the red ochre paved patio. On returning from Puebla de Acebuche's market, at three in the afternoon, Manuel Merchán piled the surplus boxes of fish into the shade of the shed, next to the edge of the well, to keep the goods fresh until the following morning. The girl found out through a crack in the door: her father urinated over the clams, obstinately closed tight, so that they would open their valves at the salty taste of urea.

'Prepare the rice, prepare the rice!... They bring me clams from Punta Umbría and I'm running out of them, I'm running out.'

Juana devoured that reduced world with her eyes, quietly, she took down notes of her impossible desires on pieces of brown paper – the same paper her mother used to roll up handfuls of clams into paper cones at the market – and hid them in the cracks of the pigeon loft out of the pleasure of finding them unfulfilled and absurd later on. Her desires smelt of rotten fish.

Juana and her mother hardly ever spoke. Juana was disturbed by her mother's permanent bitter smile on the corner of her mouth and by her bulging belly. Juana looked at her out of the corner of her eye; she had learnt that it would be in the fifth month of pregnancy when her mother needed to fasten her drill skirt with a wide-mouthed safety pin: her lower stomach, melon-shaped, removed from the rest of her ungainly body, would endlessly swell. Juana and Isabel were taken up to the pigeon loft with Chachachica when they began to ask about the sobbing coming from her mother's bed.

Carmen took being pregnant as destiny's punishment or the whim of a cruel nature that had chosen her with a fertile womb where seeds spontaneously germinated – suspended in the air, in the dry plain of her bowels – with only a rub, the sweet and sour smell of a man, or the light breeze of desire. Juana looked at her mother out of the corner of her eye, and secretly; when she returned from the market dragging her feet and thinking nobody was watching, Carmen chewed parsley leaves and punched at her stomach with reddened and scale splashed hands after having moved around codfish and sea bass. Another sister, a blue-black oarswoman rowing in the lukewarm humidity of the maternal placenta, and there was nowhere for her to sleep. In the pigeon loft there was not enough air. In the tenement house on Alpechín Street you could not breathe.

It was Chachachica who prepared lunch on the coal cooker. As she cooked the esparto curtain cushioned the burning sunlight, Setefo's monochord hammering and the refrying of garlic on the stove Balbina had brought out onto the patio. Matías Iruela's hearing became finely tuned as his lung tissue dried up. Broad bean pod stew puffing steam. Ration book bread, heavy and worthy, on the stone kitchen top, precise incisions made by the point of a knife into its black crust: Chachachica checked the sharing out three times. Juana's father always ate standing up, his nose in the stew. He chewed with anxiety and with a puppet's grimaces.

'How much?'

'Nothing, Chacha. Two pesetas at most.'

Softened looks in the suffocation of August. At the Merchán s' home there was no talk at lunchtime; in reality they never conversed because the lead certainty that everything had been said gagged their mouths.

'We can't go on like this; like this we can't go on... Tomorrow, at first light, I'll go to Nueva Square to see if the foreman of Dueña Alta will choose me for the unripened olive picking. And I'll take Juana with me.'

Chachachica's grave voice resounded off the empty, grease shiny, bowls.

'Don't be stubborn, Chacha. Olives, no. The Maldonados don't take women on to do day long shifts, and they'll only pay you for half a day. Anyway, the Maldonado family don't even want to smell us near their lands. Remember what happened with me.'

'Whatever you say, Manuel, but we aren't getting anywhere like this. What'll I put in the cooking pot tomorrow? Go on, tell me. What'll I put in it, air and a lump of stale lard? And meanwhile, may the Christ of Paño forgive me, you two fucking every night in bed.'

Juana's sharp eyes caressed her father's weak and grieved profile. Her mother, head bowed, swallowed without chewing a rasher of salt pork; only her mother had salt pork because she was pregnant and needed food, because her mother and her belly were one, her mother multiplied the same as God, one and three. Her mother repeated herself in girls. Juana would have preferred to have been a man, snatch the knife out of Rafael's hands, the barber's eldest son, and in one slash cut off her tits – timid, pricking, strange to the touch – in front of everyone, like Saint Agatha of Catania, and offer them to her father and the village on a blond lace pewter tray: two wobbly crème caramels with caramel nipples. To be a man with reinforced iron muscles instead of breasts, leave for the fields before dawn, work on an empty stomach until dropping exhausted onto the dried earth and return home with your existence justified in a miserable day's work. To be a man, raise your voice and thump the bare kitchen table until your knuckles bleed. To shake her father. Both her breasts amputated and wobbling like El Mandarín crème caramels. At the Mercháns' home they never bought powder for making crème caramels. Never. At Antonio's grocer's shop boxes were piled upon the shelves. The Chinese man smiled against a cobalt blue background with his plait of hair lank across his shoulder.

'Go on, Juana, get the basket and go to Antonio's for some chickpeas.'

'Antonio, my mother wants a handful of chickpeas.'

'Your mother already owes me four pesetas, girl.'

The panic of returning home empty-handed.

After lunch the leaden kingdom of the siesta unfolded. It was then when time became stagnant and the relentless stifling heat consumed your will. With prongs of fire the sun lashed the land marked out by olive trees, a vast green and ochre area gently rolling into the dust-swept distance, of air without air, of blinding light. The tongue of heat scorched the flat white roofs, the broken windows of the oil mill, the church bell tower, the still lime trees of Nueva Square in front of the club, the whitewashed side streets of old baroque splendour and the counterpoint of the cicadas lancing the silence with wire cutter snaps. The smell of pressed olives impregnated the air. The tenement house on Alpechín Street slept with rhythmic breathing. Juana, lying on the straw mattress, heard the muffled crying of her father climbing up to the pigeon loft. Merchán sat on the bulrush chair under the vine, his elbows dug into his thighs, his face sunk into his hands. Nobody except Juana seemed to hear her father's wails, the pain of a shattered adult man, an anguish that the women dare not risk feeling, not even with their fingertips.

'I don't want to work in the fields, I don't want to work in the fields, I don't want to work in the fields...'

The fields meant hunger. The day labourers broke their bodies harvesting tobacco and reaping; advancing through paddy fields with water up to their ankles; scratching their hands on the jagged corollas of cotton; grape picking, at the end of September; olives, with the first of the cold weather. Sleeping under the shelter of the stars and walking from village to village with sore feet. Identical faces carved by misery crowding together in village main squares, waiting for their daily wages under the rumour of a dry storm. Men with the same weight on their weakened shoulders, without complaint, fallen, trained to understand, in collarless shirts and hemp rope-soled sandals that fell apart on the muddy paths when the gang hurriedly returned as the December rains threatened to fall on the olive groves owned by others. In Nueva Square, Julián Ortega, the foreman of Dueña Alta, pointed to those chosen with his riding whip without dismounting his mare. Julián Ortega never picked Merchán: he did not even look him in the eye. After the selection had been made, the foreman lashed at his horse's dappled flank and returned to the country estate through the blue shadows of a still intact dawn.

'I don't want to work in the fields, I don't want to work in the fields, I don't want to work in the fields... The fields are for wolves.'

41

Merchán hated farm work since childhood. When the flu epidemic took his mother, his father got him a job working with a swineherd at the manor house of a country estate owner from Malaga who lived between Madrid and Seville. The young Merchán pulled skin off the chilblains of his ears as he tricked hunger watching the pigs chew carob beans. Bitter carob beans, fought over by elbowing with the animals. The miracle of satisfying his stomach.

'Take care, pigs have got filthy tempers. I saw one pull the arm off a kid like you. In one bite. Like this, crack!'

One late night in February, a pig escaped and the foreman deducted it completely from his daily ration of salt pork. One day after another, after another, after another and then yet another: imagined cuts made into a pig's dewlap, into the nape of its neck, the pig's ear, into the jaw, while the lips of the others glittered with fat shine. At night the young Merchán wetted himself in bed from pure loneliness and from panicking at the howls of the old greyhounds that prowled around loose until, at last, when dawn broke, he could leave the stable and shake the blades of straw off his rags. He would move close to the kitchen fire to warm himself where, with his stench of reheated urine, the day labourers avoided him, holding their noses. Curro Merchán went to rescue him from the manor house drunk on manzanilla and smelling of a poor woman.

'Son, it's just that when I sing well my mouth tastes of blood. I lose my head.'

The young Merchán then learnt the secret of song at brothels and parties, from bar to bar, from fair to fair, from boarding house to boarding house, from where they would escape in the early hours of the morning through the back windows because they did not have the money to pay the bill.

'The young masters like good old flamenco.'

Often his father was hired for the binges organised at Gavilana's brothel. Curro Merchán awaited his turn to sing in an adjoining room with his son, with his wide-brimmed hat between his knees. He coughed the type of cough he wished he did not and finished off the drink to warm his voice.

'The most difficult style is the *soleá* for singing. The mother of all songs. A mixed tempo of twelve beats. Like this, listen: one two *three,* four five *six,* seven *eight,* nine *ten,* one *two –* his hands, shaking from wine, tapped the table top.

The young Merchán dozed between the corridor and the broom cupboard, curled up in a dark crimson velvet armchair. At Gavilana's brothel there were mirrors and an incomprehensible coming and going of water, linen towels and washbasins. It was then when Chachachica met Curro Merchán and his son. Then she still had black hair and a pure heart; and was never to separate herself from the child.

'What a poor little thing... It's your living portrait!'

'And he's inherited my voice, he's inherited my voice. Even though I didn't want him to... In art you go through many hardships.'

Gavilana's protégées gave the young Merchán sweets – honey-coated doughnuts, cream-filled fritters during the clientless tedium of Lent, sugar powdered cream sponge cake served on a porcelain plate with a spoon – and they taught him to roll cigarettes.

'Hold the smoke in your lungs and say: three black rooks. Then breathe out. Phoooooo.'

Nights of song and wine. The young masters were tall and had mouths full of teeth. They had not lost a single one;

43

matching white pairs of teeth. They talked, always talked. Sometimes they laughed.

'What are you saying, my good man... How am I not going to agree to land reform, Don José Joaquín? With the acres I've got and those that I'm due, well, figure it out...'

It was in the early hours of the morning, and it was winter; they had just proclaimed the Republic. Leaving Gavilana's place, Curro Merchán was talking loudly and brandishing a fistful of notes. Death, swift and astute, was awaiting him. The man who killed him had one arm thinner than the other.

That time the binge at the brothel, paid for by the big landowners who spent their time on their arable lands in Seville, on their hunting grounds and doing business in Madrid, ended at dawn, soaked in wine and the racket of broken bottles. Chachachica – at that time only the young Merchán called her that – took care of cleaning the rooms at the brothel, washing the sets of matching bed linen and towels, taking washbasins when the bells rang in the bedrooms and doing the shopping and cooking. The woman who ran the brothel was called Teresa Almenara, but she was known as Gavilana, the sparrowhawk, because of the vehemence with which she defended the brothel's interests; she called herself a widow. Gavilana's nieces woke up around midday and, still dishevelled in their nighties, helped Chachachica fold iron damp bed sheets.

'What grub are we having today?'

'Fried bird nests. With what your boss gives me for shopping, what do you want me to come up with?'

Gavilana calculated how much she expected to pocket that party night, and the amount filled her with so much generosity that she gave a pair of silk stockings – smugglers transported them on the back of mules from the borderlands of Gibraltar – to each of her protégées, whom she had taught how to discreetly show off their thighs across the worn velvet of the large armchairs.

'Girls, nerve frightens men... Whores yes, but not so they can tell. Important people are coming tonight and I want all Seville to know what class my nieces have got. The rest of them don't even come close to you at all; get it into your heads.'

The brothel smelt of ammonia and cheap tobacco despite Gavilana making the girls air the rooms when the house awaited the arrival of wealthy clients.

'Doña Teresa, you've had us with the windows wide open since first coffee; if our private parts freeze, your business will be ruined and then see what you'll do. We're shrinking.'

'Listen, my little delicate one: in this house what they want are women, and not trade unionists or ailing nuns. If you're cold, get dressed and move your bum over to the salamander.'

The binge ended at the break of day. One of the clientele's stomach, bad from amontillado and olives, exploded over the platter of ham, a blunder the rest greeted with laughter, thigh slapping or disgusted expressions. Chachachica cleaned up the vomit with a hessian floor cloth, with the acidity of her own nausea and the looks that egged her on like a fleshless shadow, too slow. Gavilana sprayed the lounge with false laughs and eau de cologne.

'That's enough, it now smells of lemon. It was nothing and the party goes on. Right away I'll get you a cup of pennyroyal tea, Don Emilio. Or would you prefer some broth to liven you up? I'll filter the grease out of it through a cotton gauze and you'll see how good it'll make you feel.'

Behind the boss's back, Chachachica washed the slices of

ham in an earthenware bowl with a lot of soap and water;
she rinsed them, dried them with a clean linen cloth and hid
them in a sack. The young Merchán was asleep in a wobbly
armchair, hidden from the visitors in the broom cupboard.

'How disgusting; you're turning my stomach.'

'Well go back out there, love, you haven't missed anything
here in the kitchen... The ham is for my Curro, for the boy,
who's growing, and for me too, because tomorrow I won't
remember where it came from.'

That early morning when death came looking for him,
Curro Merchán sang cherishing the promise of the seventy-
five pesetas Gavilana had given her word to. The masters
wanted a big party and among those who rhythmically
clapped along with the songs was an individual he had never
seen before in his life; Curro Merchán thought Gavilana had
hired him without telling anyone.

'Heredia, and that one, who's he? The one clapping, sitting
next to Perrachica... He's got one arm thinner than the other,
have you noticed? He looks crippled, but he's not bad at
keeping time with me.'

'He's called Rafael and he's a blacksmith. They say the
furnace ate the flesh off his arm.'

The binge ended drowned in alcohol and a pool of blood.

'Give me mine?'

'And you, where did you spring from?'

'I was hired the same as you; you to sing and me to keep
time. And to each his own.'

'Well reach an agreement with Gavilana.'

'I'm telling you to give me what I'm owed. And don't make
my blood boil; I know how I can get... People say I get nasty
all of a sudden.'

46

'I've never seen you before in my life. Who are you?'

'I'm a member of the Carmona family, the blacksmiths. I don't want to talk to you; give me what I'm owed and that's that. I know they call you Curro Halfshit and I know where to find you.'

'I don't even owe you a good day, you bastard. I was allowed to sing, nobody asked you to butt in. If you agreed anything with Gavilana, settle it with her.'

The dullness of dawn threw glints of light like salt onto the blades of the sheep shears pulled out of the blacksmith's belt. Fate tinted the fast twist of his wrist violet, blood gushed out and filled the zigzags of the gaps in the paving stones, and clumsy hands tried in vain to stop the throb of intestines. Protected in the hallway, the young Merchán saw Chachachica kiss his waxed dead lips and heard glass-like splashing coming from the cistern, where the man with a useless arm washed his hands and cleaned the sheep shears before escaping into the shadows of the night.

'I don't want to work in the fields, I don't want to work in the fields, I don't want to work in the fields... The fields are for wolves.'

At siesta time Juana heard the muffled crying of her father among the patio hydrangeas. Nobody in the tenement house paid any attention to Merchán's suffering, except Juana, given in to idleness, to the softness of her body that refused to move stiffened in the white heat, in the impossibility of getting close to her father, of caressing him, of trying to understand his silences. What could she talk to her father about? Where were the certainties, where were the strong, secure arms that hugged and invited you to rest in them? The impossibility of talking to her father.

'The end of the war caught me in Almadén, in the province of Ciudad Real. We withdrew by train to the city of Seville, Armas Square Station. We were stuck in the wagons for four days.'

The blue Moors tattooed on his forearms performed a belly dance, trying to distract the kids from the whiplashes of an empty stomach.

'In the war the Moors wore baggy trousers the colour of chickpeas tied around the back of their knees and had willies so long they rolled them into their belts.'

'Merchán, you have no shame nor have you ever known it! How can you say such a thing to the girls?'

Juana observed her father with huge eyes, he was holding Isabel in his arms. Very thin, like a green cigar, with spider legs, helpless, flirtatious, sick with pleurisy. Juana's father remembered all the stations passed in the withdrawal, from Almadén, in the province of Ciudad Real, to the city of Seville.

'Come on my girl, try to sleep. If you learn them all, I'll buy you an egg and lupin seeds and hawthorn berries and roasted quince jelly. Get well. Let's see now, repeat after me: Almadenejos, Los Pedroches, Belalcázar, Cabeza de Buey, Almorchón junction, Zújar, La Granjuela.'

The liturgy of names tricked illness and the pangs of hunger.

Peñarroya (muddy rain falling on burnt fields).

Bélmez junction (women in black at the station).

Cerro Murriano ('They say we've won the war, Merchán').

Cordoba ('Victory? What victory? Whose?').

Los Rosales ('I became a fascist for a plate of whiting. But in the trenches I only ever fired into the air!').

In the heat of the siesta Chachachica, also given in to thought-lessness, sat on the kitchen bench. She slept very little; only keeping her eyes closed for half an hour – her pulse throbbed under her eyelids – was enough rest for her tiny body used to exertion. In her misty drowsiness the voices of the dead mingled with her in a dance of flashes briefly returning from the past. 'Captain Díaz Criado, remember: you're to die like a dog.'

The end of July in thirty-six. The young Merchán's absence spurs the night on with the buzzing of a bumblebee. It is impossible to keep a young man on a short leash when he has recently turned seventeen, without a trade or money in his pocket and with hunger built up in his memory. Manuel has not returned yet and it is beginning to get light; in the room there is no clock. Chachachica crosses herself and lights two tea lights – one for her mother's soul; the other for her disembowelled love – so that the wandering dead watch over the young man. Someone bangs on the door.

'Where have you been, you scoundrel?'

'I got held up with Laureano the Bottle, with Juan, Tomasa's boy, and with some of their friends.'

Merchán speaks with his mouth full. He gobbles down cold chickpeas from the cooking pot.

'You're stinking of wine... I asked where you've been and not who with.'

'Well if you know who I was with, why do you need to ask more? We went to the Dueña Alta manor house.'

Merchán dips a crust of bread into the bottom of the pot. He eats standing up and hungrily.

'Your eyes are full of fright... What have you done? And the sack? What have you got in the sack?'

'Open it and take a look.'

'Holy Christ of Paño! What do we two want with a silver

49

candelabra? Tell me, what for? What have you done? You're looking to get us into trouble, Manuel.'

'They must have told the Civil Guard by now.'

The boys drank brandy to give them Dutch courage. On the walls of the wrought-iron gate, Laureano – the only one of the gang who could write – scratched clumsy letters with a pole: 'Less Holy Week; we want bread and work'. They set the stables at Dueña Alta alight with paraffin. The horses neighed in pain and, tied to their feeding troughs, breathed the stench of their own burnt skin into their nostrils. The manor house foreman, dressed in long johns, blocked their way with a shotgun. His arms were shaking and the weapon went off, hitting Juan in the thigh. The gush of blood and the screams frightened Bottle; he knocked the foreman down with a stone and, when he had him on the ground, stuck a pitch-fork for winnowing straw between his ribs.

'Bastard, fascist. You're going straight to hell.'

They tore his long johns off and left him to die on the pipeclay ground, death rattling like a fish. Flames joined the delirious orgy of destruction. Tomasa's Juan fled through the low olive trees leaving a trail of blood behind him.

Manuel Merchán had to spend twenty days and nights hidden in the same den he shared with Chachachica at Puebla de Acebuche's school in exchange for her sweeping the classrooms, refilling the ink pots and doing the washing and making lunch for the school master, Don Agustín. Chachachica and Manuel slept in the same bed. Twenty days and twenty nights with the fear of a hangman's noose around his neck and with his torso naked. Merchán only had one shirt, coloured red. The piece of clothing, soaked in bleach to fade it, came out of the earthenware bowl in shreds.

'Chacha, Manuel can have this, it's hardly worth you sewing it. Just look at it: it's older than me and I hardly ever wear it... And tell the boy to be on his guard, bad times are on their way.'

The school master's shirt rolled up to his elbows and tucked into his trousers. Manuel always dressed in dead men's clothes.

It was a Saturday, midday, a burning July Saturday, when a neighbour's voice broke the false calmness. The man's shouts rebounded off the silence and the whitewashed walls. A rattle of Persian blinds and heads looking out of opened windows.

'The Foreign Legion in Morocco has mutinied! The Foreign Legion in Morocco has mutinied!'

The city surrendered at the feet of General Gonzalo Queipo de Llano. Triana and the *Sevillian Moscow* neighbourhoods were gutted, brick by brick, to annihilate the 'Marxist swine'. The horror took hardly a week to reach the countryside.

'They say there's been a massacre in Morón, they've hanged the day labourers that had occupied the marquis's estate in the bell tower square. They've hanged them from their necks with butcher's hooks, and nobody dares bury them. The dead dance from the avenue's acacias.'

Paths and plots of land littered with corpses rotting in the sun. Fear gathered around the only radio in the neighbourhood at eight in the evening when Unión Radio Seville broadcast the general's speeches.

'Silence, for fuck's sake; there's no way to hear.'

'I'll remind everyone that, for every honourable person that dies, I'll have at least ten shot, and there are villages where we have exceeded this number. There can be no hope for leaders saving themselves by resorting to escape, for I'll bring them out from under the earth if need be.'

They came late at night.

'We've come for Manuel Merchán.'

'At your service.'

'We've got orders for your arrest.'

'Where are you taking him? For the Christ of Paño's sake, where, where? For whatever else you want, tell me where.'

5

Since her arrival in Barcelona, Sunday evenings are all the same, walking up the Rambla, walking down the Rambla, after meeting up in Cataluña Square with Isabel, her father and her father's friends: two men from Écija, a monumental mason from the El Perchel quarter of Malaga and a Cordovan, Lucas Naranjo, who Merchán met on the scaffolds. The same route repeated every Sunday evening, walking up and down, from the square to the statue of Christopher Columbus, from the motor launches at the port to the Canaletas fountain.

'If you can last out a year in Catalonia, look this is what I say, only one year, even though it's hard. Wouldn't you like to return back to the south? I give you my word. No one misses dried bread. You've got to remember what I'm telling you.'

Juana's ears are still ringing from the words of a young boy who got on the train in Alcázar de San Juan. His onion eyelids flooded with tears. With the rattle of the moving train, a flowerpot of basil, giddy in the net rack above, sprinkled earth over his dozing temples. An endless journey. The sight of the sea swallowing the mandarin sun on the horizon. The sea that now does not move her.

'Chacha, what's the sea like?'

'Salty and never ending. It's like the sky, but it's below.'

Chachachica's last words on the platform to the two teenage heads sticking out of the window.

'Girls, take care. And the scrap iron basket, don't let anyone touch it.'

When Juana and Isabel got off the train at Francia Station, their father, who had promised to pick them up, was not there. Rain poured down onto the two girls, onto the big city and the unknown break of day, enormous in its greyness, and sad. Neither of the two sisters dared open their mouths: the taxi driver had to put on his glasses to read the sender's address torn off a letter: Conde de Asalto Street, number seventeen, first floor, second door. Their hair and the suitcase with cinnamon-coloured edgings dripped; water from the downpour had soaked Juana's toe-holed kitten-heeled shoes. The landlady came to open the door with a steaming cup in her hand and shouted out for their father, who came to the threshold in a vest, still wearing his pyjama trousers – short, irredeemably short – and with soap sticking onto the flares of his nostrils.

'But weren't you due at eight? I was shaving before leaving to meet you...'

The first night of exhausted sublet-housed bodies, in a place where they could not use the kitchen. The crumbs of a dried sandwich sketched drawings on the oilcloth. The landlady, Doña Victoria, brought two foam-rubber mats rolled in the night dew of the balcony; the men helped her to move the pine table and the chairs into the corner. Juana and Isabel slept in the dining room, next to the snoring and breath of the other tenant.

'Is it true, señora, that at the market they give information about places that need girls to serve?'

Identical Sundays, walking up the Rambla, walking down the Rambla. Juana and Isabel walk arm in arm this evening, separated from the group of men shouting a few metres behind. The black lines around Juana's eyelids drawn with a scalpel steady hand and borrowed colours.

'On Wednesday I started work at the house on San Gervasio. Two children, a grandmother and tons of ironing. And, on top of that, the lady wants starch. Her husband is an engineer, and yesterday he took me shopping in his three-wheeler that stopped every five minutes in the middle of the road. You should have seen me pushing that piece of junk in these high-heels...'

A flirtatious remark comes from behind them on the corner of Hospital Street.

'Now that's what I call meat, and not the kind my mother tosses into the pot!'

'Shut it, animal, they're the type that don't have hot dinners... A lot of rouge, but even their armpits smell of bleach. Can't you see? They've brought the whole family following on behind. Look at them: *charnegos* – dirty southerners – go everywhere together, like ants.'

A dignified clicking of heels on the cobble stones.

'Why are you pinching me? I'll have a bruise, you brute!'

'So that you don't turn and answer them back, Isabel, I know you...'

Their father's friend from El Perchel suggests having a drink. The group enters a dismal looking bar in the fifth district with the floor carpeted with sawdust, snail shells, spit and the whiskers of boiled prawns.

'A bottle of Mirinda fizzy orange and two glasses for the girls.'

A bottle of light red wine and large olives dressed with fennel and oregano for the men. Although he cannot write, the Cordovan wears the silver arrow of a Parker fountain pen sticking out of his jacket pocket.

'Lucas, what're you going to write for us today, son?'

'Don't pester me, Merchán, don't pester me, you're such a big piss-taker'

'What a bad temper you've got, Cordovan.'

Juana took short sips of her soft drink – her bag resting on her kitchen maid's knees – and looked out of the corner of her eye at her sister Isabel, both sitting at the table with the reserve of two sparrows on an empty washing line. Broken glasses of conversation cracked under foot like snail shells.

'Merchán, how many points do you say you've got on your pay?'

'With seven children and as a widower, you count it... nineteen. When they find out how much they've got to pay me, foremen don't want me on the site. I've got to trick them to take me on, and then see if they sack me or not.'

'They pay my points the last Saturday of the month.'

'Can you believe what that nasty piece of work said to me: "Andalusians are lazy". I had to bite my tongue. But I was quick to answer back: "Well, don't get like that; one chickpea doesn't make a stew".'

56

'Andrés, my sister Reyes's eldest, has got a job at the Mono factory.'

'Mono anisette, the cocky one's drink from Badalona!'

'Germany is the place to go; there you can earn bucketfuls.'

'Germany or Belgium. My brother-in-law insists on calling his son Baudouin, like the king. Baudouin, can you imagine it?'

'They looked at the teeth of a guy from my home town as if he was a horse and they drew a syringe full of blood from him, this much. He told me that once he walked into a restaurant with a friend and when the owner realised they were Spanish he told them to please don't take the forks away with them.'

'Guv, have a tapa of snails on me.'

'Do you remember the hardships of forty-five?'

'Jesus, how am I to forget! The things you say...'

'Right now wouldn't you eat some Utrera macaroons? And some dressed eggs? And a bowl of gazpacho?'

'Like the flamenco singer Marchena, there's no one; with Tómas Pavón's permission, of course.'

'The most difficult style is the *soleá* for singing, my father used to say, who sang like an angel. The poor wretch didn't have any luck. He was killed in front of my eyes.'

'Guv, have a glass of you-know-what on me.'

Drinks of you-know-what when there was little money in their pockets: wine from the washing bowl where the leftover drops from all the glasses in the bar ended up.

'Merchán, sing something, it's like a wake in here.'

He clears his throat and begins with *bulerías*.

'Over the Lújar mountains / they're coming down / the most valiant band of smugglers. / And in front is coming, / and in front is coming, / boss Carmelo who is their leader, / who is their leader.'

Time is kept with empty palms and on the sticky table top. Juana looks at her sister: the squared neckline enhances her bust; white suits Isabel. She has not seen the dress before: the lady on San Gervasio must have given it to her.

'It's two in the morning, / it's two in the morning. / On cotton clouds / the moon makes its bed, / on cotton clouds / the little moon makes its bed.'

The same song repeated all evening. The same route perpetuated every Sunday.

'Jesus, Merchán, don't you know another?'

Sunday evening falls imprisoned in a violet cellophane shell. Juana returns to Salud Monterde's flat, walking down the Rambla towards the sea through a green tunnel woven by the recently opened banana tree crowns. Summer is anticipated in the salt dragged in by the damp breeze and in the doorways, where couples rush furtive kisses before night and the grey omen of Monday fall. Brilliantined hair, tightly knotted ties, little gypsy women, card-sharps, soldiers using up passes and an obstinate sheen of silence over the city's flat-roofed houses. In taverns the sneak thieves impatiently long for the connivance of darkness; prostitutes and lottery sellers wait between yawns for the first and the last of their clients.

Juana's feet walk slowly, prolonging the barely quarter of an hour left until nine o'clock. The two clocks will chime in unison in the flat on Carmen Street, on the corner of San Lázaro, suffocated in the half-light by vinegar and Chesterfield butts. The evening is agony. Her small feet, her pencil skirt, her low-cut white blouse, her young untouched breasts. Juana advances slowly, not wanting to arrive. Perhaps the Monterdes are not at home. The lady and her two daughters also work on rest days; there are always people with money who can go out and enjoy themselves on Sunday nights. Salud Monterde and her daughters only rest on Mondays, when there is no performance at the Liceo or at the Theatre Principal and the bars they go to are closed: Boadas, Tabú, Villa Rosa, Moka, Brindis, Montecarlo, Rigat, El Charco de la Pava... Juana knows these names from interwoven threads of dialogue over dinner, when she is taking dirty plates from the dining room to the kitchen sink. Juana knows what the Monterdes do: they sell jewellery. At dusk they go down to the street elegantly dressed with their shoulder bags worn across their chests, inside of which are jewels in pieces of black felt; what they call 'blankets'. Juana has seen them wrap valuable pieces with ecstasy and with porcelain carefulness. Señora Monterde – her black hair taut over her temples and collected in a high ponytail – presses her bag against her bloated belly when she walks down the stairs holding onto the handrail, raised up in blue varicose veins and high-heeled shoes. Is it stolen jewellery? Juana turns right into Carmen Street. On one side, Belén church; in front, the jeweller's. The uneasiness of arriving on the corner of San Lázaro.

The Monterdes are not at home. They have left their dinner plates – reheated paella leftovers – submerged in the sink; grains of rice float on the surface of the murky water. Juana savours the pleasure of going to bed without having to greet them. Señorita Mercedes is a crook. Last night it was way after ten when she left with her sister Montserrat. Both wore their bags across their chests and they seemed nervous.

'Have you kept the emerald safe? Don't let your attention wonder, Montse.'

'They'll have to touch my tits up to take it off me.'

59

Señorita Mercedes came home when it was already morning. She arrived haggard, without her keys and accompanied by a man a lot older than herself, fat, with his eyes swollen from alcohol and a late night. When Mercedes knocked on the door Señora Monterde and her youngest daughter were still asleep.

'Good morning, señorita.'

'Good morning, Juana. Make me a cup of coffee, I've got a slight temperature. Do you want anything, Feliu?'

Juana knew then that he was the man who had lunch on Sundays at the Monterdes' flat.

'No, coffee no. Perhaps a little Vichy... Is there any Vichy, girl?'

Señorita Mercedes brought a paper cone of flour fritters swelling with oil and *La Vanguardia* newspaper. The man accompanying her walked through the corridor – he must have been there before – he untied his bicoloured shoes and collapsed onto the sofa with his velvet jacket undone and his blue socks rolled down over his ankles. Juana made some coffee and a camomile tea for Señor Feliu. She took the tea and coffee sets to the dining room table and, coming and going, heard threads of conversation.

'How much did you say you got out of him in the end?'

'Twenty thousand pesetas.'

'That's not bad, my little Mercedes, that's not bad. Times being as they are...'

'The American was no fool.'

'Yes, I figured that.'

Feliu took off his socks and sniffed them. He lay down again on the sofa. He said:

'And me, how much are you going to give me?'

Mercedes poured three teaspoons of sugar in her cup. She took her time in answering him.

'What we agreed.'

'Ten percent? That's not much, Merche. And on agreeing, talking about agreeing, we didn't agree anything. I did all the preliminary work and, also, I had to wait almost two hours for you while you took the American up to the room. Merche...'

'What?'

'Did you sleep with him, you little whore?'

'You're a pig, Feliu, a dirty old man. You make me sick.'

'And you're drunk.'

Feliu fell asleep on the sofa. Señorita Mercedes did not even touch the flour fritters. She yawned, softly sang and sometimes talked to herself as if there were nobody else in the dining room.

'*Tu vuo' fa l'americano, mericano, mericano... Ma si' nato in Italia...* Oh, I'm so tired. Even my eyelashes hurt.'

'Go to bed for a while until midday.'

'What are you making for lunch today?'

'Your mother told me to measure out the rice and water and to leave the fried onion, garlic and tomato base ready for the paella. Señor Feliu is staying for lunch, isn't he?'

'My mother's got a lot of imagination: every Sunday, rice, tedium... And it remains to be seen whether this ball of fat will be capable of getting his bum off the sofa; his hangover will last until Tuesday, at least. You've got the afternoon off, haven't you?'

'Yes señorita, like every Sunday. Until nine.'

'And what will you do?'

'Nothing. I'll go out for a walk with my sister and my father.'

'Haven't you got a boyfriend yet?'

'No señorita.'

'You're very pretty; you'll soon have one. Are you still a virgin?'

'Yes...'

'And tell me, do you touch yourself there below?'

A drunkard's laugh. Señorita Mercedes went to bed in her clothes; she only took off her high-heels and seamed stockings, leaving them fainted over the back of a dining room chair.

Juana repeats Sunday's nightly ritual. She takes her make-up off with cold cream, she smears her damaged hands with olive oil, turns the gas off and recounts the money she keeps in the crocheted bag, inside the suitcase with cinnamon-coloured edgings. Her father told her this evening that he is thinking about renting a flat with his Cordovan friend.

'We have to do all that we can to save, Juana. When we bring the kids from the village we can't continue in a sublet. What landlady will have us with so many children? And the Cordovan is an uncomplicated man; also they're only two, him and his wife, because their only son is doing military service in Africa.'

Save, save, save.

'Do you touch yourself there below?'

Stolen jewels. Crooks. Who cares?

Sunday languishes in the hallucinating gargoyles of the Gothic quarter and in Liberto Pech's windows. The Persian blinds are usually drawn even during the day in this humble flat on Baños Nuevos Street because Liberto Pech hates both natural light and what is happening beyond the rust of his balconies: the street stinks of death and damp rubble, and in it nothing ever happens. Nothing. It has been more than ten years since the world and its illusions stopped interesting him. Liberto does not leave his flat much; just enough to go shopping and refill the demijohn of Gandesa wine at the wine cellar in front and, once a week, to go to his compulsory appointment at the Vía Layetana police station. He only finds comfort in work and in the coming of Sunday, for the football and because he has a shave. It is the only day of the week when he shaves, unscrewing the jar of Floïd massage cream with a palace ceremonialism – one of the few whims he permits himself – and taking his time slapping his face; sometimes he chafes his face from the blows. Some neighbours avoid him as unsociable, even though they recognise in a whisper that he is one of the best craftsmen in the city and the most honest with his prices for repairs. The watchmaker frowns and shows his teeth on purpose because there is a certain satisfaction from the whispers he senses from behind his back. Natural light disturbs him: for work he only needs his office lamp and a pair of watery grey-blue eyes he inherited from his father. On insomniac nights he takes advantage of sleeplessness to work on job orders. He washes his hands working the soap up to his elbows, he sits on his swivel chair, switches on the adjustable table-lamp and adjusts the eyeshade across his forehead. All his attention and his sense for staying alive is then concentrated in the halo of light perforating the glittering table. Night magnifies the silence and the agile dance of his nicotine-stained fingers.

The cat is miaowing from hunger and boredom at the foot of the bed. Liberto Pech has fallen asleep again in his underpants on top of the blanket and the sheet turnover, with the leather harness that holds his wooden leg fastened to the stump of his knee.

Disorientated in the half-light of the room, he opens his

eyelids soaked in wine. It angers him not knowing what time it is. He does not use a watch; when he finishes a repair he waits for the radio news to adjust the mechanism's hands. He has not had a watch since he was in prison and time stopped moving: the slow drone of the day and its routine imposed itself. Liberto hates falling asleep at unearthly hours because that is when the sharpened edges of nightmares hurt most. His fidgety eyes probe the darkness while the watchmaker tries to capture the death throes of a dream in which he still has two legs, two complete legs – bones, blood, flesh, muscle and skin – holding up a young and athletic body. In the unreal drowsiness, his Apollonian figure advances in a straight line without wavering off course: walking through walls, vegetable gardens, fallow lands, levelled grounds, marshes, stone gullies, the dining rooms of anonymous families, railway gauges, barracks, ports abandoned even by saltpetre, football pitches, churches full of people having mass, cemeteries with ordered graves and crosses, white deserts whose brilliance hurts his eyes. Walking always in a straight line, without moving off course, on two strong legs, of flesh and blood, forward, going nowhere. In the dream his robust body moves forward and he does not look back.

At the concentration camp, on the beach of Argelès-sur-Mer, the republican refugees told their dreams of the night before to dissipate the tedium and to try to open a tiny breach towards light in the absurdity of waiting. Alfredo Munárriz had tortured dreams.

'Last night I dreamt again about the cutthroat razor. A sharpened barber's razor. This time I was in a white-walled room, windowless, with other people, and all of us were dressed in white clothes. It seemed to be a hospital. I looked down to the floor and found the barber's razor with the blade open. My mouth dribbled on seeing it. I bent down, picked it up and instinctively I sliced my fingers off; it didn't hurt and my fingers fell softly onto the lino, one after another, as if made of butter. Then I cut open my face but didn't bleed. Can you imagine it? What a thing... Why are you looking at me like that, Pech? Don't you dream?'

'I've dreamt a fuck of a lot, Munárriz, this fucker has dreamt. Why don't you lot take up another hobby? What vicious dreams you have.'

On the fields of Roussillon the diabolical north wind persisted in driving men crazy; you had to be made of iron or armour-plated with luck to not lose your head. Alfredo went mad because of that perpetual wind that raised sand and blinded the corners of your eyes with howls of hinges and chains and the flapping of torn clothes between the grey sky and the frozen ashes of the sea.

'Well, Munárriz, do you like the room with a view of the sea we've reserved for you? Comrades, welcome to the hotel of a thousand and one nights. *Vive la France!*'

The Spanish refugees slept out in the open. The wind shrieked and dragged dirt and sand even under the hospital tents. The men buried their feet in the sand away from the shore line; trying to keep warm.

'The wind, it's this fucking wind... The north wind drills into your brain, it drives you crazy. Have you noticed that Munárriz talks to himself?'

Argelès-sur-Mer: a wind and barbed wire enclosure. The refugees cradled their desperation in the sound of the metallic froth coming to die on the beach. School teachers, doctors, farm labourers, soldiers, bakers, lawyers, civil servants: the ragged and humiliated horde, clothed in overcoats and corduroy jackets, walking in circles on the sieged sand. It was Alfredo Munárriz, a Negrín communist, teacher and short-sighted, who devised a system for avoiding fights during the sharing out of bread.

'Write down the names of everyone from each hut onto a list.'

'But there aren't any huts yet, Munárriz, we're still putting them up.'

'Well write down all the names of the people who are working on each hut.'

Munárriz shared out the dried bread with exquisite delicacy. He had broken his glasses and the left lens multiplied the slices into polyhedrons.

'Turn round and call out a name on the list, at random, onto where your eyes fall. And put a cross next to it.'

'Soteras.'

'Here!'

'You've got this, take it!'

'Fuck, not even if you had done it on purpose...'

'I already had the piece in my hand before he called your name... So tough on you, Soteras. Tomorrow you'll get a bigger piece; a raffle is a raffle.'

Munárriz took refuge in reading the same book by Verlaine over and over again, until the wind got into his ears and never left again: voices wandered around inside his head and they whispered impossible things to him. Alfredo Munárriz died having deliriums before the Spanish Republicans' Emigration Service could ship him off to Mexico. He went mad.

Pech's feet buried in damp sand tried to discover a trace of fossilised warmth. Pieces of worn paper, read a thousand times, from *Le Midi Socialiste* placed between his chest and his vest to protect him from pneumonia. Exhaustion and shame condensed in the water that slowly dripped off Pech's blond fringe onto his trousers and into the infected wound in his leg. The accumulated rain bombarded the blankets that served as roofs in the improvised shelters. The storm had abated and Soteras helped himself to a spade to shovel the water onto the grey sand. Munárriz said:

'It's stopped raining; I'm leaving.'

He placed his toothbrush and the book by Verlaine in his briefcase, he combed his hair and flapped his corduroy lapels. He said goodbye with a raised clenched fist and started to walk across the damp sand. He went without shoes or socks because he had sold his rubber-soled shoes through the wire fence to a Senegalese guard who wore the same size. With his glasses in four bits, Munárriz advanced towards the sea leaving behind the barbed wire fence, the doorless latrine, the first placed planks for the huts and the invented shacks. The sea engulfed him.

'Comrades, I'm returning to Spain.'

They pulled him out of the water half-drowned and delirious. A few laughs could be heard coming from his fragile body, kicking the frozen air. Liberto Pech will never forget the half-moon twinkle in Munárriz's eyes.

Waves grinded time. On the other side of the Pyrenean gorges, beyond the sad fields of Roussillon, only burnt stones remained. Gusts of freezing wind drilled their temples. A diabolical and grey north wind, tarred cardboard roofs, the grey humiliation of *The Retreat*, circles of pus under the transparent dressing covering Pech's severed knee. A grey wire fenced horizon, grey hate, grey chickpeas boiled in grey seawater on a fire of burning tyres. The Nazis were closing in on Paris.

'I'm talking to you, Liberto. You're always far away.'

'What do you want?'

'Have you read the pamphlets yet? The mobile guard are handing them out in the northern blocks. And they've hung posters from the wire fences behind, where the Algerian cavalry tie their horses, and from the post at the entrance to the latrines. Do you hear me? I'm talking about the circular that the Ministry of Interior has sent to the prefectures. They say they're going to read it out at midday through the loudspeakers.'

'I don't want to know about it, Soteras. I'm not interested. The colonel doctor told me that, sometimes, vitamin deficiency eats away at the optic nerve. I need an eagle's eyesight to work, you know? I can go without my legs, crawling like a snake, but I need eyes; both of them. And my hands too.'

'But, who the hell's thinking about work now? Pay attention, eagle eyes, for what it's worth: "The state of war, on the one hand, and on the other the need to house the evacuated French populations, makes the return of the greatest possible number of Spanish refugees more desirable than ever, and most of all of those elements least likely to add to the French economy with the help of useful work".'

Defeated muscles for the Maginot Line, cork tibias for the coal works in Gransac, congealed blood for tree felling in Les Landes. Liberto Pech was already sliced meat and an undesirable anarchist.

'Do you want me to read it to you again? Have you understood?'

'*Évidemment... La France et sa grandeur une fois encore.*'

68

A pleasant breeze blows this Sunday night, playing with the lowered Persian blinds on Baños Nuevos Street, a timid and sweet air that nevertheless disheartens the watchmaker. Liberto Pech has a dry mouth. It is the wine, the wine, the wine, the bitter poison of Gandesa wine, always the wine. He sits up in bed and with extreme slowness places his left leg and his insensible leg onto the floor tiles. The cat jumps onto the mattress and appreciates the caresses it receives by rubbing its body against the watchmaker's stomach.

'We're hungry, aren't we, Proudhon? Let's go have dinner right now.'

Liberto Pech places the frayed and dirty cushioning of the crutches under his armpits and makes his staggering way through the corridor, where the mosaic floor is warped from the mountains of yellow newspapers, displaced books and years of dust. The cat follows on behind him with its tail erect. The kitchen sink is full of dirty ashtrays and dishes, mostly glasses. The watchmaker searches the shelves for a tin of soused sardines. He picks the cat's bowl up off the floor with an agile and studied manoeuvre; his mutilated body still conserves the remains of dignity.

'Two for you and one for me, so that you know how much I like you. One's enough for me; I'm not much interested in food, you know that.'

The watchmaker pours wine into a dirty glass, sits at the kitchen table and dunks bread into the oil.

'You like sardines, eh you rascal? Eat up, eat up, food is necessary for keeping yourself strong. I've got a headache, Proudhon. How long was I asleep, two hours, three perhaps? Look, I've told you many times, you're not to let me sleep so long... But you don't take any notice as long as you get your way getting tangled up somewhere. You like doing your own thing, like me, without having to give explanations to anyone, nor anyone telling you what to do. And, now, who'll sleep tonight, Proudhon? Well now you know what you've got to do for not waking me on time: you'll have to keep me company while I work. There's only a pocket watch that needs its winder adjusted, and I'm still working on that lovely brooch for Monterde, although tonight we won't be able to work the gold because she still hasn't brought me the copper for melting... That big whore has got us by the balls, Proudhon.'

The watchmaker drinks a mouthful of Gandesa and clicks his tongue against his palate.

'That woman is very clever and knows who she's giving the work to, sure she knows, what a woman! When the bitch kicks the bucket we'll go to her funeral. Yes we'll go, we will. We'll get a taxi, like two gentlemen, to the Montjuïc cemetery with a bunch of carnations; red, for old times. I'll go clean shaven, in a tie and a mourning button on my lapel; you behind, obedient, tied to a cord with your ears drooping and nice and clean. She can't have much left now... How much gold could they have got? X number of bars, X number of emeralds, whatever, we don't know, but a lot of water has flowed under the bridge since then, and as far as I know Monterde hasn't lived on anything else since the war ended. She gets by dealing them, but she can't go to town on it, and so as not to cough up a penny she dribbles better than Kubala.'

The watchmaker lights a cigarette. Draws the smoke deep into his lungs and looks up to the ceiling. His neck aches.

'Perhaps the girl will come to bring us the copper. How nice she is, isn't she, Proudhon? By her accent she must be

Andalusian. Now those are a temperamental lot. Hmm, Andalusians... You didn't see it, brother, but, then, the Andalusian and Murcian riffraff were at the fore of the revolutionary vanguard... Oh, yes! I still remember the day we seized a house on Gracia Avenue, on the corner of Caspe, and they followed on behind with their eyes burning with hate. They knew no fear.'

'But what have you done, you bastard? Per què l'has mort? – Why have you killed him? – Did you know him by any chance? Answer me, did you know who that man was? The poor bugger was crying from pure fear. Ets un porc, un salvatge – You're a pig, a savage... You've killed him in cold blood. I should shoot you in the balls.'

'He looked like the master of my village... He poisoned my father's health. That's why I had to come here.'

A sardine and a crust of bread satisfies his stomach. The watchmaker pours himself another glass of rough wine to flood his senses and memory. He drinks every night, especially on Sunday, until the outline of objects blur and his head weighs heavy on his glass vertebrae. Liberto Pech is used to the hazy dulling of alcohol and to move staggering about his flat. He is even convinced that he could reach his room with his eyes closed and without crutches, hopping on his good leg and with his arms crossed.

'Proudhon, I think I'm drunk. Why have you let me drink again? You're a bad friend.'

One false move in the dark, his crutches bend like reeds. A dull thud, a gash on his forehead, a taste of earth from the blood in his mouth. The cat miaows next to his unconscious body, spread out face down on the cold floor tiles of the hall.

6

In winter the cold sharpened the concentrated stink of brazier on the overcoats hanging in a line off hooks on the far wall. The political geography map hung from a hook above the blackboard, between the Generalissimo's uniform jacket, buttoned up to his Adam's apple, and a cross, and the crooked portrait of José Antonio Primo de Rivera, which had an insect pressed under its glass. The school teacher – in a nun's skirt down to her shinbones, sunken cheeks, her breath smelling of lard and barley water – walked with her shoe heels clicking about in a resigned way on the dais and she unrolled the map with trembling fingers when suddenly she decided to write resounding phrases on the blackboard so that her pupils would perpetuate them in blue blotted spider handwriting. The chalk screeched between her teeth and over the surface of the blackboard.

'Knight, knot and knee are spelt with a K. Knife. Knuckle.'

To Juana the map of the Iberian Peninsula seemed like a

dizzy head, pulled off from the rest of the world, dripping blue snot at the mouth of the Tagus. A big tear in the cloth allowed a glimpse of its hemp innards and suspended the provinces of Salamanca, Avila and Segovia in a limbo of shredded dead flesh.

'In the north Spain borders on the Pyrenean Mountains, the Bay of Biscay and the Atlantic Ocean.'

The girls had to pronounce the word ocean with a stress on the penultimate syllable and in an enthusiastically false accent so as to rhyme the same old song. The Canary Islands withdrew frightened to the bottom end of the rectangle behind a fragile red line. The pointer thickened boredom; Doña Amalia's voice bounced off the ceiling beams and dragged with it the shipwrecks of phantom geography.

'In Africa Spain has the possessions of Rio de Oro, Spanish Guinea, the Annobón Island, Ifni and the Morocco protectorate.'

Against the window light the teacher pulled out chin hairs with a pair of tweezers and with each trophy she allowed herself to lower her gaze onto the lime trees of Nueva Square, in front of the club, while one of her pupils read standing up from a book on the life of the saints and her clumsiness stumbled over deflowered hymens, over young flesh burnt on terrible bonfires and over wobbly breasts severed by sabre slashes. Like Saint Agatha of Catania.

When Juana first started to menstruate she stopped going to school.

'She's already pulled three, she's already pulled three hairs. And, just look at that, she's examining them against the light.'

'Her hands are shaking, do you see it? Doña Amalia likes her booze. That's why she falls asleep.'

73

At the desk in front, hair begins to grow back like a handful of ants on the shaven nape of Andrea Iruela, the carpenter's daughter.

'I'm going to kill her, I'm going to kill her!'

'But, Dolores... Why do you let her run stark naked across the patio in this frost? The angel of God will give you pneumonia.'

'I can't believe I've got lice again!'

On hearing the shouting the neighbours opened windows and doors. Andrea sobbed naked in the middle of the patio, with everyone seeing, with her legs in a zinc washing bowl; her bony knees hugged by cold and shame. Rafael Falcón, the eldest of the barber brothers, gave a sadistically incisive smile leaning his elbows on the upper balcony rail.

'Lousy, lousy!'

Andrea covered the beginnings of her pubic hair with both hands and stared at the ground, at the flowerpot left in pieces during the chase: the white geranium contemplated the sky with its roots in the air, awaiting certain death on a carpet of scattered earth and bits of baked mud. The well water, sharp like a February morning, bit into her calves. Dolores Iruela pulled a pair of impressive scissors out of her apron pouch. Black locks of hair fell onto the flagstones between metallic snaps. Before leaving for the barber's on Agua Alley Rafael Falcón guided his cutthroat razor over Andrea's skull.

'Keep still or I'll make you bleed... How on earth could I charge you, Dolores? I'd never dream of it. If one can lend a hand, you know. That's what neighbours are for.'

Leaning on the workshop doorjamb with an awl in his hand, Setefo – an uncommon bulge under his leather apron –

looked with delectation at the adolescent body with two budding still green medlars.

'Girl, stop bawling... I'm going to get my red Carlist beret that I've got somewhere in the wardrobe for you to wear to school. You'll see how between your mother and me just how lovely we'll make you.'

The cobbler's sarcasm sharpened the smell of petrol rubbed into Andrea's scalp.

'Now you'll see how you won't get nits again, you pig.'

Juana and Isabel waited for her sitting on the church steps, on the corner of Alpechín Street with San Pedro. The air sandpapered Andrea's shaved nape, sitting with her back to them, she did not look at them and could not even open her mouth. Rabid, she began to rub gravel out from the gaps between the slab stones with the soles of her shoes.

'Don't cry Andrea... Your hair will quickly grow back.'

The words came from her mouth without will, with their own life, electrified; Juana wanted to take her friend by the shoulder, hug her, protect her, lock her into an invulnerable cuirass, caress her shiny, insulted skull, kiss her perhaps. But she could only swallow saliva; Juana did not dare, she could not: no one had taught her to walk along the wire of affection. Her mother never caressed, her father only knew how to sing.

'I'm not going home; I don't want to see my mother, I can't see her yet. I hope she suffers, cries and thinks the Salado currents have dragged me off.'

Juana had seen them: they pulled the drowned blue bodies out of the river, the colour of the water stuck to their skins and hair tangled in a mess of slime and weed; the intensity of blue was concentrated on their bellies and in their swelling lips. But it had not rained for years and when the River Salado flowed through the red lands carrying pebbles and silt with it, it deserved more pity than respect.

Juana was convinced that it was she who invoked the drought after months of devastating storms when the boats on the coast of Cadiz and Huelva could not go out to sea to fish. Even so, her father stuck to his routine of getting up every morning at his usual time. He combed his hair without a mirror on the patio, with his head leaning over the hydrangeas, he buttoned his previous day's shirt up to the neck and, sitting on the bulrush chair next to the carpenter's workshop, rerolled in rice paper the cigarette butts Chachachica collected from the club. He closed his eyes at the smell of glue Matías had begun to heat.

'Merchán, you're not going to the market today?'

'The fish haven't arrived.'

'So what are you going to do, son? Patience and card shuffling?'

Juana's father smoked and modulated his voice with broken, inconclusive and clumsy fragments; when he began to cry the sobs rose up as far as the pigeon loft room.

'I don't want to work in the fields, I don't want to work in the fields, I don't want to work in the fields... The fields are for wolves. God damn the day I was born. God damn it for ever. Me, I became a fascist for a plate of whiting, God damn me too.'

In the year of the rains, Juana's father invented impossible businesses, while her mother dozed with the fragility of a perennial pregnancy. Sitting at the kitchen table, Juana, Chachachica and Isabel helped Merchán in silence to overcome the tiredness closing in under his eyelids at each stitch, through a sleepless night sewing cushions for the bullfight made out of newspapers and filled with straw from

76

the market that smelt of ripe melons (it rained ferociously with thunder and lightning over the region and the bullfight had to be suspended). Juana's father also bought a cart full of chrysanthemums which an old and lazy mule carried from the fertile plains of Granada for All Souls' Day (the sky, opened like a canal, flooded the cemetery and no one remembered their dead; the flowers – drowned, withered, their petals torn off – agonised in a corner of the patio next to the cobbler's den). It continued raining all winter: bunches of soft grapes, patiently selected from amongst the rotten soggy ones, for New Year's Eve in forty-eight.

'But, Merchán, son, don't you know that leap years are unlucky? You have to spend them on tip toe, in silence, without festivities. Look who's bought a cart full of grapes...'

Juana's father's crying, crumbling and impotent next to the goldfinch cage, only rang in Juana's ears, who wrote down her conspiracies against the storm on paper used to roll up clams into paper cones, and hid them in the cracks of the pigeon loft.

'Mother, it was me. I've stopped the rain.'

Her mother's fingers left red marks on the skin of her cheeks. Juana was stung more by her dark terrifying stare than by the unexpected slap, the treachery of it.

'Chacha, it's your fault for putting bad ideas into the girls' heads. The last thing we need is you and your prophesies. And leave the dead in peace for once.'

And the rain did not return. Don Ignacio, Puebla de Acebuche's priest, and his bunch of lay sisters – sloes, tiny, sticking together like rosary beads – brought out the Virgin of the Abandoned for a procession so that the sky would take pity on the dry plains marked out by olive trees and on the day labourers, desperate under the lime trees in the square, in front of the club, scrutinising the cruelty of a sky taking pleasure in burning the flesh of olives.

'Chachachica says that drowned people announce storms.'
  'Well it hasn't rained for months.'
  'Your Chacha is nuts... Are you two coming with me?'
  'Where to?'
  'To the cemetery to pick mallows. I'm not going home. I don't want to see my mother.'
  The three girls climbed the stony village hills, leaving behind the large houses abandoned to weeds and nostalgia, the all-enveloping smell of pressed olives and the old dusty corners. They reached the cemetery by way of the streets furthest from the club's awnings and the lazy looks of Nueva Square. On the whitewashed cemetery wall lines in black paint, faded from accumulated sun glare, could still be read:

FRANCO!

FRANCO!

FRANCO!

The mallow buds eased the anxiety of hunger and covered their tongues and palates with a floury fine skin.
  'They taste the same as a block of dried figs.'
  'You've never tasted a block of dried figs in your life.'
  'At home we call them bread rolls.'
  'Chachachica says eating mallows that grow in cemeteries is like swallowing the souls of the dead.'
  'Always going on about your Chacha. She's far gone... They say that when she was born they cut off her fingernails and threw them into the fire, that's why she went mad.'

The three girls chewed the flowers' bitter aftertaste sitting on a marble gravestone darkened from years of being weatherbeaten. The quince-coloured light on the last evening in October blended into the undergrowth that grew among the graves, crosses and the cypress trees' dried cones. The east wind cracked the skin of their lips.

'Chachachica speaks to the dead.'

'People invent lies to distract themselves. They have nothing else to do.'

'Your Chacha's crazy.'

Juana – her father's silences knotted around her neck in a blue scarf – read aloud the inscription of the gravestone they were sitting on.

'Sebastián Maldonado (1875–1936). Your blood lives on in our memory.'

'Doña Amalia says Juana is the best reader of all her pupils.'

'They killed this one during the war.'

'The Maldonados are the masters of the Dueña Alta manor house, aren't they?'

'That's it, play stupid, Juana. Why do you ask? You know the Maldonados' story better than me. Your eyes follow young master Eduardo around at mass, or do you think we don't notice? Well learn once and for all: no Maldonado would even look at you; for being poor and snotty-nosed, though you're as pretty as your Chacha says.'

'You're the one who's snotty-nosed, Andrea. Juana's had her first menstruation; she had it the other day.'

'And you, why don't you shut it, you big fool?'

'The little missy's getting cross because I said she's had her period.'

Juana would have preferred her place to have been among men, on the benches to the right of the presbytery, close to the entrance. And to play with a shabby hat on her lap.

'Put a cloth down there below.'

Serapio, the slow-witted sacristan – invested all his capabilities into sweeping the church steps in the morning and in greeting the lay sisters with congealed saliva on the corner of his mouth – had placed a bronze vase of dahlias, chrysanthemums and autumn flowers at the foot of the main altar for the twelve o'clock mass. The men sat on the benches to the right; in the first row, their collars stiff from starch and their hair combed with brilliantine, men distinguished by the surname Maldonado – masters of the Dueña Alta manor house – followed by the Palacios stock – owners of the La Dehesa country estate – the chemist, the scale fee doctor and the regular patrons of the club, those who talked about the drought and their plant beds, sipped manzanilla with raised little fingers and sucked on king prawn heads with mystic rapture when Juana, Isabel and the carpenter's daughter returned from school. The women sat on the benches to the left with ornamental combs as finishing touches and mantillas embroidered with finest tulle that became transformed into simple headscarves for wiping sweat as poverty pushed them into the back rows. Disinfectant by the ton poleaxed the outpour of old wood that the confessionary and the baroque carvings gave off.

'Come, I'll straighten your hair; how are you going to go out with your hair dripping wet? Don't you come down with pleurisy like your sister Isabel.'

'Are you coming to mass, Chacha?'

'Every Sunday I ask myself the same question.'

Manuel Merchán also never set foot in the church. Juana

sat on the back rows, close to the main door, next to her sister Isabel and Andrea, the three dressed in immaculate rags. Shame and disgust made them feel dirty; Juana was apprehensive of the new dampness in her vagina.

'Mother, I've stained my knickers... I think it's from my belly, only a drop; without me meaning to. I didn't notice.'

'Let's see, show me.'

Her mother examined her from a distance, lying on a fluff mattress, with a child hanging from her exhausted nipple and her hands red from using the skin and bone above her nails for washing. A barely audible voice emerged from her windpipe.

'Now you are a woman, Juana... Come on, go up to the pigeon loft room. In the bottom chest drawer you'll find some rags, put one of them there below. And listen: from now on you're not to go close to boys; playing in the street is over, you hear me?'

In the bottom chest drawer her mother kept pieces of bed sheets and old rags, and her father, stripped of words and memory, a tin box with his military campaign record, an unfired bullet, a watch with its face crushed and various pages from the Bible. The watch hands were stopped at half past four. The pages torn out belonged to the Book of Ecclesiastes.

'Go on, Juana, you read, you don't stumble.'

'For the living know that they shall die, but the dead know not any thing, neither have they any more a reward for the memory of them is forgotten.'

Juana wanted to vomit her fast over the church marble, to desecrate with a translucent slice of bread. She would have preferred to be a man and in one slash cut off the pricking yolks of her tits. To be a man without superfluous wetness and to forget the slippery threads of hemstitching and the school teacher's warnings, changing wine-and-lard-smelling breath for the dew sprinkled at daybreak over the open countryside, and to leave to earn a day's living and dignity behind the gang of farmhands; camouflaged under the skin of the last man in the line – small and invisible, with her sexual organs hidden behind a darned fly – and tread the narrow paths with the determination of a pair of worn-out boots. To be a man sitting to the right of Don Ignacio and not having to hear her father's sobbing, never again.

A piece of old bed sheet in her vagina. No explication eased her nausea, her shame or the pain that pinched at her burnt sugar areolae. Juana contracted her vagina and her lower abdomen in fear that the closeness of others in the church would give her away. The old women used to say that menstruation attracts lizards.

'*Fratres, agnoscamus peccata nostra, ut apti simus ad sacra misteria celebranda.*'

The Latin phrases dried throats. Juana looked around her; the parishioners, with drooping heads, respected without understanding Don Ignacio's sermon, stuffed into a chasuble glittering with grime and weariness. Nobody understood anything. Nobody understood anything inside or outside of the church. In the back rows and for as far as Juana could see, all, men on one side, women on the other, looked down at the marble floor in fraudulent devotion and breathed the stale perfume of incense and guilt.

'*Confiteor Deo omnipotenti et vobis, fratres, quia peccavi nimis cogitatione, verbo, opere et omissione mea culpa, mea culpa, mea maxima culpa.*'

Guilt, maximum guilt; a dense and understandable sound in Don Ignacio's monologue that melted candle and ear wax.

Juana was just able to peep at Eduardo Maldonado, who always occupied the same pew in the front row, on the bench of the moneyed families. The heir to Dueña Alta had the profile of an Arab prince.

'Get it into your head for once, Juana, you're so poor and snotty-nosed he wouldn't ever look at you.'

Coughs and the stink of fear and cheap cologne linked under the dome. Juana caught a glimpse of Doña Amalia's rigid silhouette, sitting a few rows in front, with Father Molina's missal on her knees.

'When I wash on Sundays to go to mass I close my eyes. You shouldn't cover your breasts in soap, girls. It's a sin to look at a naked body, don't forget.'

'Ideo precor beatam Mariam semper Virginem, omnes angelos et sanctos, et vos fratres, orare pro me ad Dominum Deum nostrum.'

The nausea of incense, stuffiness and red wetness in her vagina. A translucent slice of rye bread irritated her conscience, her unconfessed stomach and the bad thoughts that involuntarily perforated her maternal belly. Juana closed her eyes at the incomprehensible Latin murmuring to forget her mother's bulging paunch, in the same way as Don Ignacio raised the host over the altar and the purple chrysanthemums.

'Fructum terrea et operis manuum hominum, ex quo nobis fiet panis vital.'

The bread is the body of Christ, God is in the bread, God is truth, truth is in the bread. The bread, the body, the wine and the blood of Christ. Don Ignacio sucked the chalice blood dry.

'Benedictus es, Domine, Deus universi, quia de tua largitate acepimus vinum quod tibi offerimus.'

Christ's blood. Blood stinks. First menstruation blood

stinks of ignorance, disgust and shame, and is the same colour as raisins. Eduardo Maldonado looked like a sultan.

'*Fructum vitis et operis manuum hominum, ex quo nobis fiet potus spiritualis.*'

The blood of God is wine. If blood is wine, blood cannot be dirty because men drink wine and do not lose blood through their sexual organs. When Juana had her menstruation she could not then eat lupins on the patio in the sweltering heat of the nights when Dolores Iruela described the sinuous movements of María Félix's hips on the screen at the San Pedro cinema. Once a month Juana could not wash her hair, nor brush against the patio houseleeks, nor go walking alone in the countryside, because lizards feed on women's blood. Menstruation clouded the mercury in mirrors, rotted salt pork and made mares have miscarriages.

'*Juana, iron the clothes that are on the chest... And don't you dare go out onto the patio nor look inside the cooking pot, do you hear me?*'

God is truth. Truth is in bread and blood. God did not know how to lie, and he too loathed anchovy soup

'Your Chacha is crazy. They say she speaks to the dead.'

Mallow fluff persisted in getting stuck in the gaps between their teeth. Rabbit squeaks and the pointed tops of the cypress trees tore the fragile air of dusk and the light – ochre, green and Prussian blue – enclosed the cemetery under a glass bell.

'Juana, do you believe in God?'

'Of course I do, Andrea, the things you say.'

'Are you sure?'

'Of course I am. If Doña Amalia could hear all the outrageous things you say...'

'Juana, tell me... Do you think that if God existed, you'd wear this torn overcoat with its cloth turned inside out? You wear it every winter, since we started school. One year and another and another. Like me with this skirt; just look at it.'

Juana stretched the wizened and ridiculous sleeves of her grey overcoat as far as she could, it hardly covered her upper thighs. Spikes of wind penetrated the cable stitches tensed by the buttons at the height of her breasts and her teenage hips; the armholes bit eagerly into her armpit lymph nodes. Juana thought about God. She imagined him bow-headed, ashamed, sitting at the kitchen table, barefoot like Chacha, wrapped in a white tunic, next to her father who had not gone out to work for yet another day. God was left-handed, like Isabel, and held his spoon in his clumsy hand, away from his cotton body, a shaking hand dropping slops onto the whiteness of his beard. To God, who multiplied himself like the maternal belly, anchovy soup also tasted like camphor balls, but he concealed it; Juana read it in his eyes.

'Little miss lordy doesn't like anchovy soup. But you're fainting from hunger and you've got to swallow it down like everyone else.'

God and Juana exchanged glances when they raised their heads from their bowls. God kept quiet and Juana could not believe the tone of her own voice.

'You're a swine. And your flesh sticks to the roof of my mouth. They say it's a sin to chew your flesh. And that we're to eat no other flesh than your flesh.'

God swallowed without breathing so that the slops of broken fish did not even brush against his palate. He swallowed and kept quiet next to Merchán. Her father rarely sat at the table amongst the gang of women; he usually ate standing up and from the pan. Gazpacho with tomato dregs. Stews of large broad beans with the roughness of their pods. Fibres of transparent cod, very salty. Withered cabbage leaves sautéed in garlic and cumin seeds. Potatoes, always potatoes: boiled potatoes, potatoes with saffron, potatoes boiled with parsley. When he finished eating Merchán would go out onto the patio intoning the monochord and sad rhythm of a flamenco song between his teeth.

'Have you got any of your dead buried here?'

'I'm not sure; Chacha knows that kind of thing. My granddad Curro was disembowelled with a pair of sheep shears and they threw him into a common grave.'

'In the village there are a lot of dead people without gravestones; also in the olive groves. My father told me.'

'Does your father speak?'

'The dead frighten me... Tomorrow is All Saints' Day, and they come out and roam around here. Chachachica says the ghost of El Pernales ties his horse to the cemetery gate when he comes down from the mountain making the rounds in search of food. His horse is called Lightning.'

'Shut up, stupid, you're frightening me.'

'I want to share a secret with both of you; come with me.'

Juana and Isabel followed the carpenter's daughter's hurried pace to the far end wall of the cemetery, where the line of cypress trees became dense. Andrea bent down and searched, feeling her way along the plastered wall, parting the thicket stalks.

'I've found them! Look, down here: they're bullet holes.'

'That's a lie.'

'My father told me, and my father doesn't tell lies. Here

they executed the day labourers during the war, just like my granddad, who was leader of the farmhands. They riddled his stomach with gunshots and then dragged his body way beyond the Dueña Alta manor house boundaries. They left him among the olive trees, covered in earth and stones and with a foot sticking out. Cumin found him, who couldn't stop barking and barking when granddad didn't come home on time. My father told me, and my father doesn't tell lies. They called him Cumin because he was very small and could never keep still.'

'Chachachica says dogs howl when they smell death.'

'Cumin knew it was my granddad's corpse by the foot sticking out.'

'That's only what your father says. Ours never talks.'

'My father says Merchán is a coward.'

'Well your father will soon be eaten by rooks. His hearing's getting ever more finely tuned, just like consumptives, who can hear everything, even mice nibbling. Your father's going to die; the other day I heard Setefo say: "The carpenter won't last until May".'

'And my father says Merchán is a coward.'

Chachachica believed the first of November holiday tormented the wandering of troubled souls if they did not feel that the living tugged on the thread that still kept them joined to their earthly past. Her man's hands, hardened from gleaning in the sown fields and from the frozen water of the well, stiffened on lighting the fragile matches, and it was Juana who had to do it for her on All Saints' Day.

With one slap Chacha pushed aside the unironed rags piled onto the chest and placed in the space she made a rust-eaten tin of tuna fish with water, oil and two tea lights in memory of her mother and grandfather Curro. Juana lit the cotton wicks.

'You've got a princess's hands, those of a rich girl.'

Her two brothers, he that came out of her mother's womb dead and he who remained embraced, wrinkled like an old man, to a block of ice in the upper balcony until he could be buried in a small white box that Matías glued together, did not need prayers nor nightlights.

'They left this world with tender souls; they didn't have time to know evil.'

The blue-hearted flames danced in the treacle half-light, in whose softness floated the magnified and pulsating shadow of the chest. The only light bulb at the Merchán home, hanging from the kitchen ceiling, was switched off at six in the evening because of the shortages. The tenement house on Alpechín Street went to bed early.

'Chacha, where do the dead go?'

'They go nowhere, girl; they prowl around among us and they send us signals. Some nights I talk to my mother and to your grandfather... If the candle crackles on All Saints' Day it means the dead one left this world with the desire to tell us something. Your grandfather's tea light gives off sparks every year. In a while, when he's settled, look closely and you'll see; it commands respect.'

'Where's our soul?'

'Here, look, between the backbone and the pit of the stomach.'

'Andrea asked me if grandfather is buried in the cemetery.'

'Yes, girl, in the same cemetery, next to the cypresses by the far end wall. The doctor sewed up his stab wound with fishing line, and I had to put him into the common grave with his blood-stained shirt because I had no money to shroud him or to have a headstone engraved with his name. The silver five peseta coin Gavilana lent me was only enough to pay for the cart man who brought his body back to Puebla and to buy your father a bag of sweets. No-one could comfort him.'

'Gavilana? Who was she?'

'Nobody... A moneylender from back then. She was called Teresa, but was nicknamed Gavilana because she was very mean.'

'And tell me, how did grandfather Curro die?'

'But I've already told you a hundred times, you pest!'

'Did he sing as well as people say he did?'

'Even better; like an angel, girl.'

The dreamt image of her grandfather bleeding to death on paving stones with his eyes full of eternity absorbed Juana's imagination with a draining anxiety that was prolonged in Chachachica's pupils.

'Chacha, do you believe God exists?'

'I haven't got an answer, girl. The poor are always followed by a scythe. One has to live as though God existed.'

'And why don't you ever go to church?'

'Because I don't like priests and my shoes don't fit. I always walk barefoot.'

'Sometimes I've got things in my head I only dare ask you about.'

'And what things might those be, girl'

'Andrea says my father is a coward... Matías said so, and the carpenter doesn't tell lies. This evening we saw bullet holes in the cemetery wall.'

'Your father is your father and don't disrespect him. You're still too young to understand things that happened long ago; what happened, happened. One has to forget. That Andrea has got a poisoned tongue. Go on, climb up to the pigeon loft

89

to see what your sisters are up to. And go to bed, it's late. I'll come up in a while.'

Chachachica's profile shone in the orange glow of the oil nightlights. The blue flames of the tea lights quivered in the semi-darkness of the kitchen.

What is it to be a coward? Who imposes the limits to cowardice? Sometimes life breaks your neck with one blow and forces you to bow your head, to eat earth, to swallow pain without chewing it. Chachachica still had black hair and firm defiant breasts when she crossed the club floor on her knees in silence, at the time of day when the din of the cicadas eased and the fan blades tried in vain to shred the false drowsiness. In the middle of August in nineteen thirty-six. Chachachica had crossed the village on her knees, and her joints, bleeding since beyond the church, left behind a shadow of shutters slammed shut. An obscene trace of blood stained the spotless club marble red; her determination stopped her from feeling pain in her skinned knees. Don Jacinto Maldonado, Falange delegate in Puebla de Acebuche, sipped an anisette, leaning on the back bar as he talked to another two men sporting starched loose-fitting shirts. In the sticky heat Don Jacinto wore a white long-sleeved shirt, buttoned with cufflinks and with a black armband around his forearm. His brother, his favourite mare, Tinkerbell, and Julián Ortega, the manor house foreman, had perished two months earlier in the fire and looting of Dueña Alta.

'Don Jacinto, have mercy. Help me for whatever you want. My Manuel is ignorant. He didn't do nothing, Don Jacinto, I swear; he didn't set the stables alight nor kill the foreman. He isn't even eighteen yet, the angel of God! He didn't do nothing. They came looking for him in the early morning and

I don't know where they've taken him. He hasn't done nothing; make them take me as a prisoner in his place... Help me, Don Jacinto, for whatever you want in the world.'

'I can't do anything for you, woman. Place your trust in God.'

'You're influential, Don Jacinto... At least get them to tell me where they've taken him.'

'Woman, I can't do anything... You know better than me that your godson hung out with the wrong crowd. They would have taken him to Seville, like the rest of the region's commies, and in the city it's Díaz Criado who's in charge, the Law and Order delegate. If your godson isn't yet twenty it's probable that they won't shoot him. They say General Don Queipo de Llano spares the lives of those who join the Foreign Legion. I can't do anything for you. Go; this isn't a place for women.'

There are recollections that damage the slimy protective secretion of memory with ground chilli pepper, pin heads and alcohol for burning.

7

'The moral scruples of certain people make me throw up.'

Yes, it is the tone of voice. It is the resentment of her daughter Mercedes that exhausts her. Salud Monterde has just got up; she looks in the mirror and can hardly perceive herself in the woman observing her impassively from the cloudy water of the mercury: her face swollen, her crude flour cheeks, that bitter rind of her skin which not even rice-powder can conceal, the scathing fan of her crow's feet.

'Don't look at me like that, Mercedes; you're the same as me, blood of my blood, despite how bad you think that is... For every wrinkle, for every blunder, a rein lash on the horse's dappled flank and off to another place. That's the question, Merche: don't let them walk all over you. Never.'

Salud scrutinised the greed hiding in her green eyes, tiny, trapped in purple gelatin bags, her pointed nose shading the lines that back-stitch the insecure features of her lips and, most of all, her hair: she does not recognise herself with her hair down; it is not her. Not even her daughters have surprised her once in the helplessness of her two thin partings, dyed jet black, that now, in the privacy of the bathroom, under the slaughterhouse fluorescent light, stab the softness of her shoulders and the shining tiles, because Salud Monterde, even on the rare day when she does not go out, invariably collects her hair in a tight ponytail over the back of her head. It is a dreary morning, like many others, and only a silk dressing gown, with faded Chinese dragons and cherry tree prints, covers her cracked and freckled cleavage.

The toothpaste applied sparingly reduces the stubborn breath of alcohol encrusted on her soft palate.

Salud Monterde drags behind her a mud-dirty inventory, bloody footprints in sawdust, convictions fainting over the cotton texture of lies, promises and paper dreams suddenly uncomfortable and quickly thrown into the sewer. Smoke, Mauser gunshots and broken display cabinets.

'Up to the rooftop, up to the rooftop... Bring this bourgeois dog up to the rooftop! He carried a pistol in his armhole.'

The owner of the jeweller's, on the corner of the Rambla and Carmen Street, fell onto the paving stones burnt in the suffocation of July. He threw himself into the void, he fell faint, he was pushed, he lost his balance, perhaps he slipped. His skull split open on the stones with the crack of a watermelon.

'Hide it at home, in the rooftop water tank, under the corridor wash house, in the sewn bags behind a painting's canvass, pull out a floor tile, do what you must, Feliu, but hide it. Or under a piano lid; and if you can't practice, well bear with it and play scales on the dining room table. Your mother? But what are you saying, Feliu? Your mother can't even get up

*out of bed, what have you got to explain to her? You're joking...
The boys were right: you were always a coward.'*

Salud Monterde strokes the bags under her eyes that
persevere in their livid swelling. The years have smoothed the
pumice stone of her memory, fragmented and resolved in a
before-the-war and in an after-the-war, of the anticipated end
of the conflict in the irremissible certainty that all was lost in
the spring of thirty-seven. From the rearguard of the
barricades on the crossroads of Ronda de San Antonio and
Tigre Street to the stools in the Moka bar steep in the curse
of white heels, the jewellery wrapped in felt and tightly
pressed against her stomach. Salud Monterde knew how to
get rid of herself at the right time: the past is as circumstantial
as a wet Monday and the only truth is condensed now in the
fleeting moment in front of the mirror, in the hairpin holding
the last thread of hair, in the mature woman who has just got
up, and her reflection melts into large blobs of tired wax.

*'But how will they suspect you? You're honest you! In six
months I'll take it all from you; I promise you for my daughters'
sake. Do it for the little one, Feliu: I never asked you for
anything, I never made you feel guilty. Only six months or even
less, when it gets quieter and the streets are emptied of soldiers.
From now on we'll be respectable people.'*

Her cruel schoolgirl's hands pinch her cheeks to extract an
alm of warmth. Time pours into the spongy flesh of her arms
and into the mirror, like the silica dust falling for exactly two
minutes into the bottom ampoule of the sand-glass timing the
bakelite telephone, sleeping on the corridor wall among old
furniture and the stink of vinegar.

'I've told you two a thousand times: write down in the
oilskin notebook all the phone calls and the number of times

you've turned the sand-glass; each turn, two minutes, you know that. There's got to be control, my girls. Money is fickle, and if you don't tie it down, it'll go as soon as it comes.'

Mercedes and Montserrat are still sleeping, and perhaps will not get up until midday. The servant girl is in the kitchen ironing; she cannot be heard. Dull mornings freeze memory with the same stubbornness with which the open fissure in the symmetric centre of disgust throbs on demanding nutrition: brandy with ice and soda, splintered toothpicks, paella on Sundays, the sparkle of an emerald mounted in gold, the anxious wait for a new customer under the umbrella canopy after the Liceo, the exciting smell of sulphur that money gives off, men perhaps, anything, whatever. Nothing satisfies the voracious hole, not even the two men who left her with an imperceptible mark on her skin and a daughter from each.

'Why did my father leave you? And tell me, did you ever get married? Because you're very capable of pinching the rings off the corpse of a Falangist. But you did well, mother, what the hell. It could be said that you even look like a respectable lady with your husband and wife rings... Why are you making that face? What a small sense of humour you've got! Go on, have another brandy, we're only talking. Let's toast to us and to life. And to our customers, that they'll always be there.'

'Lower your voice, Merche... You have no shame nor have you ever known it. And listen to what I'm telling you: although you don't like recognising it, you're evermore like me; even in your gestures. Imagine it.'

Salud Monterde loved the first man – an Aragonese customs officer who loved *zarzuela*, Spanish light opera – with the fleeting passion of youth and the grief of first loss. The second

95

man she paid with her body the price of his silence and perhaps the embers of compassion towards herself.

'Do you want them to lock me up, do you want them to shoot me on the beach? They could come and search my house; who knows if someone still remembers what happened and informs on me. Someone must remember; it wasn't so long ago. Feliu, think it over, even if it's only for the little one. I won't ever ask you for anything ever again and I'll give you in new notes ten percent of all that you hide, of all that there is in the bag. Do you know what I'm saying, have you any idea of how much ten percent of this is? Feliu, listen: you only have to hide it in your house and keep your mouth shut, nothing more. If you open it, kaputt; you and me, both of us, to the grave, to hell. But how will they suspect you, you idiot?'

Some truths are so fickle and evasive that they manage to escape the impeccable trap of words: they float in the void and they cannot be heard nibbling at the shell of understanding. Salud Monterde never dared confess to her daughters that Salvador Feliu, the man who loved her with the aloofness of a stuffed bird, the pianist who lives badly on tips and who visits them on Sundays with a small apple pie edged with grated coconut, exquisitely wrapped in tissue paper and tied with blue cord for after the rice dish, is Montserrat's father, the maestro with a bald patch beaded with sweat, with shy pupils that learn jazz from American musicians, from the deaf and dumb and ecstatic faces of the marines that the red semi-darkness of the Brindis bar softens. When they slept together for the first time Salud was moved by the sight of him naked, drawing a four-four beat in the air as he hummed an easy melody, and the cigarette butt he rested on the bedside table with its glowing tip pointing towards the ceiling. Salud also does not use ashtrays.

96

'*Leave it; it'll die out on its own.*'

Tenderness is a trap, the cobweb that entangles the weak.

'*Are you sure?*'

'*Go to hell.*'

'*Well if you want, we'll get married.*'

'*Don't be stupid, Feliu. I don't want to marry you, I'm too old to dress in white, nor do you have enough phlegm to tie me down. Where are we going at this stage in the game? And what shall we do with your mother, how will you explain it to her? I'm telling you this because you should know that I'm going to have the child. Don't worry; I don't need anything from you or anybody else. I won't ask you for anything; not even a surname.*'

She was terrified of the possibility of an abortion, the furry tongue of chloroform, the turn over of a bloodstained bed sheet, of imagining between her thighs the inquisitive feel of a meat stuffing syringe disinfected in a stew pan, of going down to Carmen Street in a nightie without make-up, wrapped in the helplessness of a tight overcoat, and throwing into the gutter the monster crumpled in *La Hoja del Lunes* newspaper. And, after all, Montse, the little one, in all her peach innocence, continues calling him uncle. Uncle Feliu. Her uncle that plays the piano at the Brindis.

'*If you open your mouth, kaputt. You and me, both of us, to the grave, to hell.*'

Salvador Feliu often turns up at her flat to ask her for money for the favours he has done. Cultured, gentle, docile, the pianist's profile unexpectedly framed the door hinge, playing with the brim of his hat between his fingers, the pathetic image of Salvador Feliu any morning, without prior warning, bowed-headed, his worried pupils caressing his shoes – white instepped, brown capped – dirty from having trampled the Chinese quarter, the short and always inconclusive phrases of an old lover. The dragons yawn on the sleeves of her dressing gown.

'If it was for me, I wouldn't go through the shame of it. A little will be enough, you know that. It's for my mother. The poor thing, any one of these days now...'

'Your mother will outlive us all.'

Salud Monterde applies lipstick to her lips, dried from rage, as if hoping to gag them with brushstrokes. Grief and guilt are hindrance words, soft, superfluous, and now, at this very moment when she is perfuming her cleavage, her armpits and where her hair begins on the nape of her neck. The fifth floor on Carmen Street, on the corner of San Lázaro, will have to collapse down onto her head with a crash of debris and broken beams for her throat to emit a complaint, a lament, an outline of a plea. Salud Monterde shoulders it all – weighed down by orchids, excrement, precious stones, dust, whatever she randomly has – without reproach because beasts of burden never look back. She is only weakened by the dead weight of distrust, the need to keep her senses alert like a hunt hound, and by Mercedes' resentment.

The whisper of slippers creeping along the corridor instinctively tenses Juana's spine.

'Good morning, girl.'

'Good morning, señora.'

'Strain me a coffee, let's see if I can wake up. My head aches a hell of a lot.'

Juana disconnects the iron plugged into the light bulb cable and places it onto the corner of the table. The lady pronounces these words when she has had a bad night. The phrase is perpetuated in identical mornings: my head aches a hell of a lot, make me a cup of coffee; make me a hell of a lot, ache me a coffee. Alternating words, always words, empty words. Half truths and sock-strained coffee. The lady says 'cap coffee'.

Salud Monterde drags the back of the chair up against the wall; she sits down with tired movements, resting her bun of hair against the kitchen tiles, and places two cotton balls soaked in camomile over her eyelids. Her hair tautens her temples. Juana turns the tap on: the gush of water crashes against the marble sink with the anxiety of a punch.

'Girl, I've told you a thousand times not to leave the ironing so late; then there's no way to do it well, and creased sheets give me the shivers, I just can't cope with them. I don't sleep much as it is and the last thing I need... If the clothes are difficult to iron sprinkle a little water over them, like this, with your finger tips, stroking them. Didn't your mother teach you to iron?'

The lady has got her eyes closed, as if she were sucking the brains out of a rabbit when eating paella. She speaks with her head back with the cotton balls inlayed in her eye sockets; she looks like a corpse recently shrouded. Juana imagines Señora Monterde inside a coffin with her hair down to her knees. Chachachica says hair and nails continue growing on the flesh of the dead even after they are buried.

'*Chacha, why do you talk when you're asleep?*'

'*I talk! Come off it and don't make things up, girl. Go up to the pigeon loft and go to sleep, it's still early.*'

'No señora... In my village they don't iron sheets.'

'Today I'm the one who'll go to the market. I've got to speak to the butcher.'

'As you wish, señora.'

'You're to clean the silver Last Supper with bicarbonate; it's a shame to see it like that. Once I've had my coffee the two of us will lower it.'

'Whatever you say, señora.'

'By the way, girl, this evening you've got to go on an errand for me. Do you remember Pech? The cripple who lives on Baños Nuevos, you know who I'm talking about, don't you? The watchmaker... You're to take him the copper he asked for; he needs it for work. You know how to get to his house, don't you? You've been a few times.'

'I think so, señora. Don't worry; if I get lost, I'll ask someone.'

Leave, leave, leave. Run away from the prison of vinegar, look at inaccessible shop windows, see people, catch the last rays of light, the yellow sparks that the tramcars spit, the life sprouting between cobble stones, the colour of the flowers on the Rambla stalls... Juana could reach Baños Nuevos with cotton soaked in camomile blinding her eyes: she has memorised a sign on each corner of the labyrinth of side streets in the old quarter that leads to the house of that unsociable man.

'Girl, I suppose you won't mention it to anyone. You already know what I'm referring to, don't you? When I send you to pay the butcher with a little piece of jewellery, to settle the account with the tobacconist's or to take a packet to the cripple... You know what I'm saying, don't you? Because you're no fool. Don't even mention it to your father. Although in this house we have nothing to hide, you can relax about that. But, as you know, people are bad and talk for talk's sake. People like to lie. Don't trust anyone, girl, not even your own father. It's advice I'm giving you.'

'Don't worry, señora. My father and I almost don't speak to each other.'

100

Merchán only sings. When he is sad he sings flamenco *soleares*. And his tattoos hiccup in blue on the skin of his arms.

'I'm going as if I were a prisoner: / behind walks my shadow; / in front, my thoughts.'

'Girl, do me a favour and bring me my packet of Chesterfield. I think I left it on top of the dining room table.' Salud Monterde uncovers her eyelids. The cotton balls are hot, as if she had soaked them in coffee.

The doorbell rings.

'Feliu again! I don't believe it!'

In the morning visitors do not usually arrive because the circle of friends and the odd trusted customer with access to the flat know that the Monterdes start the day late: the jewellers do not exist before midday. The doorbell unpleasantly insists. Salud adjusts her dressing gown belt and returns the key to the sealed room to the cup of her bra.

'Juana, go take a look through the door grille, but don't open.'

Salud does not feel like talking to strangers. At this time in the morning she still has not moulded her clay words, and the remains of last night are prolonged in the aftertaste of brandy and in the biting of her varicose veins. She pours herself another cup of coffee and lights her first cigarette of the day. Morning visits tend to bring bad news.

'It's a woman,' Juana says in a hushed voice.

'A woman? So early?'

Salud advances, dodging furniture along the corridor; Juana follows her way behind. The intruder thumps at the door and shouts:

'Open the door, thief. I know you're in there.'

Salud Monterde draws back the brass catch and through the holes observes the round face, framed by tortoiseshell

101

glasses, of Rosa Armengol. She withdraws from the door grille, pulling a displeased face. The woman insists:

'Open the door or the entire building will hear about this!'

Salud motions for Juana to retreat to the kitchen.

'It's Rosita, the dressmaker,' she says hissing.

'I know you're in there, you shameless hussy.'

Salud draws back the bolts and latches and brusquely opens the door.

'Good morning, what's all this racket about?' Salud crosses her arms over the top of her stomach, where dregs of night and brandy regurgitate.

'I want you to pay me the money you owe me right now. The eight hundred pesetas.'

'Eight hundred pesetas? Have you gone crazy? I don't owe you anything; I've paid you all of it. Also, you know perfectly well that we work at night. You could have at least had the decency to wait until the eve...'

'Wait? You've got the cheek of telling me to wait? Wait for what? I've been waiting four months for you to have the decency to pay me, four months.' The guttural voice of Rosa Armengol rings out on the landing.

The noise has woken Mercedes, who comes out into the corridor in her nightie and with her head covered in hair curlers. On passing by the kitchen door her and Juana's eyes briefly cross like two night trains. Juana looks away; she always looks down at the floor in front of Señorita Mercedes.

'Calm down and remember, because I paid you down to the last penny.'

'What? You say you've paid me and that's that, what a nerve! I want my eight hundred pesetas right now. I'm not leaving here without my eight hundred pesetas.' Rosa

Armengol hits the palm of her hand with her fist.

Mercedes slowly goes closer to the argument.

'You'll see, I'll resolve this matter right now by closing the door. It's alright by me for you to stay there on the stairs until the day after tomorrow. And bellow all you want. I'm not worried by what the neighbours say, because I paid you down to the last penny. What a cheek you've got, Rosita, who would have thought it.'

'But how can you be so cynical? You owe me eight hundred pesetas and you're going to pay me, one way or another. Or is it that I work for love of art, hey? How do you expect me to feed my children, hey, tell me?'

Mercedes props herself next to her mother, on the threshold. Salud Monterde has begun to bite on a fingernail. Morning arguments give her fevers.

From the kitchen Juana concentrates on following the dispute as she irons a poplin blouse for Señorita Mercedes; it is difficult for her to do both things. She knows the dressmaker. Rosa Armengol often comes to the flat because the Monterdes have clothes made to measure: suits, loose skirts for the summer, short light jackets and cocktail dresses, because – it is another one of Señora Monterde's recurrent phrases – elegance is fifty-one percent of their work. The Monterdes go out impeccably dressed. The dressmaker comes to Carmen Street laden with samples, patterns, back issues of French magazines and a pin box. The woman lives in the neighbourhood; Juana has come across her a few times on her way to the B`oquería market.

The dressmaker is amazed by her own voice: determined, fierce, brilliant. She says:

'What's happening is that you, Señora Monterde, and your

daughters, especially this one, are villains. Who do you think you are? Film stars? Countesses? A banker's family?'

'What a nerve! How dare you speak to me like that?'

'Listen, because I'm speaking the truth by the bucketful: you pretend to live like millionairesses and spend money you haven't earned with your own hands. Wow, the flat is big: new clothes, fur stoles, shoes and luxury manicures for going out at night to socialise like whor...'

'Don't shout at me. I won't allow it.'

'All the neighbourhood knows. And, deep down, you're poor wretches dragged up from the gutter like all the neighbourhood, like all of us, as my late mother used to say. Who works here? No one. There are no men at this home. Not one. You think I don't know what you live on? Of course I know, and my mother, the poor thing, she also knew: you're still feeding off what you looted during the war. You took buckets from the basement, bucketfuls, up to the brim.

'Enough! What nonsense you're talking!'

'No, I haven't finished yet. I'd stake my life on you sleeping with those American soldiers for money. It doesn't surprise me in the least because you have no decency. Scum, that's what you lot are.'

Mercedes lunges at the dressmaker and grabs hold of her neck. Rosa Armengol tries in vain to free herself.

'Thieves, thieves!' she shouts.

Salud Monterde drags her daughter and the dressmaker inside the flat and closes the door behind her. The dressmaker is crying.

'Enough, Mercedes! Let go of her. Go to my room and bring me my purse; it's in my bag.' Salud sweats in her silk dressing gown. She looks at Rosa Armengol with the scorn of her rabbit's eyes. She suppresses the desire to stab a sharpened pick between her eyebrows, exactly at the entrance to her brain.

'Listen well to what I've got to say.' Salud holds the dressmaker by the jaw and presses her head against the wall. 'I'm going to give you five hundred pesetas, not a penny more. I'm giving you the money because I don't want to see you again and because I hate arguing in the morning.' Rage whitens the bitten finger tips squeezing Rosa Armengol's chin.

Mercedes returns with the purse.

'This is the last time you step foot in my house to insult my daughters. The last time, because I'll rip out your eyes. You know I'm capable of doing it. Don't ever think of returning. Here we don't owe you anything.'

Salud's fingers search inside the purse. She throws a wrinkled note at the dressmaker's feet. A slammed door and silence on the fifth floor on Carmen Street, on the corner of San Lázaro.

At lunchtime Salud Monterde and her daughters have hardly eaten. Señora Monterde has blamed her daughters, for being capricious and spendthrift, for what happened with the dressmaker in the morning. Chain-smoked Chesterfields and reproaches from the sofa. The lady insists that it is not a good time for squandering because customers are few and far between.

'Juana, pour me a brandy and soda. Brandy from the mesh covered bottle.'

The daughters had wanted soup and a plain omelette.

'Juana, bring me a piece of fruit.'

Not a pear, an apple, a bunch of grapes, an orange, figs, a pomegranate, a chalice of blood. No.

'Bring me a piece of fruit.'

Señorita Mercedes talks like this.

The street. The acidic smell of the street in October. The transparent air anticipates winter in the bark of the banana trees. Soon it will begin to get cooler. Juana has gone out without wrapping up properly, in a grey wool skirt and a white blouse. Her kitten-heeled shoes, also white, slide slightly on the paving, between whose gaps city flowers grow: trembling, with timid petals. The people passing by Juana walk in fits and starts, covered in a pretended hurry. Nobody cares that the girl is not wearing stockings, or that the cloth rubs the virgin skin of her thighs, or that a sticking plaster hides the hole in her toe. The passers-by could not care less that the servant crossing the street with a sackcloth bag hanging from her elbow confuses her S's, C's and Z's and imagines the soul shrunken like a bird's stomach: a mess of nerves and muscles with a little bag on the side for storing her dirty life, melancholy and half-swallowed poverty.

'Chacha, tell me, where is our soul?'

'Here, girl, between the backbone and the pit of the stomach. But it's movable and goes down to your feet or rises up to your throat. And when it hides, we walk blind, bumping into corners.'

The soul seems like a chicken's gizzard: wrinkled, trembling, its bag of greenish filth sewn to one side. The butcher at the Boquería market calls a gizzard 'quarry'.

'See you later, love.'

The butcher put the gold bracelet into his trouser back pocket. He did not even unwrap the tissue paper.

No one is interested in the fact that the servant girl carrying a bag with copper bars for the crippled watchmaker of Baños Nuevos does not know how to divide or that she has no nails on her fingers and has teeth marks of nitric acid on her skin. She still protects her hands with cotton gloves.

Señora Monterde has wrapped the copper bars in tissue paper – the same with which she wrapped the gold bracelet – and she has tied it with fine blue cord. The paper says: SWISS CONFECTIONER'S. Señor Feliu brings them cakes on Sundays.

'Thieves, you still live off what you looted during the war.'

The balconies stab each other in the narrowness of the Gothic quarter. The neighbours could pinch hands from one railing to another while watering the bracken or hanging out clothes on the wires sagging in silence. A neighbourhood of urine and damp. Number five Baños Nuevos Street. Juana presses the doorbell next to the enamelled sign – blue background, inscribed in white lettering: WATCHMAKER – REPAIRS – with an arrow pointing to the second floor. A cardboard sign – she had not noticed it before – stuck onto the edge of the metal plaque with paste, adds the note: NECKLACES FOR SALE. VALUING OF JEWELLERY.

Juana presses the doorbell again. Señor Pech takes time in opening. Perhaps he has gone out and is now turning the corner slowly, with unequal movements, weighed down with shopping bags and dragging his wooden leg. A female neighbour suddenly opens the front door.

'Where are you going, girl?'

'To the second floor, to the watchmaker's flat.'

The steps are narrow and steep, like those going up to the pigeon loft, where the cracks watch over impossible longings plotted in blue ink. Her desires smell of mackerel scales.

I hope the rain goes.

I hope the boats go out to sea.

I hope my father doesn't cry.

I hope Andrea's hair grows down to her ankles.

I hope no more sisters are born.

I hope anchovy soup doesn't taste of camphor balls.

I hope no more blood leaks out from me there below.

The wooden treads creak under Juana's very light weight. The cord that is pulled to draw back the front door bolt climbs the stairwell up to an eyebolt screwed into the loading beam in the roof. A ray of vertical light flanks the watchmaker's door: it is open. On the other side Señor Pech's cat miaows. Juana knocks with her knuckles and feels in her finger tips, under her cotton gloves, the tempting itch to retrace her steps and explain to Señora Monterde that the watchmaker was not at home.

'Chacha, I'm afraid. I don't want to leave the village.'

'You oughtn't be afraid of nothing, Juana, not even of death.'

Juana crosses herself and pushes the door.

The cat receives the visitor with a jealous snort. The transistor radio is switched on in the middle of the soulless loneliness. On the mosaic floor of the hall Liberto Pech lies on his side next to his disorientated crutches. Juana represses the wish to run, to leave slamming the door and rush down the stairs, three at a time. She gently closes the door and slowly goes closer to the bulk lying on the floor with its legs open like a pair of compasses, the wooden one and the one of flesh and blood. The watchmaker has blood on his face. With her gloved hands Juana tries to sit him up. The watchmaker breathes heavily and his greying hair smells of wine. Juana looks at the man's face with caution and surprise, his sharp and noble nose, his meaty lips, the two vertical wrinkles chiselled under his cheekbones, his eyelids protecting his shy gaze the same colour as the rain, the gash in his forehead splitting his eyebrow with a garland of dried blood.

108

Juana enters into the darkness, between piles of books and time-yellowed newspapers, feeling her way along the rough wall until coming across the light switch. She finds the bathroom at the end of the corridor. On top of a board laid across the bath tub she finds a bar of soap, a brush for scrubbing shirt cuffs, a tin of sardines in brine converted into an ashtray and a chemist's dropper with iodine. There is no sign of cotton wool, bandages, sticking plaster nor a clean cloth. She takes out her handkerchief from the sleeve of her blouse and wets it with tap water.

Liberto Pech blinks. The ceiling light bulb irritates his eyes and stops him from identifying the shadow behind the curtain of his eyelids. His ribcage hurts.

'*Què m'ha passat? On estic?* – What's happened to me? Where am I?'

Juana flicks a lock of hair away with her left hand and pours iodine over the opening of his wound. A stinging of red ants joins the feast.

'Perhaps you should go to the clinic to have some stitches. I'll come with you if you want.'

The watchmaker hears her voice but whispers flutter empty around him. He half-opens his eyes dazzled by the light.

'*Born in Barcelona, in the same province, on the twenty-second of October nineteen sixteen, master watchmaker by profession... Being found guilty by this High Court of the crime of military rebellion, under article two hundred and thirty-six of the Military Justice Law.*'

The obscene voice and the typewriter rattle jostle the white brightness.

'These papers say you're called Liberto. Liberty?'

'Yes, señor.'

It surprises him the time passed since he last heard his own voice. Liberto Pech is naked, his back leaning against the basement wall, covered up to the ceiling with white glazed tiles. His body is incapable of supporting his own weight without the prop of his crutches. More than of his sexual organs – frightened, soft, withdrawn within themselves – the watchmaker is ashamed of showing in the white light his obscene stump, brazenly dark crimson, stripped of the dignity of his harness and false leg. A plainclothes policeman unpicks the hems of his trousers; the pocket linings remain pricked, terrified, like the ears of a dazzled hare.

'Liberto? What kind of fucking name is that? Have you heard? They gave this big piece of shit the name Liberto. And his surname, Pus. Pestilent pus like an old bag's warts.'

The obscene voice sets off a boom of laughter on the other side of the blinding spotlight.

'It's pronounced Pech, with a *th* at the end.'

The tyranny of thirst parches the watchmaker's voice.

'Shut it, red trash!'

Every road is for coming and going. With his right leg amputated, the scar still fresh, and with a blister on his left heel caused by the rubbing of his sockless clog – it was July, the sweltering summer of nineteen forty – Liberto Pech had returned to Spain, together with another seven hundred and twenty-three refugees, mostly women and children, crossing the border at Hendaya, under the custody of the French police.

The Nazis had already entered Paris.

From Hendaya to Irún, dragging the painful absence of his leg with him and expecting many years in a cell – Madrid, Saragossa, Barcelona – boiled onion and cabbage and defecating in a tin can.

'Turn around, I'm going to have a shit.'

'Look how fussy you are, Catalan... It's because you've never seen your own arsehole.'

'Just turn around, for fuck's sake.'

'Listen, how come you returned? After all this time you still haven't told me.'

'You have a knack for timing, have they ever told you? All you Stalinists are the same: foul-mouthed, narrow-minded, dim, disrespectful of the individual... If you like, I returned because I missed Catalan rice and veg stew. What did you want, for the Germans to turn my good leg into animal fodder?'

Over the years built-up resentment ferments into patience.

'Where am I? Who are you?'

'I'm Juana, Señora Monterde's servant girl. I've brought you the copper you wanted. It's there, inside my sackcloth bag.'

'What's happened?'

'It's nothing. You fell over and must have lost consciousness. If you want, let's go to the clinic to get your eyebrow stitched. I'll come with you.'

'Don't worry. My skin heals up well.'

The nape of his neck woken up with cold water, the clean caress of his shirt and the aroma of thyme soup reconcile his body with his pain at this time of day with uncertain light when the seagulls and raincoat necks fly low. Liberto Pech blows on his spoon and watches the girl's back, covered in a balsamic halo of yellow flowers, as she washes up the plates and scrubs the scouring pad over the rings left by the wine on the wooden kitchen worktop. The girl has taken off her cotton gloves so as not to wet them; she has got blood stains on her white blouse. She wipes her hands on her wool skirt and hides them; she looks at him out of the corner of her eye. She says:

'Do you feel a bit better?'

'Yes, thank you. You said that you're called Juana, is that right?'

'Yes, señor.'

'My name is Liberto. My friends, I don't have many, it's true to say, call me Llibert, in Catalan, and the people of the neighbourhood know me by my surname, just Pech, or by my trade. But sit a while, woman.'

'I should go now, señor. I only came to bring you the copper. I left it in the corridor, in the sackcloth bag. Do you want me to bring it to the kitchen?'

'I must seem to you like a dead loss, but don't call me señor, please. Only hearing it makes my skin crawl... Llibert, Lli-bert. It's very easy, woman, you'll see.' The watchmaker tries out an inkling of a smile. Leaning against the edge of the worktop, the dark-haired young woman looks at him with mistrust. 'Do you know why I want the copper you've brought me? I need it for work, to melt it with gold. When these two metals alloy together the gold becomes harder without losing its flexibility. Like this I can work with it better, but one must be careful with the mixture in the crucible so that its shine doesn't become opaque.' The young woman listens to him in admiration; there is something intangible in the fragility of her feminine look that wins him over. 'Since when have you been working for Monterde?'

'Soon it will be five months, señor.'

'She'd have told you that we've known each other for a long time and that now I survive thanks to her and the odd

112

jobs she gives me. Salud Monterde provides me with the materials, the gold, you brought me two ingots the last time, do you remember? And the stones. Rubies, emeralds, topazes, whatever... But sit a while, woman. I make what she asks for and she sells it on: engagement rings, wedding rings, bracelets, earrings, the odd pendant, but most of all rings, which do best. Rings have always done best on the street. In the neighbourhood she is known as the jeweller. Doña Salud Monterde Martí. How clever that woman is! She knows in what shade to take shelter, I do believe. I know my trade well: I started out as an apprentice when I was thirteen, and before the war I was considered to be one of the best craftsmen in Barcelona. Later everything changed in this city, in all the country. That Monterde is like cork, whatever happens she always stays afloat.'

The girl's gaze does not keep still: it wanders from her damaged finger tips, to the eyes of who is speaking to her, to the tail of cat, who is licking his legs under the table, to the recently washed upside down glasses dripping water, to the cracked marble sink, to the false leg. If it was not for the purity of that anxious gaze insistently staring at his artificial limb, Liberto Pech would have wanted to fake a sudden stinging in his stump, then roll up his trouser leg and show the sawed off femur in the bulb light. But these dark eyes hypnotise and calm. Liberto Pech feels uncomfortable, he is ashamed of his fossilised stump, of the Gandesa wine that laid him out on the hall floor tiles with the limpness of a puppet, of the loneliness of a man with a cat, of the flat with the Persian blinds always closed, of his own clumsiness, of not knowing what to say.

'Why are you so quiet? Poor Proudhon couldn't have got

113

your tongue because he only likes sardines in brine; he's every bit a lover of luxury.' Again, the blush of clumsiness.

'It's just that I don't talk much, señor.'

Salud Monterde would have warned the girl, clearly.

'Don't hang about with the watchmaker, girl, and if he asks questions, don't answer. You should know that he hits the bottle and it's not even been two years since he left prison. Give him the copper and that's that. He was sentenced to death.'

What would that old bag have told her?

'During the war he and his pals went out hunting priests and they made them run naked. They dragged out pews and sculptures from the Capuchin monastery in Sarrià into the street and had a bonfire. And you should have seen him with the twelve-by-seventy millimetre machine gun on the Esplugas road when they left for the Ebro front. Ratatatata ratatatata.'

The girl smelling of wild flowers dares not look straight ahead. Her black eyes weigh like threats. She should go. The watchmaker wants to be left in peace. Liberto Pech does not need words or anybody's friendship. He lives alone and on little. He refills his demijohn of Gandesa wine every Monday on returning from the police station on Vía Layetana, he buys sardines in brine for Proudhon, goes out for the occasional slow walk to San Felipe Neri Square or all the way to Francia Station; he likes the silence following the racket of a train. The girl should go, she should leave. Proudhon and the watchmaker do not need anyone. But his disobedient tongue dares to articulate words.

'Would you like to see me work one day? If you've never seen it before, the process of melting gold and transforming it into jewellery is beautiful. Come when you want, I'm always at home working. You'd like to see it, wouldn't you?'

114

'Thank you.'

The echo of the dressmaker's voice.

'My late mother also knew. You took bucketfuls from the basement. Scum, that's what you lot are.'

'Come whenever you want, Juana... For you the door is always open.'

'I'd better be going. Señora Monterde is about to go out and will be worried.'

'Is she still making you wear gloves?'

'No, señor. It's not that she makes me, I've already told you... I burnt my hands with nitric acid; it was an accident. Now they're almost healed. I've cured myself with olive oil.'

'Call me Llibert, Lli-bert. Return whenever you want, Juana, this home is yours. And listen, don't tell Monterde that you found me drunk on the floor. Don't tell anyone, please. Don't tell anyone.'

Juana opens the door. The flat on Carmen Street, on the corner of San Lázaro, is in darkness and silence: the lady and her daughters have already gone out to sell rings in the bars and nightclubs. Juana gets undressed, puts on her nightie and once again counts the money she has saved from her weekly wages. She keeps the notes in a crocheted bag inside the suitcase with cinnamon-coloured edgings.

She switches on the metallic light in the bathroom. She closes her eyes and opens them again to make sure it is true: the keys to the forbidden room are there, on top of the stool, within arm's reach. The lady has left them. Juana imagines the scene: the rush, a shower, tiredness, the lady unwillingly putting on her make-up in front of the mirror, the row in the morning with the dressmaker, her feet imprisoned in her white high heels. When there are visitors to the flat Salud Monterde hides the keys between her breasts.

The darkness magnifies her heartbeats inside the box of her chest. Boom, boom, boom. The pulsations vibrate in her jawbone. Juana feels ice in her feet. The frosted feel of her nightie hurts her skin.

'And don't ever think of nosing around in the boxroom. Also, it's useless: I've always got the keys and the keyhole is sealed.'

Go in, take a look and leave; only that. Go in, take a look and leave. Slowly, without rushing, with her hands covered by her cotton gloves to leave no fingerprints. There is plenty of time. The lady does not usually return home until after two o'clock in the morning. When she comes back drunk Juana hears her bump into the chairs in the hall. Her daughters come home somewhat later. Boom, boom, boom. Her heart is bursting inside the urn of her chest. Salud Monterde does not enter the sealed room every day, nor every week, nor every month. Juana is always in the flat and knows the comings and goings of the three of them. And there is stale bread in the pantry for sealing the keyhole again. What if she is caught and given the sack? The lady is as shrewd as a squirrel.

'Is it true, señora, that at the market they give information about places that need girls to serve?'

A straightened hairpin is poked in and pulls out the piece of dried bread. The key enters the keyhole with the precision of a carpenter's brace. The light switch is on the right. A narrow room, closed and without ventilation, identical to the room where Juana sleeps. Inside the wardrobe, with mirrors on its doors, there are men's clothes and fur coats protected by white bed sheets.

'Who do you think you are? Film stars? Countesses?'

In the middle of the room a wooden desk with drawers instead of legs. Her gloved hands tremble on opening the drawers, one by one. The jewels are there, inside different boxes, biscuit ones, silk reel ones, cigar ones, and inside metallic soap dishes, jewels in order of colour, pearls with pearls, yellow gems, transparent ones, reddish and green ones. In the last drawer six small gold bars wrapped in cellophane and a pistol with lettering engraved on its barrel: LLAMA. GABILONDO & CO. Elgóibar (Guipúzcoa).

On the desk, a cardboard-cover notebook and a fountain pen. On the left of the page, dates written in sloping calligraphy. The first: 23rd of July nineteen thirty-six. In the centre column, under the credit side, it says: 'pearls', 'ingots', 'emeralds', 'rubies'. Next to the words 'diamond' and 'sapphire' there is a question mark between brackets. In the right column, names, crossings out and numbers getting smaller as they get closer in time: thirty pieces, twenty, eight, three.

'You're still feeding off what you looted during the war.'

Juana's hands shake as she tries to repeat the same pattern made by the key and chain on the stool from when she found them.

'Think that not even my daughters go in there.'

And the flat on Carmen Street, on the corner of San Lázaro, is filled with imagined noises.

117

8

In those days death had a smell. Juana associated it with the aroma of freshly cut rosemary. It smelt of creosote pearls for stopping a river of blood and for preserving meat from putrefaction, of disinfectant, anise and sesame seeds for funeral wake sweets. Of burnt cotton. The breath of death smelt the same as the rags kept in the bottom chest drawer.

'Juana, go up to the pigeon loft and put a rag there below. And don't you dare go close to the clump of hydrangeas. And don't touch the knives, they'll go blunt, do you hear me?'

The bottom chest drawer, the cesspit where old rags for menstruations and the residues of a paternal memory are hidden from the world: an unfired bullet, a watch with its strap broken, a military campaign record and various pages torn out of the Ecclesiastes.

'Come on Juana, take the tin out of the drawer and read the Bible to us.'

'Always the same. How boring!'

'Well read something else. What else is inside? Take a look, search well.'

'Here's a piece of paper.'

'Let's see... what does it say?'

'You're going to tear it, you brute! Leave it to me... It looks like an address: "Rosario Atienza. Second-hand Bookshop in Argüelles Square (opposite the law courts), Seville".'

Death also smelt of lime and summer.

Matías Iruela, the tenement carpenter, and Carmen Merchán died and were buried in identical smells, in the same midday sun, confused over time, and in the suffocating heat, both led on by the same whiplash of fate.

Matías made his own coffin. Between sawdust coughs he planed down the wood with a jack plane as far as his strength would allow and, when his breath failed him, he sat out on the patio to sway himself in the rocking chair rhythmically swinging to the cobbler's slow hammering. He left the coffin half-finished, vertically leaning against the wall covered in photographs of bullfighters stuck into place with pine resin, amongst tools, planks, brooms and his earthenware drinking jug.

'It's incredible, but with just a drop of anisette the water is cooler.'

The carpenter shut up his workshop with a padlock and chain and he sat to chase lizards out of the corner of his eyes.

'Pepe Luis Vázquez is the greatest. He avoids the bull with a half-turn, how he avoids it! The greatest.'

Matías Iruela could hardly support himself on his tin legs. Tuberculosis had moth-eaten the organdie of his lungs and at the end of his life, like a sparrow with its wings covered in mud, it reduced his existence to the miracle of being able to inflate the bellows of breathing. At nightfall in summer, when the lull fell, it was pleasing to sit next to the jasmine in the belief that its syrupy perfume lubricated his gasps of air. In each stamen, in the wasps knotting buzzes amongst the vine shoots, in the speed with which the lizards popped their heads out of the cracks and climbed up to the pigeon loft, in the sizzle of onion scrapings which Balbina Falcón fried on the stove, in the small talk of the female neighbours embroidering behind the scenes, a tiny miracle lay in ambush for the carpenter to cling on to without strength, amazed, with the will to absorb the instant and extend it, like stretching out a definitive goodbye in a station canteen. His wife took him out onto the patio even when it was getting cooler because, she said, clean air did him good, and she then took the opportunity to air the bed sheets over the balcony rail and sweep the room, freed of the omen of a new fit of coughing. Like this, in the slow evenings in front of his locked up workshop, Matías, reclining in a low rocking chair, swayed and deciphered the enigmas that the clouds sketched in the stretched canvas of the sky or half-closed his eyelids and lay his head back to concentrate on his goldfinch's warbles.

'What a darling little bird. Have you heard it, Merchán? It even seems to sing Andalusian songs for me!'

With the dew of nightfall Dolores covered his knees with a soldier's black blanket which Merchán had given to the carpenter a little while after he became ill. The blanket stank of paraffin and was scarred with cigarette burns.

'Ay, Matías, if only this blanket could tell all it has seen! I can remember off by heart all the train stations of our withdrawal, all of them: Almadenejos, Los Pedroches,

Belalcázar, Cabeza de Buey, Zújar, La Granjuela... You didn't go to war, did you?'

'I missed it because I was too young. My father, who was leader of the farmhands, was executed against our very same cemetery wall when the Falangist Movement started... Now you'll be taking me there.'

When she hung the washing out on the patio wires Dolores Iruela made sure that her husband did not catch her out of the corner of her eye checking the spittle floating in his spittoon at the foot of his rocking chair. The phlegm with traces of blood contrasted with the whiteness of the spittoon. The carpenter wasted himself away in the simple effort of rocking and breathing.

Amongst the women who came to the tenement house on Alpechín Street with mouth-opened shoes for Setefo to repair, there were few who dared ask him about his health, and those that did scrutinised from a distance those pupils of his fluttering the ephemeral sparkle that announces death.

'How you doing, Matías?'

'Well, as you can see, girl; patience and card shuffling.'

Matías Iruela's phrases formed lumps in his throat; he lacked air to conclude them and he came out with them crudely and in short flight, as if he were talking to himself. The carpenter wasted away on the patio among red geraniums and girls' laughter.

'Dolores, go warm my bed. I'm chilled to the bones.'

One evening, soon before dying, Matías gripped hold of the arms of his rocking chair to rouse himself enough to shout.

'Get the girls out of here, get them out. For God's sake!'

Juana watched him paralysed through the kitchen window overlooking the patio: two of her sisters were playing next to the sick man; Consuelo was lying face up next to his rocking chair and the spittoon, and Elvira laughed, covering her mouth. Juana could distinguish their voices.

'Lie down on the ground, Elvira... He isn't wearing anything under the blanket and you can see his prick. Dolores hasn't put underpants on him.'

Juana absorbed the rudeness of the scene rigid behind the oily patina of the glass. Nobody heard the carpenter's wailing. Her mother, oblivious to his pleading, lay defeated on the flock mattress, domesticating her tiredness, her unassailable pain, the tedium and the unnamed desperation of a new pregnancy. Her mother did not get up. Juana remained trapped in the cruel fascination of that game on a draughtboard of red floor tiles and consumptive expectorations. She was hypnotised by the embers of dignity of the man who, given up to the servitude of fate, hung on with tired bones to the very roots of life and tried to form a shout so that someone would take the girls away from him and the vapour of his illness. Matías was hurt not so much by the infantile mocking of his body naked from the waist down, with the soldier's blanket hiding the deflated bag of his testicles, covered in fuzz like seaweed smeared across the faces of those drowned, as by the horror of dragging out the miasma of death.

It was Juana who washed the hands and tongues of her sisters with a piece of caustic soda soap.

The carpenter passed away in his sleep; his shattered lungs wore him out from breathing and he never opened his eyelids again. He died in a dream fragranced by cherry tree and lignum vitae shavings, houseleeks and goldfinches that sang him flamenco. The female neighbours of Alpechín Street shrouded him on the workbench of his workshop. The sawdust crackled under their rapid feet. They combed him with splashes of cheap cologne, parting his hair in the middle, they washed his skinny body with cloths soaked in freezing water from the well; his armpits, his chest as if gnawed at by spiders, his flabby arms, his scrotum populated with gulfweed. They shaved his angular face with the apprehension of catching something, they dressed him in a clean white neckband shirt and in his wedding trousers which they tied with a cord around his hips because of the extreme thinness the tuberculosis had condemned him to. His cold uncovered feet, sockless. Not even Chachachica dared cut his toenails.

During the wake Chacha placed a plate with salt on top of him so that his stomach would not bloat. The carpenter seemed even smaller inside the crude wooden box, under the orange light of the oil lamps. His wife, Dolores, dressed in black, surrounded by black wailing, dug her nails into her flesh. She cried not out of pain but out of the fright of her own thoughts.

'Matías, I've bought you five cents worth of salted pork lard.'

His greasy lips chewed without appetite, now without strength. The immense pupils of the man swallowing the ball of fat and breathing laboriously in the small hours of breathlessness. Food to nourish death.

In Juana's infantile eyes, in the commotion of percale housecoats, shone her fascination for the greying hairs breaking through in Matías's beard.

'Chachachica says hair and nails continue growing on the flesh of the dead.'

It was the same flesh that the day before rocked on the patio, the same flesh that throbbed, that still sustained a thin line of subtle air between its fingertips until the black bird

123

ascended to heaven with a rabid flapping of wings and with the fish of death trapped in its beak.

Juana's father went to the funeral wearing the dead man's oversized shoes. He had to fill the toecaps with newspaper.

'For all the walking the poor man will do now, Merchán should make use of them.'

Setefo, the cobbler, tied up the feeble pine coffin with a rope so that the corpse would not fall out on its way from the tenement house on Alpechín Street to the cemetery. The carpenter did not even have time to coat his own coffin with aniline.

Carmen Merchán died two months later. She passed away accepting her own death, and she did not cry or feel sorry for herself, not even the few times she was left alone in the room separated from the kitchen by an esparto curtain. Her postnatal haemorrhage after giving birth to her only male child and the septicaemia which she later caught submerged her into lethargy during which she talked in a whisper – and evermore less – about everyday affairs to trick death's astuteness: the honeysuckle in flower, the boxes of fish sold at the market stall, the latest brawl in the tenement house, the prank of one of her daughters, the lateness of the rains, the money hidden in the curtain fold. Chachachica licked her index finger each time she recounted the notes. Without knowing how to add up, she was never wrong.

'Monday, Tuesday, Wednesday...'

The closeness of bodies in the tightness stopped Carmen feeling vertigo, the sentiment of profound loneliness, of being at death's door. Only during the siesta, the house silent, the rope-soled sandals bewildered at the foot of the bed, the buzz of heat beyond the window shutters left ajar, only then did

Carmen feel the uneasiness of having lived in vain, for nothing, to languish at the wrong time and in silence like a candle flame. She died with a devastating sensation of tiredness.

Carmen Merchán went into labour one evening at the end of July. The patio's female neighbours alerted themselves by shouting from the upper balcony.

'Carmen has broken waters. Hurry up, Balbina!'

'Don't be in such a hurry, that one's a veteran and gives birth easily, like a rabbit.'

Manuel Merchán had not yet returned from the market and they sent Rafael, the eldest of the barbers, to tell him. The shouts of Balbina Falcón, the carpenter's wife, and Chachachica resounded among the pots of boiling water steaming over the house. Juana's mother was keeling on the uneven floor of her room and blood accumulated on the skirting board like still hot little livers. The baby was imprisoned with an old man's eyes in the purple lips of her vagina. Juana and Isabel, holding hands, scrutinised the women's comings and goings behind the esparto curtain, their eyes terrified and fixed on the secure arms of the midwife.

'Lay her down, lay her on the floor! But what are you doing? Have you gone mad? Carmen's bleeding to death, we're losing her!'

The umbilical cord floated in the spittoon with the grey sadness of drowned anchovies in a cooking pot. The razor blade on the overhang of the cupboard, its paper sheaf torn by haste and nervous hands, bitten by blood and fingers, a wrapping with a silhouette of the Giralda – the Seville cathedral tower. SEVILLIAN KNIVES.

The midwife washed the fragile body of the newborn child in a washbasin.

'It's a boy, a boy! Carmen, do you hear me?'

The only male child to survive her was baptised with the name José because adversity – the tender skeletons of the two Manuels lay in the cemetery – had rejected the possibility of baptising him with that name. After giving birth, Juana's mother wasted away pallid on the flock mattress. On entering the room only her eyes could be distinguished, sunken in the pillow. Juana's father could not even sing to alleviate himself, and pity shrunk him in the passing of the days, one identical to the others.

'I can't do anything for you, Merchán. Her infection is now very advanced. Ask a member of your family for a loan or pawn something, a ring, I don't know.'

'A ring? But what ring? Are you aware of just what you're telling me?'

Chachachica unpicked the curtain fold with determination. The rolled up notes smelt of rancid horse mackerel.

'Why do you save money in the fold?'

'To buy your father a grey worsted suit, nosey.'

The little curtain that covered the pantry's lower shelves was blue polka-dotted. It was made from a cutting of cloth that the delegate of the Female Branch of the Falange had given to Juana at school. A cutting of cloth, a veil for wearing to mass, a set square or a wedge of American cheese for Doña Amalia's obedient pupils. Whatever was given.

'Mother, I want a frilled skirt. Blue and polka-dotted. A skirt for wearing to the village fête.

The penicillin arrived smuggled from the port of Algeciras, originally from Gibraltar on the other side of the bay, hidden in a grouper's stomach, shortly after Manuel Merchán had agreed a price at the club. Chachachica slit the fish's stomach and pulled out from among its guts four transparent ampoules full of white powder. Death smiled in her toothless mouth. The voracious infection engulfed Carmen's body. Juana's father, felled by pain, awaited her end under the flowering clusters of vine with his face plunged in his hands or else doodling on the patio floor with a twig. His voice choked in his throat.

'Lemon and cinnamon, / mixed with jasmine, / that's how your body smells to me when / you snuggle up to me.'

During Carmen's agony at the Merchán's' home words were ambushed by muffled noises, by looks that were fish hooks, by whispers, by the moaning of objects. Chachachica earnestly devoted herself to doing the housework and, at night, although she was exhausted on the straw mattress, anguish thwarted her from resting. Her voices between dreams swirled down the pigeon loft stairs.

'Captain Díaz Criado, I hope to God you never find peace... And the evil you long for will lead you to the grave, the evil you long for will lead you to the grave, the evil you long for will lead you to the grave.'

The carpenter and Carmen died in a slow summer of dust and cicadas.

'Juana, run and tell Don Ignacio to come to the house with his holy oils. Go in through the vestry. And hurry, girl. Run.'

The ghostly sound of the handbell accompanying the viaticum could be heard from the beginning of Carmen Street, before crossing Quijada Street, under a sun trailing incandescent over the line of midday. Don Ignacio sweated in his chasuble. Some passers-by knelt down on the cobblestone ground as the priest passed with his altar boy, who walked ahead with a chalice in his dirty hands and a surplice tightened from starch. Others took off their hats and slowly crossed themselves, the hat brims held against their chests. The tinkle of the handbell rang unreal in the silence of the dusty streets. The heat and the light – mostly the furious light reverberating off the whitewashed walls – produced a sensation of strangeness: it was impossible to die in the amber blaze of an August midday.

The priest left his things on the overhang of the cupboard and after anointing oil crosses on Juana's mother's dried lips, palms and feet he burnt the cotton ball. Exhausted, drained of blood, hardly a hint of a smile on her lips, Juana's mother lay on the double bed and her complexion blended in with the whiteness of the pillow. Her nightie covered in flies, its lace edging faded, her breasts still full of milk, her ankles gaunt. Chachachica had intertwined her hands with a rosary and a sprig of rosemary. Freshly cut rosemary in dead hands that had never learnt to caress.

'Mother, it was me. I stopped the rain.'

And the memory of a dry slap on her cheek.

Juana watched the extreme unction from aside, protected by the firmness of an esparto curtain. The Latin prayers fell like rotten wood onto the oblique glare of the room.

'Sacrosanta humane reparationis misteria te omnipotens Deus et omnis presentis, future vite penas perdixit misteria sempiterna perducat.'

The horror of seeing fulfilled her desires hidden in the cracks of the pigeon loft.

I hope the rain doesn't return.

I hope Andrea's hair grows down to her waist.

I hope no more siblings are born.

Fulfilled desires that smelt of fish. Blue and terrible desires.

'Chachachica says rocking an empty cradle brings bad luck.'

During the wake Juana could not take her eyes off her

128

mother's lifeless body, her immobile mouth that had put up with the punishment of pregnancy, quarantine and hunger in silence, with an expression carved in her cheekbones that was one not of sadness but of anguish perhaps, a grief that penetrated when felt. When Juana's mother laughed – the handful of times she had laughed – her laughter cracked intimidatingly into the air. She laughed and her laughter was a whip lacerating misery's back. Chachachica fanned herself with eyes closed sitting on the bulrush chair while the female neighbours of Alpechín Street talked in whispers, were coming and going and looked after the men. Juana, her terrified eyes on the corpse's stomach, rescued a tiny memory stabbed into her bosom that glinted.

Juana is seven years old and is the girl pressing her eyes to discover stars and fluorescent spirals on the black curtain of her eyelids. She is the girl throwing pebbles into the well and believes that the whines of the pulley are the wails of blue dead men that do not rest in peace and are wandering groping their away along in the damp darkness of the shed, among flowerpots of aspidistras, on winter nights in the howling east wind, under the pigeon loft beams, among the gelatinous drowsiness of hunger. Juana hugs Azucena's crunchy body, the doll stuffed with wood shavings picked up from the carpenter's workshop. Azucena has a black embroidered ball-eyed sad look. The girl hugs her doll while she prepares her tea: stones, shiny fragments of brick, dried leaves, sour grapes, geranium petals, comb teeth, broken buttons. The girl hugs the body of cherry tree sawdust now without fragrance, hears shouting out on the patio and stiffly observes the scene: Setefo, the cobbler, is facing his shack door with his red

Carlist beret and the open bowleg leggings held up by his paunch. Setefo holds the tied opening of a sack he had shoved a cat into and he is beating it with a plank. The cobbler is biting the tip of his tongue to perfect his cruelty. The cat miaows, screeches, spits, curls its back into a ball, tries to escape the pain by wriggling, scratching the sack cloth until it is left exhausted. Setefo says he is going to make himself rice with cat. The seven-year-old girl is asked if she wants a plate of rice with cat.

'Cats are the cleanest there are... Chickens are dirtier, they eat their own shit.'

'Hang it to air, hang it, leave it skinned to air.'

Setefo skins the animal with a cobbler's knife and hangs the still steaming meat from a rusty eyebolt to air. The man with the red beret laughs with his mouth wide open, surrounded by adults talking with raucous voices. Juana's mother also roars with laughter with her head back. The cobbler has a few teeth missing.

'Hamito the Moor sucked threads of cheap tobacco with his palate. He was gap-toothed above and on the lower gum he only had two teeth left. He'd walk through the trenches without fearing the bullets and repeated the same phrase: "Cold water, cedar, girlfriend writing paper." Over and over again. Enough to make us crazy.'

Juana is paralysed by fear and loathing.

'Girl, do you want a plate of rice with cat? We'll add chilli peppers to the fried onion and tomato base. And garlic.'

Juana is frozen with panic, incapable of answering. The same as her father, words get stuck in her throat. Her mother roars with laughter and holds her pregnant stomach with hands red from washing. A vulgar laugh, cynical, intimidating. Juana closes her eyes to hide the horror and begins crying. A humiliating smack on the back of her head, and her mother's circular voice. 'Fool, you big fool... You're very fussy for one so poor.'

The gravediggers waited outside, under the patio vine, with a bottle of brandy submerged in water in the sink. From the wrought-iron gate Juana, with the baby in her arms, watched the cortège walk off to the cemetery down Alpechín Street flooded by sunlight. The coffin without iron fittings wobbled on the bony shoulders of the two buriers in shirt sleeves and rope-soled sandals. Merchán walked, head bowed behind them, dragging his too-big shoes in the tow air, with a black arm band on his jacket. The procession stopped to catch its breath in Salitre Square, on whose stones the gravediggers rested the coffin to wipe their sweat with white handkerchiefs. The heat pulled cellophane tape off the prickly pear leaves.

Life resumed as before after the maternal absence.
'Girl, help me peel potatoes.'
Chachachica and Juana peel tiny potatoes, cutting off their shoots with a surgeon's expertise, cutting out the frost damaged bits and placing the slices into a white enamel washbasin. The knife blade glides swiftly in Chacha's mannish hands. Juana works carefully with long nails painted the same colour as morello cherries.
'What's up with you, child?'
'Me, nothing.'
'You couldn't trick me even if you tried.'
Chachachica wipes off the starch covering the blade of the knife on the corner of her apron. Juana looks out of the corner of her eye at the old woman's spider-like movements and

131

reproduces the image in her memory, the same scene folding in on itself from back in time, towards the past. Two women peeling potatoes in the stillness of the kitchen, boiled potatoes, slow-fried potatoes and green pimientos, potatoes with saffron, plain potatoes. And a bowl of lard on the table, presiding over hunger.

'A letter has arrived from your father in Barcelona. Rafael, the eldest *falcon*, has read it to me.'

'And what does he say?'

'Nothing.'

In infancy, gestures centred on the mechanical act of eating hid no messages. With time, however, pans began to speak a ciphered language that adults only managed to intuit through silence and habit. The olive oil bottle and the frying pans talked in a whisper of the joy of peeling very poor potatoes, of chopping an onion with sore eyes and of hearing it sizzling away lively as the zenith light of summer fell across the rooftops. They talked about the happy anticipation of the act of eating in the oil boiled on the stove, of the clatter of plates and forks placed in disorder onto the table, of the number of pots and pans uselessly dirtied in preparing the same meagre stew every day. Cumin seed, bay leaves and thyme for perfuming hunger. Eighteen eyes around the table followed the conscientious sharing out by Chachachica's hands that prolonged the implicit language of the pots into the quantities: manliness and paternity sat at the head of the table, Juana's mother's new pregnancy, perhaps a punishment, the illness of one of her sisters.

'Angel of God, give her a little more; we almost lost her to pleurisy this winter.'

'Isabel, you green cigar, eel, long fingers, spider legs.'

The violent contrast between the before and after of eating.

132

The empty bowls – miraculously steaming a millisecond before – renewed their conversation after the cheerful ritual of making the food and swallowing it. Whispering, they then said that the food never filled them and that their stomachs should be satisfied in the hope of waiting, in the effort of not thinking about food, in the insufferable melancholy after lunch, only interrupted by a quick gesture, an insignificant remark, an occurrence, by the use of repetition.

'The end of the war caught me in Almadén, in the province of Ciudad Real.'

Juana had been waiting in silence, in the certainty with which one awaits the inevitable. In that house stripped of words, the fateful conversation took place one morning at the end of February.

Isabel is washing down the patio floor. In the kitchen, behind the esparto curtain, Juana and Chachachica are shelling broad beans and an uncomfortable silence separates the two of them.

'What's up with you, girl?'

'Me, nothing.'

'You couldn't trick me even if you tried. For days something's been on your mind'

Jet earrings swing from the old woman's elephantine ears.

'This morning Damián brought a letter from your father in Barcelona. Rafael, the eldest *falcon*, has read it to me.'

'What does he say.'

'He's working on a big building site and he's waiting for you and your sister Isabel. He's already found accommodation for both of you in a boarding house. There's work, mostly for servants. He says they give information about places that need girls in shops and at market stalls.'

Juana stares at the tip of her rope-sole sandals. The recently pronounced words cut an apprehension until this moment cottony, vague, shapeless, without attributes or contours: to be living on the tips of your toes, like a shadow, in a place where you now do not belong.

'There's nothing for it, Juana. You know you'll have to leave the village. That's the itching you've had these last few days.'

'If there weren't so many mouths...'

'Everything in this world, when shared out, turns out to be less for everyone. But there's one thing, just one, that means there's more for everyone: hunger. Leave, you've got to try to leave the village.'

'I'm afraid...'

'You oughtn't be afraid of nothing, Juana, not even of death. All roads are uphill, and in this life you've got to keep on moving on without looking back, always forward, always, even if you have to prod the side of your horse with paper spurs.'

'So many mouths, so much hunger, why?'

'You've got to try to leave the village, girl, you've got to try, even if it breaks your heart. You must go to Barcelona because your father needs you there. I'll stay with the children until you can take them.'

'And in a few years who will look after you? You'll be alone in the village.'

'I don't need much. The ox only licks itself well alone.'

'I'll miss you... Don't ever die on me, Chacha.'

'Well, my time will come, girl, like for everyone. Nobody stays to tell what it's like.'

'I'd like to be at your side to close your eyes. I want it to be me. Will you send me a signal?'

'I'll send you one.'

'And how will I know it's you?'

'You'll know, girl. You'll know.'

The vague sensation of living in the past.

'Why when we were little did Andrea say my father was a coward? When she took us to the cemetery there were sparks in her eyes, she parted the thicket with a swipe and she showed us the bullet holes in the plastering. She said that during the war they executed the day labourers against the cemetery wall. Her father had told her. She repeated it to make me furious.'

'Lower your voice, Juana... That's just idle talk. Old things.'

'You always do the same; you swallow your words without chewing them.'

'And who cares about that now? Who wants to remember? For what?'

'Is it true that my father was in the gang that killed Don Jacinto Maldonado?'

'Who told you that?'

'Andrea; the carpenter told her before dying. They thrust a pitchfork into the foreman's stomach and they shot Don Jacinto. They set fire to the Dueña Alta stables and painted the wall of the wrought-iron gate with their blood: "Bread, work and less Holy Week". The mares neighed crazy from pain. Her father also told her that the stink of scorched flesh could be smelt from beyond the manor house boundaries.'

'Shut up, girl, shut up. I'll tell you just one thing. Your father isn't a coward... Hunger was to blame, bloody hunger.'

Part Two

9

Captain Díaz Criado Gavira stretched, as was his habit, at the lethargic hour of the siesta wrapped in a yellow laziness that stuck toothpicks in his eyelids. With one swipe of his hand he removed the bed sheets, damp from his own sweat. He sat up and blood returned thick to his pulse. He studied the covering of his body with exactness, as if each member pleaded for the spur prick of his gaze to restart life: the accordion fat of his belly, his thirsty tongue, his aching testicles – he lingered looking at the straw-coloured stain on his underpants – the stiff musculature of his nape and shoulders. His headache hindered the superhuman effort of putting on his socks, sweaty from the day before.

The balcony of his room overlooked Jesús del Gran Poder Street. The trickle of water being poured into the ceramic washbasin was a mere murmur in the heat of the room, shielded against the glare of the sun by an esparto Persian blind. The captain looked at himself in the mirror which was criss-crossed with veins of decayed mercury. He pinched his cheeks with thick, short, hairy-boned fingers. He belched. He forced a tight jawed smile and sniffed the hollows of his hands that retained the sweet and salty smell of a vagina. He reluctantly washed them in the basin.

'Aurora, you whore, you bitch... You want to ruin my life.'

The contact of his face with the water, warmed in the muggy heat of the room, hardly managed to wake him up. He wetted his hair, combing it back with his fingers, and positioned his peaked cap over his receding hairline. The captain did not use brilliantine.

He descended the marble stairs holding on to the banister. The stifling heat and the alcohol still undigested blurred distance and volumes. He crossed himself twice in the hallway and with a mechanical gesture, without looking at it, he checked that he had his gun in its holster. He stepped out into the white fire of the street.

In July, at the end of that torrid July of nineteen thirty-six, Seville was the rotten mouth of hell. The shadow of heat drew liquid crystal arabesques in the air. The city pretended to sleep an impossible siesta of terror and esparto, while the captain advanced in the sultry afternoon heat with his eyes fixed on the caps of his boots impeccably shined the night before at the Las Siete Puertas flamenco venue.

'Aurora is one real woman and very suave, Don Manuel. Ay, that hair and that little porcelain face of hers! Don't trust her, captain, don't trust her.'

The shoeshine man's drooling and servile face invited the delirium of grabbing him by the scruff of his neck and burning his corneas with the glowing tip of a cigarette, of going deaf from his blind cries and getting drunk on the arousing stench of his burnt flesh.

'Don't trust her Don Manuel, there's a reason she's called the Knife, there's a reason.'

Díaz Criado opened the shutters to the only balcony his office had. An arrow of light pierced the polished mahogany desk. The inkwell, the letter opener with its bull horn hilt – the captain used it to clean his finger nails – the telephone, the black folder with the list of prisoners and, to one side, a skull on a wooden base where it said in Gothic lettering: 'This is how I see myself for being a bad Spaniard.' Everything in place. The familiar presence of objects, the austerity of the office and the smell of old wood marinated into a balm that seemed to alleviate his migraine. The naked walls, the wooden armchair and the coffee table, the four-seat leather sofa for visitors and a clothes wardrobe on whose shelf the captain rested his peaked cap and where he hung on a coat hanger his uniform jacket with three stars encrusted in its cuff.

His hangover pierced his gums. The fried baby birds for supper still floated in Moriles oloroso wine inside the puddle of his stomach. The black and white tiled floor shrank and stretched capriciously, at the mercy of the shooting pain striking at his temples. The floor throbbed and the captain was calmed by immersing himself into the obsessive draughtsboard of the floor and covering the room with big strides, stepping on the black tiles – only the black ones – without even brushing against the gaps that separated them from the white ones. He began to make himself dizzy and laid himself down to sleep on the visitors' sofa.

The captain pressed the buzzer as he searched for change in the pocket of his khaki trousers. He went to the window

141

to distinguish the coins. The air, heavy with the heat, slowed the rhythm of his breathing. A man in a corporal's uniform, extremely thin, opened the sliding door and made a military salute.

'At your command, captain.'

'José, go to the bar and bring me a cup of white coffee and a piece of toast. Also bring a bottle of brandy. And get rid of everyone. Today I won't receive visitors; give me a rest.'

The captain forced himself to gobble down his disgust and the bread smeared in oil to settle his stomach and absorb the alcohol that flooded his gut. Díaz Criado only ate hot food over dinner, which he invariably had at the Pasaje del Duque restaurant.

He hung the holster strap onto the back of his chair. The light brushed the spiders off the dossiers copied on carbon paper. He pressed his eyes. He returned to smelling his hands stained with oil, searching for the memory of Aurora the Knife amongst the blurred remains of the night. He rested the weight of his body on the back legs of his chair, made his neck comfortable on the head rest and looked up at the ceiling. He unbuttoned his shirt; the heat softened his will and his movements. The hotchpotch of dossiers bored him. The captain preferred the list of corpses removed by the military investigating judge in the working-class neighbourhoods – Triana, El Pumarejo, La Macarena, San Julián – or at the entrance to country villages to be read to him.

'Corpse of a man about 45 years old in the clothes of a rural postman and the initials J.S. on his trousers; wounded in the left temporal bone. Corpse of Andrés Vázquez Gaitán, identified by his neighbours, with a gunshot wound in the right cheek. Corpse of a man about 25 years old with the face destroyed; identification impossible.'

He paused in delight at the fantasy opened up by the details, in their precise morbidity, in the precision of objects stripped of identity but palpable: the tobacco pouch found in a pocket, a peseta and twenty-five cents, the Montepío notebook stained with blood or the payment book from the cork factory, the foundry, or the olive warehouse, the tattoo on a chest – 'Long live anarchy!' – the Red Aid coupon, the handkerchief with the initials R.R.

'Ricardo Ramos. Rafael Robles. Ramón Rodríguez. Ramiro Ruano, perhaps. Red Rat.'

Compassion made him sick. The captain could justify any human weakness, but compassion gave him nausea.

He heard the corporal's characteristic tapping at the sliding door. The little man stood to attention once again at the threshold. The captain felt uncomfortable by his fluttering gaze and his nervous cough. He knew his ticks.

'Captain, a woman there outside insists on seeing you.'

'I've already told you I don't want to see anyone. I don't feel well.'

'The woman's looking for her godson. She doesn't know which prison he's in, she hasn't been told. She says she's come walking all the way from Puebla del Acebuche... She's pretty. She's got sky-blue eyes.'

'And you, what's up with you? Have I got to repeat it to you? If you want to fuck her, take her down to the basement or take the afternoon off; I don't need you. I've already told you José: get rid of everyone, all of them. I've got a horrible headache. If you're so interested, tell her to come back tomorrow. Or the day after. Today I'm not here for anyone.'

143

10

Escaping through the windows without Persian blinds or
curtains are the fumes of a breakfast fry-up and the guttural
voice of Antonio Molina interrupted by an advert for Titanlux
paints. The neighbourhood of one-floor hovels climbs the side
of a hill that rises in the city's imprecise limits and sketches
a labyrinth of untarmacked slopes, flooded in mud when it
rains or carpeted in stubborn dust that stiffens your palate
and the cavities of your nose on dry days. A Sunday off work.
The damp December morning stabs the sky. The wind whips
up dust clouds that scratch the corners of your eyes. Juana
walks holding her sister Isabel's arm and notices the
increasing pressure of the gradient in her calves. Isabel trips
against the stones in her high-heeled shoes – she has no other
pair – and clumsily climbs the slope, leaning her weight
against Juana's body. A few metres ahead Manuel Merchán
and his Cordovan friend Lucas Naranjo go up the hill

accompanied by a man who was waiting for them in the square, his hair combed back with brilliantine, a green scarf knotted around his neck. He was wearing a pair of brown leather buckled shoes with straps stretched by his bunions. The three men talk. The Cordovan, Lucas Naranjo, wears the top of a Parker fountain pen sticking out of his jacket pocket.

The two girls walk in silence. Juana looks at the unknown landscape, at the recently invented streets with the names of fish and planets, and at the cardboard signs hanging from improvised walls: 'LA MACARENA WINE CELLAR BAR', '*SPUNG* CAKES AND FRITTERS', 'SHEET METAL, CHIP-BOARD, FRAMES AND STRIPS FOR SALE'. A canary sings trapped inside a cage. A ring road hugs the base of the hillock. Seen from the top of the mount is, at its feet, a lunar gully, naked of trees, the rust of old drums and smashed tiles glinting over the coppery land and, beyond, car tracks corroded by saltpetre and a carpet of cement crashing into the sea. Following the profile of the coast, on the horizon line, the panorama is populated by grey chimneys, factories, slums and corrugated asbestos and cement roofed warehouses.

The gloomy loneliness of the slums on the edge of town.

The man with the leather buckled shoes stops when they come to a green painted door. He looks behind him, at the girls, and takes out a set of keys from his pocket.

'We've arrived. It's here.'

The group go out onto the patio, an empty rectangle with a greenish cement floor crossed in the middle by a sewer that drains out into the slope of the hill. Two doors open out onto this soulless patio. The man with the buckled shoes mistakes the keys. The smaller door – an aluminium sheet with holes at the top for ventilation and fixed into the plaster of the wall with two eyebolts and a padlock – opens into the cesspool and the latrine, separated from the neighbouring back garden by a wattle fence.

'This was put up by my brother-in-law Paco a bit at a time, on holiday, whenever he could get away to Spain. He built this house with his own hands. My brother-in-law has lived in Germany for three years; in Hamburg, I think it is. He works in a tinned food factory and because you can make good money there, he's been able to build this to have somewhere to live should he ever return. But, as they say, Paco would never dream of returning because he's got a good job. My sister Remedios also found work out there.'

The man with the leather buckled shoes says the house is rented furnished. Three amber-coloured duralex glasses rest upside down on the worktop, next to a coal stove. On the wall hangs a plate rack and an out of date calendar with printed letters that say ESPUNY WORKSHOPS, red crossing outs and the image of Mount Montserrat. At one end of the kitchen three chairs and a foldable table are stacked aside against the wall.

The smell of enclosed dampness forces Juana to screw up her nose. Lucas Naranjo and Merchán look at each other; the Cordovan shrugs his shoulders in a gesture of tired acceptance. Juana projects the image of her father and his Cordovan friend at the foot of a scaffold, with metallic lunch boxes on their laps, back broken and chewing cold meatballs. She closes her eyes and gives up: four cardboard walls on a slope for giving up being the servant of a thief who sells stolen jewellery.

'How much are you asking for the place?' Merchán asks with his hands inside his pockets. His trousers are too short for him; his bony ankles can be seen.

'Two hundred pesetas a month for the rent and four

hundred down as a deposit... Well, about the deposit, we could reduce it if we reach an agreement.'

Merchán does not know how to do sums in his head. The monthly rent, the deposit, the train tickets for his five children waiting for word in Puebla de Acebuche... Merchán and his daughter Juana briefly look at each other: what they have got saved, is not enough.

'Tell me, good man, if we give you a payment and a deposit, will you keep the house for us for a month?' Merchán whispers. Words leave his throat, being pushed out.

The man puffs out and looks down at the cement floor. Red socks can be seen through the gaps in his shoes.

'A month is a long time. You've got to think that others will want to take this place off my hands. There are a lot of people looking for a place to live in the district, as you know. If you give me a fortnight, we can still reach an agreement.'

In twenty days Manuel Merchán and his Cordovan friend will have to come up with enough money to put down a deposit and buy an additional second-hand mattress. Their families waiting in Cordoba and Seville, in their villages of origin, will have to wait a little longer. The man puts two hundred pesetas in his back trouser pocket. He seems to be trustworthy. Lucas Naranjo pulls the top off his Parker pen. The landlord tears three pages off the calendar and writes three times in pointed letters his first name and surnames, the amount received and the address of the house he is renting. Three copies, one for each. Manuel Merchán practices a clumsy flourish on the back of September. His Cordovan friend signs with three Xs in the margin of the paper, three intimidating crosses. Juana's father and Lucas Naranjo promise to meet the man with the leather buckled shoes in three Sundays' time, at the same hour, in the square. Merchán calculates that he will have to jump out of bed at four in the morning to arrive at the building site on time. Two buses, at least, and a lot of shoe sole.

Sunday extinguishes itself amongst banana tree leaves. When Juana reaches Carmen Street, on the corner of San Lázaro, she sees light on the fifth-floor balcony and outlines a grimace of displeasure on her lips: Salud Monterde will not go out tonight. Juana is annoyed that the lady stays at home on Sunday nights, depriving her of a few hours of relaxing alone, when she could wash up the dinner dishes her own way, with the radio on, putting up with the light weight of her melancholy and without feeling observed.

'What can I do for you, señora?'

'Girl, do me a favour and prepare me a washbasin of warm water and salt; my feet are swollen like barrels. I went walking with Feliu to the Ciudadela Park and from there we went to San Juan Avenue and all the way down to Generalísimo Avenue. What a really long walk! I won't go out this evening, Lord no. My daughters can take charge of business. I'm not in the mood for bars and late nights.'

Señora Monterde says she is worn out, but Juana knows that the truth is otherwise, they are selling little. It is ever more difficult to sell jewellery and the Monterdes cannot even find customers for the most simple of rings, those thin ones like noodles that Señor Pech makes. Business is not going well. Juana hears them arguing from the kitchen as they eat after she has served them.

'Girls, I want you awake; like two hares.'

'The fears and scruples of certain people make me sick.'

148

They are always quarrelling. Señorita Mercedes mashes her peas on her plate before eating them and when she speaks her words have the pungent taste of bitter apples.

'Here's the water, señora.'

'Oh, good! Let's see if I can ease the pain a little... Sit down at my side girl.'

Juana withdraws within herself; she is surprised that the lady wants to strike up a conversation and fears that the reason is that she has found out about her imprudent violation of the intimacy of the sealed room, where the gold and the gems are hidden. Salud Monterde places her deformed feet into the warm water.

'Ow, how my feet hurt! It's as if my big toe's been crushed by a hammer.'

Juana mistrusts the relaxed tone with which the lady begins the chat. Stroking her back and, later, when she has relaxed, a heavy blow to the back of her neck. Salud Monterde has tucked up her silk dressing gown, printed with dragons and discoloured cherries, up to the middle of her thighs where blue varicose veins snake. Juana looks at her hands: she has still got white flaying from nitric acid.

'Where were you today, girl?'

'Walking with my father and my sister Isabel. We went to visit a man from our village who lives in Casa Antúnez.' Juana avoids looking at the lady. Juana's lies are transparent.

'In Casa Antúnez? There where the shantytown is?' Salud Monterde slants her green eyes; she bites the skin of her thumb and chews on it. 'That's incredible... They arrive from the south by the tonne, so many there's no room for us all. And all these people from Andalusia and Murcia breed like rabbits. They say the Civil Guard wait for them at the Francia

Station and from there they take them to Montjuïc Stadium until they've got enough people to fill another train and they then send them back home. There are those who come with their earthenware drinking jugs and cuttings for planting on balconies... How very narrow-minded!'

Juana looks down at the floor. She fears Salud Monterde will corner her against the truth and force her to confess that yes, she did enter the forbidden room and that she will stop serving at her home as soon as she has saved enough money for her siblings to move to Barcelona. Her thoughts flutter over the grey hill and shacks on the edge of town.

'And you, girl, how many brothers and sisters did you say were left in the village?' Salud Monterde lights a Chesterfield with her head leaning back.

'Four girls and a boy, the little one. They live with my great-aunt. Well, she's not related, but she's always lived with us, and we love her a lot. All the people in the village know her as Chachachica, Little Nanny, because she's short and always ready and willing. Only Isabel and I have come to Barcelona.'

'Seven children, that's incredible!'

Juana looks at her damaged hands.

Night falls beyond the balcony overlooking Carmen Street. Juana wants to go to bed. The lady's eyes intimidate her.

'Seven children, with it being so hard after the war and all! But, at least, I'd say that in the countryside you could still steal a melon once in a while or go gleaning. But in the city, here, in Barcelona, oh mother! I was a fully grown woman when the war broke out and I thought I'd seen everything. Oh, girl, if I were to tell you! One day there was a rumour that a ship filled with oil drums had docked in the port and the people threw themselves out of desperation into the sea not knowing how to swim, girl, without knowing how to swim, to raid the hold. Several drowned and they had to be pulled out with ropes... Seven children, that's incredible. I had enough with two. And, to tell the truth, better none at all.'

Juana listens in silence, looking at her damaged kitchen maid's hands. She is confused by her excitement: she fears and at the same time wants Señora Monterde to confess in a moment of distraction where the jewellery she keeps in the desk of the sealed room came from.

'Thieves, you live off what you looted during the war. My poor mother said so: you took buckets, bucketfuls.'

But the chat advances in lazy meanderings. The lady speaks and speaks and speaks. About the war and her first husband, about her daughters and her exhaustion. She speaks for herself in a loud voice. Juana only needs two ears that pretend to hear and agree.

Salud Monterde has gone to bed early. Juana undresses in her room. Naked except for her knickers that cover her belly button and her woollen socks, she goes to the cardboard suitcase to comply with her nightly ritual. Before going to bed she takes comfort in counting the money she has saved.

'Good man, if we give you a payment and a deposit, will you keep the house for us for a month?'

Only her nocturnal counting, alone in the room with the small window ventilated by the kitchen, justifies her living in someone else's home. Juana keeps the money in a crocheted bag with its opening tied with a cotton thread cord; Chachachica crocheted it for her. She pulls out the rolled up notes, counts them and money is missing: two one hundred peseta notes. She recounts the money, this time more slowly, to convince herself that she has made a mistake. But money is still missing. Terror freezes her to the marrow. She tries to remember and reconstructs the morning step by step. No matter how much she goes over it in her mind, when she went down to Carmen Street she only carried a five peseta coin rolled in her handkerchief which she usually kept in the cuff of her jersey. Two hundred pesetas are missing.

Juana cries naked, under the bed sheet, with her eyes open in the blackness of the room. She has no more energy to put on her nightie. She cries out of rage, out of pity or out of humiliation or out of all those minced up confused sentiments. When she was a girl Juana believed that sky-blue eyed people, like Chachachica, cried blue tears.

'Crying is good, girl, because it cleans your eyes and makes them bigger.'

Her almond and brown eyes cry mud. Juana bites on the corner of her pillow so that the lady does not hear her sob. She has never had the freedom to cry alone, freely, to stamp, shout, run away, to hug and console herself.

The evilness of the Monterdes perturbs her: her money has not left Carmen Street, on the corner of San Lázaro. Juana imagines them rummaging through her clothes, bent over her cardboard suitcase. Could it have been Señorita Mercedes? She imagines her wobbling on her stiletto heels when she returns home in the morning with her mascara having run, her mouth furry and a newspaper under her arm.

'Tell me Juana, do you touch yourself there below?'

And that drunken laugh of hers.

Juana cannot begin to understand how the Monterdes have been able to rob from her. She would wish to remain sleeping and wake up somewhere else, far away, away from the world and all that surrounds it, away from the grey and gagged city that scrutinises the servant's hands scorched by nitric acid. She knows she will be incapable of raising her voice and she will stick her nose to the ground like a basset hound, like her father, like her mother did, like Chacha would. They called Doña Rosita, the dressmaker, a liar and beat her from the flat. Señora Monterde's small green eyes spit evilness.

'Girl, do me a favour and prepare me a washbasin of warm water and salt; my feet are swollen like barrels.'

The lady has had the nerve to ask her for a washbasin and, as if nothing had happened, then began talking about everything, about life, her memories, her daughters, as if she, Doña Salud Monterde, the great dame, the respected neighbourhood jeweller, on airs on her white high-heeled shoes, had not entered into the room of that silly girl who hand-washes her slip stinking of tobacco and sweat and had not rummaged through her things with fat fingers like leeches fattened with blood. Juana would not dare to reclaim her money. She cries. She will go from the flat and leave her to her wheeling and dealing, her cigarette butts squashed into her bowl of soup and her red hangnail fingers. She will leave her, her and her daughters, with their white and polished skeletons, because the three will wake up one day dead, devoured by woodworm and those little silvery wood fish, with their eyes emptied by termites that spring up in beams, drawers and chests. Yes, she will leave the flat that smells of reclusion and vinegar.

She is terrified of telling her father she is missing two hundred pesetas.

'How could the lady take your money? Where has such a thing ever been done? Have you gone off your rocker?'

Juana's father would click his tongue and would scrutinise

her from head to toe, from her hair down to her shoes, snooping to discover a lie or a new finishing touch to her clothing. Her father would not say anything.

Juana curls herself into a ball under the bed sheets, closes her eyelids and rocks herself into a sickly sweat swaying that calms her. A woman matured by force, on the wooden planks of a train. Her infancy and adolescence severed with a slash. The sea, the sight of the vast sea through the train window.

'*Chacha, what's the sea like?*'

'*Salty and never ending. It's like the sky, but it's below.*'

After washing up the lunch plates Juana asked for the afternoon off with the excuse of resolving a family matter. Salud Monterde has let her go without asking for explanations, with an untrusting arc to her eyebrows, hastily painted with a brown pencil. Her kitten-heeled shoes set course on the polished cobblestones of Carmen Street. Juana walks forward with her eyes suspended in the void, with a pretended determination because she does not know where her walk is taking her or she does not wish to recognise it, and she lets an unconscious impulse carry her away. The city smells of silence and damp ash. The grey raincoats she crosses on the street look down on her. She stops at the traffic lights and in front of her a tramcar leaves behind a trail of averted faces. The voices around her echo empty. She feels blue lead dust over her shoulders and eyelids and her pulse pumps feverishly under the skin of her temples.

Juana stops walking in front of number five Baños Nuevos Street, where the watchmaker lives. Juana rings the bell without wanting to ring. The grimy cord draws back the front door bolt with a metallic click. The wooden treads creak again

154

under her soles. The watchmaker's door is wide open. The tall man, with eyes the same colour as rain, comes hobbling towards her with an outline of a smile. Juana cannot open her lips; a tong of acidic saliva squeezes her throat. Liberto Pech studies the scared eyes looking at him.

'What's wrong, girl, have you been crying?'

Juana goes up to the watchmaker and slumps her face against his white shirt front. She breathes in the incense of vanilla and aftershave that envelops her, and again she is crying without wanting to cry. His strong hand strokes her cheek and the sore skin of her eyelids. Juana wants to cut up time, dismember it, chop it up into pieces, rip apart the moment condensed in a shirt that smells of tobacco and invites her to rest without questions.

The boldo tea tastes of iron and alfalfa – not even sugar calms its bitterness. The watchmaker has nothing else to offer the woman sitting in front of him, with her face misted behind the cup's vapour. Liberto Pech has poured himself a Gandesa wine and watches as the young woman concentrates her vision on the surface of the liquid concoction.

The dining room smells of violets – yellow violets, if they exist – of light, of peaches on the branch, of broom picked on a hill. The watchmaker feels too coarse and distracted to open his mouth and say something soothing to the woman in front of him, with her head bowed, with a blue vein on the bridge of her nose hinting at her beauty. She looks away and notices his books, piled onto the chest of drawers, on the floor, in the dark silence of his den, books of poetry covered in a velvety coat of dust. Her eyes involuntarily pause on the spine of *El poema de la rosa als llavis*, by Salvat-Papasseit. Liberto takes

155

another sip of wine. The girl's hands caress the hot cup; small slender hands, with cuts that multiply their softness. The watchmaker picks up his cat by the scruff and places it onto his lap; his gentleness oozes out finally in angora caresses.

'I'm sorry, Señor Pech, I don't know why I've come. I didn't know where to go.' Juana breaks the web of silence. She had not said a word since she entered the watchmaker's workshop.

'Why do you say that, woman? You know you are welcome in this house, isn't that right Proudhon? And call me Llibert, how many times have I told you? Drink the herbs. It hasn't got a pleasant taste but it will make you feel good, and when you've calmed down tell me what's happened to you.' The watchmaker notices a ridiculous tone to his voice that he resists recognising; the wine tastes bitter. 'What's happened to you?'

'The Monterdes have robbed me, I don't know which one. Before going to bed I count the money I've saved and last night two hundred pesetas were missing. I need the money: it was to send to the village, for my brother and sisters and Chacha. My father will kill me when I tell him; he'll never believe that the lady has robbed me. We are saving to rent a house, stop serving and bring my brother and sisters to Barcelona. My father won't believe me, he won't believe me, he won't believe me...'

'Take a breath, woman, calm yourself. You don't have to tell him. I think I've got about two hundred pesetas, I'll go and have a look. I'll lend you the money and you can pay me back a bit at a time. But don't cry again. None of the Monterdes deserve your tears.'

Liberto Pech slowly gets up. He walks down the darkened corridor and the loose floor tiles creak under his tottering weight. Proudhon follows him.

'I'm twenty-five pesetas short of two hundred, but we'll fix that. Don't worry.'

The watchmaker rests his crutches against the chest of drawers covered in books and before sitting down notices the perfect curve of her ankles, fragile, like green reeds, that are hugged by a pair of white shoes with a sticking plaster over one toe.

'Doña Salud Monterde. You call her lady? She's as much of a lady as I am a marquis. Don't trust her, Juana. What can I tell you? As you can see she's capable of robbing someone who lives under the same roof and you've earned your money honestly. Don't keep your savings in that house: hand over your wages to your father as soon you get paid, or a friend can keep if safe for you, or bring it here to me if you want.'

'I haven't got any friends.' Juana looks at her burnt finger tips.

'Friendship isn't a matter of just one day, Juana. You too will make friends in Barcelona, you'll see... I'm going to tell you some things about your lady, as you call her, so you'll see what she's really like, but promise me you'll never say a word. That viper is capable of informing on me and leaving me without work, although it would make her worse off.'

'I promise.'

'I've known her for many years. To her, ideas, sentiments, the most profound convictions of a human being are malleable like clay and are moulded according to how the wind blows. You should have seen her during the revolution,' the watchmaker instinctively lowers his voice. 'She looked like Agustina of Aragon, with a CNT armband and giving orders to men like me who could have cracked her skull with just one punch. In those days we all knew each other, I believe that now. Salud came with us when we raided the Beristain gunsmith's, which was close to here, on the Rambla, right on the corner of Fernando Street. We took all the shotguns and cartridges while poor Llofriu took the time to open the cash register. He set fire to all the notes that were inside it. We were young and believed in the revolution, in a new order where there was no room for money or greed. And perhaps we were free for a while, during a few months, who knows; freedom crumbles like pillars of salt when you try to define it. Over the first few days the streets in the centre, the ones you have walked through coming here, were covered in dead mules and horses piled up acting as barricades. We frightened away the bluebottles off their flesh with rifle butts. The heat fed on the rotting flesh and we had to cover our mouths and noses with handkerchiefs and pour disinfectant because the stench was unbearable. We believed in the revolution. Imagine it, bonfires everywhere, lavish furniture piled up in the street, paintings, pianos thrown from balconies, religious images decapitated and burning...'

'Were the churches burnt? Señora Monterde says that you... Well, sorry, I...'

'No, don't be afraid, Juana. What does the viper say?'

'You forced the priests to run naked.'

The watchmaker lights a cigarette and strokes the back of his neck.

'The smell of blood makes you drunk.'

'Is it that you don't believe in God, Liberto?'

'I never had the need. Now I don't even believe in man, only in my hands and perhaps in the ground I step on. And that I step with only one foot.' The watchmaker looks down at the floor and observes the floral sketch of the tiles, the rubber tipped finish to his right leg and the slipper covering his left foot.

'The dressmaker that does the Monterdes' clothes says those bandits live off what they looted during the war... They threw poor Rosita out because she said they owed her money. The lady didn't want to pay her.'

'When you return to the Monterdes' flat notice the corner of the Rambla with Carmen Street. On one side you'll see Belén church, which was burnt during the war and, opposite, a jeweller's. We raided it during the first few days of the revolution. She had one eye on the cause and the other on her pocket. I don't know why, but Salud Monterde and her husband ended up taking custody of the looted stones and gold; he died before the war ended. The stuff must have remained hidden for years.'

'How long? Where could they have hidden it?'

'I lost trace of her. I didn't see her again until I returned from France and they captured me. By then she was all of a respectable unblemished widow.'

'Why did you return?'

'Another war, the Nazis, my attachment to this land. Perhaps tiredness. Loneliness. I don't know. What use is a mutilated man in a country at war?'

'Señora Monterde keeps the gold in a sealed room. She goes out with the keys hanging from a chain around her neck because she doesn't even trust her daughters. But the other day she left them in the shower and I couldn't resist the temptation of entering the room... Perhaps the lady pinched my two hundred pesetas as punishment, to teach me a lesson so that I don't do it again. I still don't know where I got the courage from. The lady seals the lock with soaked breadcrumbs.'

'She can't have much booty left. It's been twenty years.'

'I was too nervous to start counting. My legs shook. She

keeps the stones in boxes, ordered by colour, and the ingots wrapped in cellophane. Don't you have any qualms about working for a thief?'

'It was Salud who came to find me when she learnt I had left prison. They caught me in Madrid and condemned me to twenty years and one day's imprisonment. They let me go halfway. I was luckier than others, executed by firing squad in Campo de la Bota. They moved me to Barcelona and when I left the Modelo Prison, in the neighbourhood everybody knows this, Salud came to find me and offered me work. I couldn't refuse: I know my trade well and have got good hands but nobody would give me work, nobody would take the risk. At a workshop they offered me a job as a messenger, imagine it, as a messenger, crippled and at my age, and what's more, so that the police wouldn't see me, I had to be the last in and the first to go and have all the work done. The boss was a good person, *"No em comprometis, Pech*, don't compromise me," he said, but I only lasted a few months. Nobody trusts a victim of reprisal with a mutilated leg.'

'But you could inform on her...'

'And who'd believe me? Salud was a gift from heaven. She pays me what she wants, but I don't complain: I don't need much to live on and I like my trade... Juana, be careful of Monterde, don't trust her, she's a very clever woman, with a nose for things. In nineteen thirty-seven we all knew the war was lost but we continued like blind dogs; she didn't. After the Ebro she got off the train.'

Juana, the Monterdes' servant, has just left. She has promised to return his two hundred pesetas right away, as soon as she can. Liberto accompanied her to the door and, holding onto the banister, watched as the girl with slender ankles went down the narrow staircase onto ground level at number five Baños Nuevos Street.

The void on closing the door. The smell of yellow violets among the dust and the mess of books. Those big pure eyes of hers.

Liberto Pech sits at his work bench. This evening his hands are not shaking; the watchmaker says that wine makes his hands shake. He switches on the adjustable table lamp and opens the top drawer of his desk. He puts on his eyeshade and places his eyepiece over his right eye. He takes out a stone and carefully undresses it of its protective fragment of black velvet. The watchmaker holds the *padparadscha* in a pair of tweezers under the beam of light and studies its shades. A pure state of beauty. The Sinhalese call it *padparadscha*, which means lotus flower, this crystallised piece of loveliness, this freak of nature: a freak sapphire because chance has denied it the colour blue. A cluster of aluminium and oxygen atoms without a brushstroke of titanium which would have turned it blue. A stone cut into a cabochon. Nine points of hardness on the Mohs scale. A weak dispersion of colour, double light refraction. The watchmaker is in ecstasy contemplating the stone, a ritual he performs when alone, away from the world. He has read all he has found on the *padparadscha* in magazines and in libraries, and he is still looking. The Persians believed that the world rested upon a giant sapphire and that its reflections coloured the sky with all the tones that this gem could have in the bowels of the Earth: the indigo of a star-filled night, the sky blue of a radiant midday by the sea, the redness with igneous spots in the line of the horizon of a summer's nightfall over a wheat field, the mauves and violets at dusk. Or this prodigious lotus flower with its stains salmon-coloured like a sunset: orange, pink, yellow. *Padparadscha*. The watchmaker keeps notes and cuttings in his worktable drawers. The ancient peoples believed the sapphire to be a powerful talisman, a protective guiding star for lost travellers and pilgrims. To those searching without finding. *Padparadscha padparadscha*. The watchmaker stresses the musicality of the word. Lotus flower. A mistake of nature that owes its beauty to millions of years of rock pressure. An accident, an error. The beauty of a mistake. Of failure.

'Pech, you and I both know you can't deny it. You haven't got a place to drop dead in! We both need each other... Tell me, this salmon-coloured stone, what is it? A topaz perhaps? There's no other one of the same colour; it's the only one I found in the bags. The only one.'

'How strange... Topazes never have this tonality between orange and pink. Let me see it. Hummm. This isn't worth anything, Salud. Crude corundum.'

'Don't ever think of ripping me off!'

'Take it if you want, but this stone has neither value nor virtue, save its extreme hardness, almost like a diamond. Perhaps I could use it for cutting and engraving, I'll try it... You wouldn't get anything for it and it'll be good for me for cutting.'

Liberto Pech has never asked himself how much he could get on the street for the *padparadscha*. Only an expert would appreciate its worth. He does not care. He only wants to be cast under the spell of its rare and eternal beauty, to be able to contemplate it every evening on his work bench.

When he was a child his father took him on spring Sundays to look for minerals and fossils in the countryside. Little Liberto was hypnotised by the immutable silence of stones.

162

Alone, silent, thousands of years old. They were always there, under the relentless sun or suffering wind and rain erosion since the confines of eternity.

It rains on the watchmaker's memory, a heavy rain that soaks and sticks clothes to their bodies stiff with cold. Under the downpour Liberto and his companions wait out in the open, surrounded by hungry women, in Le Perthus, while the French government discuses the legality of opening the border to Spanish refugees. No one complains. The freezing Pyrenean paths become cluttered with objects that are useless in their humiliation: a trumpet, a pair of high-heeled shoes, a trunk, China cups, disembowelled suitcases with their contents scattered over the ground. The feat of conserving their dignity and hopes. A girl caresses a headless doll. Liberto Pech tightly grips his crutches. Without antibiotics or sulphonamides, the pain bites at his leg: the wound has opened from the superhuman effort of walking from Figueras to the border crossing, and it has been bandaged with cloth and cotton to soak up the blood.

In the end the French open the barrier in the early hours of the twenty-eighth of January nineteen thirty-nine. They separate the men from the women. It is raining. Liberto bends down with difficulty and picks up a fistful of wet soil. Soil, so as not to forget. The men pass in single file and throw their pistols or Mausers onto a pile of guns in a muddy ditch. The mobile guards search them.

'Lève les mains!'

Liberto Pech raises his arms with the fistful of soil tight in his right hand.

'Que caches-tu dans le main?'

163

'Nothing.'

The rain drenches the scene. His companions watch. Nobody dares protest. Tiredness and pain has sewn their lips. The guard raises his voice.

'Ouvre la main!'

'Leave me alone.'

'Je t'ai dis de l'ouvrir! Est-ce que tu en m'a pas entendu, salaud?'

The mobile guard grabs the young refugee's stubbornly obstinate wrist. He hits him on the forearm with a wooden truncheon to force him to open his hand.

'Terre! Terre! Stupide... Jette-la ici! Maintenant tu vas voir combien de terre tu va manger. Allons-y, ne reste pas ici immobil, marche. Allez, allez.'

Liberto throws the fistful of soil into a puddle and begins walking, dragging his pain and open wound along with him.

The dining room still smells of yellow violets.

11

The man responsible for the daily cleaning of the lorry was nicknamed Dog. Every morning the prisoners watched him on the coal wharf, which was formerly the straw wharf, when he washed the cab out with a hosepipe. The Dog was ugly, lean, with sallow sunburnt skin, thick black hair, long at his nape. He moved slowly – perhaps quicker than his thoughts – dressed in dark overalls – bottle green or Mahon blue – and since childhood sniffled with a wet nose at whoever came up to him. He listened defensively with his chin raised; it was because of this that the prisoners on the *Cabo Carvoeiro*, a cargo ship of the Ybarra Company, called him Dog. The mutiny on the eighteenth of July had surprised the ship docked at the port of Seville, and it was converted into a prison ship and used as a place of punishment for prisoners from the provincial gaol.

During their afternoon walk, at about midday, when the

sun reached its zenith, the prisoners on the *Cabo Carvoeiro* who had asked for permission to leave the line to smoke studied his movements on the dock from the starboard bow, their hands acting as shades. There below, always at the same time, the Dog whistled and, wearing fisherman's boots that went up to his knees, climbed into the trailer, helping himself up on a pile of coal sacks. As he scrubbed the floor and walls dirtied by blood and excrement with a bristle brush he threw curses into the air. The condemned men simulated barking from the deck and the Dog insulted them back by bellowing at them through trumpeted hands.

'You smell of death, you sons of bitches. Of death.'

The Dog was paid twenty-five cents for each corpse. According to the route he was told to take, he picked up bodies out of ditches on the country roads, at the entrance to villages and from the working-class neighbourhoods and took them to the closest cemetery. When there were no witnesses he searched the pockets of the dead and opened their mouths to examine their teeth. If in twenty-four hours the dead had not been identified by a member of their family – often, before the time was up – they were thrown into anonymous graves with quicklime. The Dog tied a handkerchief over his nose and mouth and looked the other way.

'What explanation are you asking for? The only thing I'm interested in is filling my belly. I don't know who's inside the lorry. I don't know and I don't care.'

The Dog slept in the lorry which he parked on the Delicias Wharf or close to the Alameda de Hércules stands. Sometimes they shook him awake in the early hours to urgently move those sentenced to death.

'Wake up, Dog, wake up! There's been a call from Captain

Díaz Criado's office. They say they'll wait for you with the lorry at the Variedades club. Hurry up!'

He disliked driving at night; he also knew what a dawn 'removal' meant. The Dog preferred a silent cargo, although he had to recite ballads to the dead and tell them funny stories to shake off the slight start of his fear. He preferred them dead because they did not cry. When he was ordered to transport live prisoners the Dog poured a double layer of sawdust into the trailer to make it easier to clean later.

'These swine have no balls. Some throw up or shit themselves.'

The prisoners called it 'the meat wagon'.

The greenish water of the Guadalquivir smelt of rot. At the time of day of their morning walk the surface of the river shone with brown reflections of oil and tar. The prisoners walked in two-file, without the right to stop, following the same course over the deck with their hands held behind the back of their necks. During their walks they were allowed to take it in turns to smoke; they could also talk.

'Boy, raise your hand and let's leave the line to smoke a fag.'

'I haven't got any tobacco.'

'Raise your hand, boy, or we'll miss our turn.'

When it was time for bed a corporal tied the prisoners' hands with a hemp cord; they were crowded together in the hold, the bilge, the engine room and the cabins. The day labourer Manuel Merchán Vázquez, seventeen years old, had been arrested in Puebla de Acebuche by the Civil Guard and moved to the *Cabo Carvoeiro* in the early hours of the twenty-seventh of July. Merchán shared a rickety old bed with a second-hand bookseller who was old enough to have been his father; from how he looked, because he never asked him his

167

age. In reality it was the youth who enjoyed the straw mattress because Celestino, the bookseller, had his sleeping pattern reversed: during the day he linked dreams and naps; at night he tormented the rats peaking their noses into the hold as he read the Old Testament. The guard did not tie the bookseller's hands; Celestino had given him a little gold medallion and occasionally offered him a cigarette.

'If you hear three taps in a row, put that thing out, hide your hands and pretend to be asleep. I don't want to get into trouble.'

Celestino had made himself an oil lamp with a tin of sardines and a rolled up page from the Bible that served as a wick.

'Boy, they say this is the truth; smoke it.'

'You smoke the Bible?'

'I've run out of papers, what do you want me to do... It's the only thing they've allowed me here inside, the Old Testament. We're smoking Exodus, boy. "And the Lord said unto Moses, Stretch out thine hand over the land of Egypt for the locusts, that they may come up upon the land of Egypt, and eat every herb of the land, even all that the hail hath left".'

'You know it off by heart.'

'Almost, given I've nothing else... And you, do you know how to read?'

'No.'

'Smoke, smoke... My mother brought me tobacco on Wednesday. This scum crumbled up my wad, and I'm certain they've kept half of it.'

'Sure they have.'

The prisoners on the *Cabo Carvoeiro*, the majority detained in country villages, did not receive visitors. On Wednesdays, however, their families could hand in food and tobacco to a guard, who, installed on the dock with a foldable table and chair, made note of the names of the receivers in infantile handwriting on lined paper. The women handed over their loose bundles with infinite sadness; sometimes weeks passed before they heard the fatal phrase.

'It's not necessary for you to continue coming.'

On Wednesdays when they handed in their packages the women could communicate with the prisoners that thronged on deck. They yelled, gesticulated and waved handkerchiefs to attract attention. It was a feat rescuing a coherent phrase through all the hubbub.

'Some socks, mother. Bring me a pair of socks.'

Manuel Merchán never heard his name amongst all the shouting.

The bookseller's eyebrow hairs took time to grow back. Without them his face had a hallucinated and cold expression. Once late at night Celestino Alquézar Atienza had returned hand-tied to the hold with his skull and eyebrows shaved. Even when that was a punishment reserved for women, the soldiers shaved his head and forced him to swallow a glass full of castor oil.

'Shout louder, poofter, louder. So that they'll hear you in Cordoba, shout like this, like me: "Long live Spain".'

The prisoners respected that little quiet man who shat himself two days running and who, with stained trousers, still looked ahead. On the third day he was given a clean change of underwear.

'Boy, would you like me to teach you to read?'

'What's the use, they're going to shoot us.'

'It's only to pass the time.'

'Leave things as they are. I'm very slow.'

'You've still got fear in your eyes... What have you done?'

'We looted the manor house in my village and set the stables and chapel alight. The foreman came out with a shotgun. We left him there with a pitchfork stuck in his belly, bleeding to death among the olive trees. Young master Maldonado also fell... I was drunk. Drunk on brandy... And you, Celestino, why did they shave your head?'

'For reading, thinking, defending the Republic and for selling Marxist novels; that's what they say. We'll get out of this, boy, you'll see. Catalonia, Madrid and the North resist. Only in this desert of priests and big landowners does the rebellion thrive... Boy, put your hands behind the back of your neck, we should return to the circle.'

12

The diffused light penetrating the barless little window spills onto the headboard of the bed where Merchán abandons his body to the warmth of the sheets. He sleeps in his undershirt and underpants and from under the printed bedspread a thin but muscular shin peeps out. The tattooed Moors on his arms – one with a beard, the other touched up with a turban – quiver in rhythm to his calm breathing. Although normally he opened his eyes at four in the morning, Manuel Merchán succumbs to the soft murmur bordering between sleep and wakefulness until midday. Sunday is a godsend for his back. It is the only day of the week when Lucas Naranjo, his Cordovan friend with whom he shares house and toilet on the last levelled grounds of the city, does not tap on the windowpane and make his usual signal; twice, always twice. Although they sleep under the same roof, the Cordovan is embarrassed to cross the kitchen and the dining room to knock on Merchán's bedroom because he imagines his six daughters crammed there inside, still asleep and half naked. Lucas Naranjo prefers to go out and call him through the window opening onto the little patio because this way he nurses a false sense of intimacy.

On working days Manuel Merchán counts the thirty-six wagons of the freight train crossing the edge of town little before five in the morning, following the line from the coast to the gas factory.

'Clack, clack-clack, clack, clack-clack, clack, clack-clack, clack.'

He makes sure there are thirty-six and awaits the Cordovan's signal lying down as he watches through the skylight how dawn clouds the sky a dirty colour. The only alarm clock in the house is a wind-up one, with two bells, and it thunders in a metallic cry an hour later when Merchán's daughters, the eldest ones, get up to clock in on time at the textile cloth manufacturing factory situated at least an hour away from the neighbourhood.

Routine domesticates his tendons despite his tiredness and obliges his ruined body to break the web of sheets, straighten up and put his skinny calves, one after the other, into his trouser legs. Once standing his limbs act alone, without the need of his will anticipating each of his movements. Lucas Naranjo tends to wait for him on the patio with a cigarette in his mouth and his back leaning against the whitewashed wall. The Cordovan smokes Bisonte – bison – and when he lights his first cigarette a herd of wild oxen kick in stampede inside his chest; Lucas violently coughs as the beasts head butt and uproot the pasture of his bronchial tubes by goring.

On winter mornings Merchán and the Cordovan have a *barrecha* – a mixture – of Cazalla brandy and muscatel in the

La Macarena bar behind the plate glass smoked with grease and the menu written with ground chalk. Tomás, the owner, serves the same everyday drink without the men needing to ask for it. The toilet key hangs from a frayed cord tied to a nail in the wall. Merchán and the Cordovan drink the concoction in one gulp, without breathing.

'Medicine for wringing the damp out of our bones.'

They drink the same potion on summer mornings.

'Medicine for disinfecting our blood.'

Lucas Naranjo arrives at the building site with his slum cough, his walk light, his hair combed back and, although he does not know how to write, with the top of his false Parker sticking out of his jacket pocket. At this time in the morning Merchán's fingers are still too stiff to dust the lime marks off himself; sometimes he has to urinate over his hands, sore from unloading bricks, to cure them with urea. The site foreman says 'tomes' instead of bricks.

Both men walk down the slope of the hill in silence. The slippery blur of dawn blends over the plots of coppery land and the still asleep slums. To their backs, on the lifeless horizon, the grey line of the sea mingles with the mist, the outline of factories and the gas factory tanks. In the square the two men wait for the trolley bus, joining a line with other shapes of sleepwalking flesh carrying loose bundles with their lunches under their arms. Nobody talks.

The worst has been left behind. The loneliness of living in a boarding house in the Chinese quarter, without friends and without the warmth of females, the shame of having two daughters working as live-in servants and of having left the rest, the youngest, in the village under Chachachica's care, too old for so much bustle. During the first months Merchán got up early, at the hour when the whores went home and hoses washed away what was left of the night. He walked on an empty stomach up the Rambla until Urquinaona and, on the last corner, before entering the square, he rubbed saliva over his frayed trouser knees to hide the noticeable wear. Men like him, skinny with sunburnt faces, waited on foot, walking around in circles, for the contractors to arrive and take them on to do a day's labouring at some building site. If he returned to the boarding house empty-handed, he would throw himself fully clothed onto the dirty bed sheets and kill time and resentment until the next morning. Or he would go out for a walk around the neighbour-hood until the soles of his feet were burning. On those kinds of days his sandwich of leftover sausage tasted of venom, of purge, of guilt, of obstinate bad luck.

'I don't want to work in the fields, I don't want to work in the fields, I don't want to work in the fields... The fields are for wolves.'

It was in the circles of day labourers in Urquinaona Square that Manuel Merchán met the Cordovan, a timid man with a dry expression, with whom he did not need words to be understood. That stranger spoke up for him and talked to a building site manager. Life got harder from then on and now Merchán even considers himself lucky in having his seven children under the same roof. What is important is staying together, whatever happens.

On Sunday mornings, for a change, Manuel Merchán sleeps until his head becomes dull or the shouting of neighbours and transistor radios wake him. Sometimes it is little José who jostles him until he manages to drag him out of bed. Merchán and his only male child, who is almost eight years old, sleep together on the same mattress. A grey blanket held up on thick rings to a transversal cord fixed to the living room walls divides the bedroom into two parts and separates the men's bed from the area where Merchán's six daughters are heaped together, divided into a bunk bed, a chrome-legged bed base and an uncomfortable deckchair, which they draw lots for once a week. The eight bodies breathe the same nocturnal sweat, slum humidity and exhaustion.

The house lacks running water and it is necessary to carry it up from the fountain at the foot of the hill for their Sunday bath. Merchán thoroughly washes his body in a zinc washtub next to the little patio's narrowest low wall, crowned with a trimming of green broken glass. If there is washing hung out to dry on the line, he makes use of the intimacy of the clothes to undress his thinness behind them, his arms and legs blackened by the scaffold sun and his torso white. When there is no washing hanging out, he places his printed bedspread over the cords. Between wet clothes fragments of his tired body can be seen. Merchán soaps his face, sings and concentrates on getting out the hardened cement from under his finger nails with a brush.

Juana and her five sisters spend Sunday morning tidying up the house they share with the Cordovan couple. Housework is done according to an implied code: sweep the dust matted into clumps and the reddish earth accumulated under the beds – the windows do not fit their frames and the wind brings it in through the cracks – scrub the cement floor on their knees, scrub their father's work clothes mummified in cement, wash their blue smocks with letters embroidered into the pockets – Casals' Cloth Manufacturers – and cook for the week ahead. Juana is assigned the stove. Isabel washes Juana's clothes because nitric acid had burnt her hands and left her with open flesh wounds.

The March sun reluctantly illuminates the neighbourhood with a garlic soup weak light. Juana looks at the sky and fears that her white blouse will not have dried by four o'clock. She takes a stool out onto the patio and sits next to the Cordovan married couple. The herb bushes grow dishevelled at the foot of the wall and on the sides of the sewage pipe drain crossing the paving. Lucas Naranjo keeps some newspaper pages folded on his lap for Juana and has his head bowed forward. His wife, Soledad, passes a razor blade over the nape of his neck.

'How are you, girl?' Soledad greets her.

'I've finished... I've just put the cooking pot on the fire.' Juana rests her sight on the greying hairs lying on the cement ground, a stiff and sad ball of fluff contrasting with Sole's secure movements. Everything makes sense in the Cordovan woman's hands. The silhouette of Juana's mother – her bitter profile, her pregnant stomach – strikes shooting lightning in Juana's memory.

'Here you are. Take it.' The Cordovan passes the pages torn out of *El Caso*. Juana unfolds them and skims through the headlines.

'What do you prefer, Lucas, the sentencing of the Las Ventas gypsy or the Villarroel Street mystery?'

Lucas Naranjo weighs up his answer with half-closed eyes.

'Read me the one about the mystery, let's see what it's about.'

Juana begins reading aloud. When she stumbles, she makes herself start the paragraph again from the beginning.

'According to our sources, the young man was found dead in waters of the maritime port, supposedly having fallen into the sea from the Barcelona wharf. The forensic report states that he must have died at ten or eleven o'clock the night before. We are giving the incident all the attention that such findings, easily mistaken as suicides, tend to require.'

The Cordovans have only one son who is on military service in Ifni and who occasionally writes them postcards linking set phrases. It is Juana who reads these to them. In the evening, before Merchán's daughters return from the factory, Sole keeps an eye on little José and Cecilia, for whom there is no school in the neighbourhood. The girl is ten years old and already knows how to warm up her brother's lunch, multiply and divide, and to read the sign, handwritten, on the school door.

'There are no more places.'

Soledad Naranjo listens to the reading of the newspaper, but it is an effort for her to concentrate on the slow and distant voice, and her thoughts flutter beyond the toothed walls enclosing the patio. While Lucas pays attention, entranced, and underlines the pauses, full stops and new paragraphs with emphatic head movements.

'Well I never. I don't know what things are coming to.'

'For a year now Pedro has had a formal relationship with a young lady called Montserrat Alonso, a twenty-year-old, who has been working for four years as a servant for a couple living at number 467, Generalísimo Franco Avenue.'

Some Sundays Lucas asks Juana to read him a crime he has already heard. The Cordovan never learnt to read.

Juana walks down the steep slope of the hill with a shred of anguish nailed into the pit of her stomach, with the vulnerability of one who has nobody to confide in. Her lies are transparent and she fears that her sisters suspect, especially Isabel, who knows her best. They have grown up at the same time; born twelve months apart.

On Sundays after lunch the Merchán girls go out together to the city dancehalls – Venus, Novedades, Cibeles, La Pérgola – wearing the same clothes every week, which they swap around to hide their poverty from friends and hopefuls. Worn, flounced petticoat dresses, sewn and resewn again, with their colours washed out, timidly ironed as if eyes would unpick them. However, when together they descend the muddy slopes, a perfect line on their eyelids marked with the same pencil, dressed up in starched rags, the neighbours look out of their windows to see the slum's princesses go out. From one Sunday to the next Juana excused herself from going to the dance with her sisters.

'With a girl friend?' Isabel looks at her suspiciously. 'And what friend would that be?'

'She's called Azucena.'

'Azucena? There's no Azucena at the factory.'

Juana's legs shake. In a fraction of a second she resists the temptation of throwing herself into her sister's arms and telling her all, to pour out into her ears the inexplicable happiness she is brimming with. But she has never been intimate with Isabel, despite the bodily closeness between the two of them, of poverty's suffocating proximity. Juana bridles her desire.

'She doesn't work at the factory... I met Azucena serving at the Monterdes' house, when you were in San Gervasio, in that house with so many children. Do you remember the Monterdes? Yes, woman, those bitches who lived on Carmen Street, on the corner of San Lázaro, the ones who traded jewellery. Azucena served in the same building, in the house of a Catalan couple, they were elderly and very good people. I told you about her, woman. She is from Murcia, thinnish, there's not much of her and very discreet. We'd run into each

178

other at the market and in the neighbourhood shops, one day yes, the other too, we became good friends.'

'Well I still fail to understand why you two don't come to the dance with us. You're not ashamed of your sisters, are you?'

'Ashamed? What are you saying, Isabel? I don't know what there is to be ashamed of, Azucena is Murcian. I've already told you, she's a plain and simple girl and has deformed knees from so much scrubbing of floors. What it is is that she's highly imaginative and prefers the cinema to dances. She's asthmatic, get it? She gets very bad when there are clouds of smoke and a stuffy atmosphere. This afternoon we're going to the Rex. They're showing one with Tyrone Power.

'And how come you're so dolled up for going to the cinema with a girl friend?'

'Isabel, cheap cigar, lanky, long fingers, spider legs.'

Juana slowly walks down the hill. She has left early enough, when the one-floor hovels of the neighbourhood doze in a misty silence, card games, over dinner talking and dirty plates. She has dressed in a white blouse – the armholes still damp – a grey wool skirt, a faded raincoat, kitten-heeled shoes and a pair of sheer stockings secretly bought out of the money from her wages put aside for transport. When she reaches the square, at the foot of the hill, Juana goes to the fountain and takes out of her bag a cloth rag which she soaks under the flowing water. She sits on a bench and cleans the mud off her shoes with the wet cloth. Dirty shoes give away poverty. In her raincoat pocket she carries a piece of white sticking plaster to hide the hole in the toe of her shoe.

The trolley bus energetically pops round the bend and burns the neighbourhood's cloudy melancholy with yellow sparks. Juana sits on a wooden bench with impatience and relief. From bus stop to bus stop the seats are slowly taken in the unpleasant Sunday afternoon: couples, groups of noisy well-combed boys, the occasional solitary person, bored married couples. A changing human landscape: the journey refines the lustre of faces and lessens the tense gestures of the passengers in measure to her neighbourhood and its blurred limits being left behind. Juana has a borrowed book on her lap – *El poema de la rosa als llavis* – but her restlessness prevents her from concentrating on reading it. It is difficult to understand Catalan and she searches between the lines for meaning, a ciphered message that would place her in the world. She understands some words.

'Lips, white rose, arrows and silk, thief, sacred flesh, almond oil, friend, twig of mint.'

A week has passed since Juana last saw the watchmaker. She does not dare recognise the fact that she is waiting for the reunion with anxiety, that at the end of her day's work, returning home on foot, she is surrounded by a shapeless sadness, like the houses on the edge of town, that only the passing of the days and the closeness of Sunday dissipates. Then, her spirits transform her and she laughs for no reason, her factory workmates' doings and gossip distract her from herself, as she checks buttonholes and lets herself be rocked by the metallic thunder of the looms and the darning machines. She has doubts about this strange sentiment that spurs her on and, even so, she goes barefoot deep into the unexplored, bramble-covered territory. No, she is not in love with that man who, at his age, could be her father, who is watched by the police and has an artificial leg fixed to his knee stump with leather harnesses. How could she be in love? No. And, at the same time, she longs for

180

Sunday to come and to see him, talk to him, listen to him. Juana has no one to ask advice from. Only Chacha could help her; she thinks about her and guilt bites at her head: alone in the village, with only the company of a climbing jasmine and lemon balm plant pots, Chachachica keeps absences like old rags.

'I'd like to be at your side to close your eyes. I want it to be me. Chacha, will you send me a signal?'

'I'll send you one.'

'And how will I know it's you?'

'You'll know, girl. You'll know.'

Juana gets off the trolley bus and starts walking towards number five Baños Nuevos Street. The watchmaker's silences, his circumspect inward concentrating profile attracts her with the fascination of a black angel, of a solitary wolf ruling over an infinite plateau. His hands: beautiful, delicate, sensitive, agile; she could spend hours watching their movements. They are lovely although his fingertips are yellowed from nicotine. Liberto Pech only abstains from smoking when he is working, and then the world and its illusions disappear. She is fascinated by seeing him wearing his shade and eyepiece, his face serious and elsewhere. In his worktable drawer, wrapped in black velvet, he keeps a stone he pinched from Salud Monterde. He says that he will never sell it: he only wants to look at it in silence, contemplate its splendour for hours, take pleasure in its vitreous brightness and capture the twelve-pointed star that light draws out from the middle of its vertical centre. The watchmaker explained to her that the stone is an accident of nature, a sapphire dispossessed by chance of traces of titanium and iron oxide that would have coloured it blue. One Sunday he showed her how to look at it under a beam of light. And Juana, with a magnifying glass to

181

her eye, saw that it was true, that in the centre of the crystal there was fire, flames of an orange colour with rose sparkles. The watchmaker says that in the East they call this gem a lotus flower because of its unusual beauty.

Juana never tires of watching Liberto's hands when he is working; she imagines them smooth and strong to the touch. The watchmaker has a halo of mystery that hypnotises and at the same time frightens you off. He is a pit with crystals at the bottom, and you have to bring them to the surface with the help of a rope and pulley. Sometimes he seems sad, melancholic, lost, a wandering being expelled from somewhere only he knows, and he locks himself in his silences. Then Juana feels forced to speak and tells him how her new house is and what work at the factory is like. Juana adorns the truth: she has forgotten that she lives on a hill where the city loses its features, in a rented house shared with a Cordovan couple, on a landscape of corrugated asbestos and cement roofs and tar, without a sewer system, where the neighbourhood faeces and slops descend the hill in view of everyone. She has not told him either that the patio drain is sprouting green-coloured leaves with the spring rains, as if the slum still had to be conquered hand to hand from nature. Poverty humiliates when one does not have anything to hide it with.

Juana feels ridiculous explaining silly little things about the factory girls. She does not feel that her words heal, that the man with eyes of rain finds solace and comfort in listening to them, that there is something relaxing and new in her voice. When Juana manages to get a smile from him, the watchmaker's face transforms: the vertical lines framing his mouth disappear and the edges on his forehead and between his eyebrows diffuse. He smiles and he is another person. But Juana prefers to listen to him, learn from him how to unbury beauty crushed under the lead slabs of the days. Liberto speaks to her of strange and lovely things. About light. About gratitude. About the dignity there is in working with your own hands. About colours.

'The purest blue is that of steel.'

The watchmaker explained to her that it was his father who chose the name Liberto and who taught him his trade. On spring Sundays he would take him to the countryside to collect pieces of granite, pyrites and fossilised snails, which he keeps labelled with dates and names in a wooden box with compartments. On occasions the watchmaker seems withdrawn within himself, as if he were searching for stones inside himself. He has told her he was exiled in France after the war and on returning he stayed in prison for more than ten years, during which time he did not eat anything other than cabbage and rancid sea bass soup. But if Juana interrupts him to ask about something she did not manage to grasp, Liberto Pech immediately repents and yields to the desire of erasing his recently pronounced words. It is Juana who then responds sparingly to his questions: at the Mercháns' they don't mention the war. Her father never talks; not even before, in the village, when he had plenty of time and hunger turned the hours into cotton.

'I became a fascist for a plate of whiting.'

The watchmaker hates the wind. On his Sunday walks when he goes as far as the sea and the breeze blows and shakes the tarpaulins in the fishermen's quarter, Liberto cringes scared, as if past misfortunes catch up with him and the gusts of wind stir his memory. The watchmaker's eyes are of an unusual colour, changeable, ambiguous, between grey and blue, with brown markings, like the sea in winter. The colour of rain and steel.

183

'The purest blue is that of steel. It is the colour of sadness, greyed and somewhat paler than the intense blue of the sea.'

Sometimes those eyes look at her without daring to speak. The last few afternoons Juana has noticed that Liberto wears an ironed shirt, he shaves and perfumes himself with Floïd, the same lotion that Señor Aiguadé, the manager of the textile factory, who keeps his bottle in the metallic toilet cupboard, uses. The memory of those Sundays smells of mint, of a chest of drawers with linen sheets, of cinnamon, of vermouth from the barrel, of an unmarried godfather's sugared almonds. Of a recently ironed shirt.

The doorbell is shrieking tears into the semi-darkness of the living room. For more than an hour the watchmaker has been waiting for the bell to ring and, nevertheless, he is startled when the noise shatters the peace of the afternoon. He goes out to the stairwell and tugs on the grimy cord to unlock the front door. Despite his limp Liberto Pech moves more quickly than usual; he opens the balcony door, rolls up the Persian blind for light and fresh air to enter and ties the cord to the balcony rail. He looks at a watch: it is five past five. The watchmaker straightens his shirt front and goes to welcome her.

'Good afternoon, Liberto.'

'Come in, please, come in.'

The watchmaker stumbles over his own clumsiness. The words he has just pronounced feel too poor for receiving the girl with a face full of light who is crossing the threshold.

Juana sits on the edge of her seat. She places her bag on her lap and does not take off her raincoat. The provisional nature of her gestures disheartens the watchmaker.

'Do you want a cup of coffee?'

'Alright, a little, if possible... But don't put yourself out, tell me where you keep it and I'll make it.'

Silence expands elastically in the kitchen under the light of a forty-watt bulb. Liberto puts a saucepan of water onto the flame. He has his back to the girl who cannot see his face and, in this timid intimacy, he grasps the edge of the sink and closes his eyes to breathe in the impossible aroma of yellow violets again. He only hears the gas's blue hiss.

Juana does not know how to strike up a conversation; she looks round the cleared kitchen, the empty ashtrays, the worktop free of pots and pans and, most of all, at a plate of sugar-coated buns. Juana cannot quite define the tenderness of the buns that patiently await her on a ceramic plate.

'They're for you; I don't like sweet things.'

The silence also makes the watchmaker stiff. Juana fixes her eyes on the cat.

'Proudhon, you're getting thinner by the day... Don't you give him sardines any more, Liberto?'

'He eats little and does his own thing, like his master. Bad habits are contagious.'

'You're looking better.'

'Thank you. You take sugar, don't you?'

'Yes, two teaspoons.'

Juana sits at the table and takes pleasure in the deliberate movements of the watchmaker's hands.

'On Sundays the trolley bus takes an incredibly long time. I had to wait for more than half an hour for it to come. That's why I'm so late. Fortunately I've got the book you lent me in my bag. But, in the end, it's not important. We've still got a long time left to chat.'

The conversation sounds fictitious, getting pin-stuck into pauses.

'You're very pretty today. Your change of life suits you well.'

'Thank you.' Juana looks away. 'The water's boiled, Liberto... The truth is I can't complain. I earn less than working for the Monterdes, but I certainly prefer working at the factory. And with overtime I even manage to earn more. The manager, Señor Aiguadé, is happy with us, with the whole group of Merchán sisters, because we take the work load off him. Almost all the girls at the factory are Andalusians and we agree to do overtime; it goes without saying that it suits us... By the way, I've brought you the fifty pesetas I still owe. I think that pays off my debt.'

'Don't worry about it, woman. Keep it; you can return me the money some other time.'

'Thank you once again.'

'That's alright, Juana. You know I'm here to help in all you need.'

Juana feels a slight shiver on hearing her name on the watchmaker's lips.

'On Wednesday Salud's eldest daughter was here, the Marchioness of Monterde's daughter, as you call her. She came to bring me a copper chloride solution, as you know I need these concoctions for work. We hardly exchanged words, what an unfriendly woman! I was surprised Salud sent one of her daughters and not her new servant... Or things are going bad or she hasn't found anyone who wants to live in that lair.'

'They were always arguing. And the house stank of vinegar.'

Again, the rough density of silence.

The watchmaker, still with his back to her, has not got to sitting down yet. Juana burns her lips on the reheated coffee. Her uneasiness magnetises the soles of her shoes to the tiles.

'Juana...'

The watchmaker's voice drags a sack of rocks. Liberto grasps the corner of the sink once again to regain his breath and continue.

'Juana, you see, I don't know how to tell you... I don't think it's a good idea for us to continue seeing each other.'

Liberto takes a pause. He wanted the girl to understand and to continue the reasoning from where she wanted, saving him the effort of transforming his anxiety into words. But Juana does not open her mouth. The watchmaker does not even hear her breathe.

'Juana, I don't know how to tell you. Since I met you... Well, it's been in a slow way. You'd say I've lost my senses, and perhaps you'd be right. I think it would be best if we didn't see each other again. Juana, I don't know what's happening to me...'

The watchmaker slowly turns and quickly looks at the face staring at him, but he does not dare fix his eyes on her. He hobbles to the table and takes a seat. He would swear that he feels sap running through the severed veins of his artificial leg.

'You'd say we hardly know each other; and you'd be right. As things are you'll leave through that door and I'll miss you until next Sunday. It doesn't make sense.' The watchmaker looks at Juana's disconcerted face, looking at him with knots of salt in her eyelashes.

The words get stuck in Liberto's throat. He does not dare confess to her that, without meaning to, without knowing it, he has begun to think of her day after day, desiring her to suddenly appear, with any excuse, to tell her that just her presence makes him happy and fills his life with light, that the aroma of her skin leaves a trail of yellow violets.

'Forgive me... What stupidity! I've been shrouding myself

in the fiction of waiting for you, of longing for Sunday as if I lacked air. What stupidity! It makes no sense. It's best that we didn't see each other again. Don't come back, Juana. I'm just a coward, a loser.'

Silence covers them in a cloud of cold ash. The watchmaker pours himself a glass of Gandesa red wine and sits down again; his hands are shaking. The man is hardly able to look at the girl out of the corner of his eye; she has her eyes fixed on her damaged hands. Liberto closes his eyes and tries fitting Juana's profile in with the clear image of another female face that now does not exist. That woman was called Emilia and had some lovely features, also full of light, ruined by horror and death. Alcohol soaks his memory in ether and stiffens his tongue.

'Man is a despicable being, Juana... I'm finished, I'm an impostor. Now I don't believe in anything, not even in myself. I have no right to hope; nor do I pretend to. I don't deserve you Juana. It's best you don't come back.'

Silence spiked with nettles. Saliva thickens with a bitter aftertaste.

Juana breathes in deeply and is relieved by the air filling her lungs; she wishes to retain it inside the box of her chest. She does not understand why the man with eyes of rain wants to push her aside. What has she done wrong, what mistake has she made, why do his lovely hands push her away, why do they shove her from his warmth?

The lighter slices the kitchen's stillness with a crack. Tobacco smoke places an impenetrable curtain between the two of them. Juana places an elbow onto the table, supporting her head on her left hand, and with the index fingertip of her right draws a determined square over the surface of the table, branding the square's four sides, again and again, with rage and determination, as if she wanted to lock up the dregs of dead words behind four bars.

The watchmaker places his hand onto Juana's and stops the stubborn drawing. Juana closes her eyes. Liberto's hand stays still; Juana only feels its warmth. Slowly, his hand insecurely explores her burnt skin, her nitric acid scars and the soft web between her fingers. Their hands talk in silence, and the remains of the shy Sunday afternoon are concentrated in touching.

13

Captain Díaz Criado scattered the cards with a slap; some of them fell to the floor. The player who was winning the hand gave a start and hastily began to pick them up. All of them except the jack of spades that had fallen face up: Díaz Criado was stepping on it with his heel. On his knees, under the table, amongst trousers and breeches nervously shaking, the player did not even dare brush against the polished leg of the captain's boot. He sat down again and placed the incomplete pack to one side. The captain tapped at the butt of his pistol in a mechanical gesture that usually relaxed him. The thump knocked the tallow candle over onto the card table and the liquid wax bit at the fleshy web between his thumb and index finger. Díaz Criado swept the table clear in a reflexive act, perhaps because the strong summer heat got on his nerves, perhaps because on the third hand he had become bored with the game – he was losing thirty pesetas – or because jealousy and wine vapours clouded his cards. The game was over. One of the habitual choristers at the captain's table clapped in the air.

'Hey, we're out of coal, let's cook on wood... Paquito, clear all this away and bring us half a bottle of Imperial Toledo and a plate of ham. Put it on my tab.'

Díaz Criado clenched his jaws. As he pulled off scabs of wax from the edge of his nail he thought of Aurora the Knife's rosy and rebellious nipples. He looked at the clock again: there was barely four minutes to midnight. The Knife was taking her time, even though the captain had sent his official car to pick her up.

The bar's atmosphere was dense, a sour mix of Tabú – a perfume much in vogue, sickly-sweet, like faded spikenard – sweat and tobacco smoke that dyed ochre the walls, decorated with a mounted block of Sevillian glazed tiles, finished with fillets of indigo ceramic. The La Sacristía flamenco venue's private room where Díaz Criado went to enjoy himself almost every night was separated from the rest of the customers by a glass-beaded curtain that tinkled amongst all the dull scuffle of voices, godet skirts, empty bottles and guffawing. Behind the glass beads the listless strumming of a guitar could be heard. At the back, at the bar, three prostitutes chatted, slapping themselves on their thighs. Pallid, their sadness on the point of hysteria, black-eared, the women drained glasses of anisette and showed off their teeth in forced grimaces, the same pretend smiles they used when they went to the captain's table and let themselves be groped by their fans.

'You've got to remember what I'm telling you: here in twenty years time there'll be no room for anyone.'

'He was brilliant today on the radio. Did you hear the general?

I'll repeat it from memory. Perhaps it's not exactly what he said, but what a pair of arguments Don Gonzalo has! And what wit! He said, and perhaps I'm mistaken, because I'm repeating from memory: "If those red and anarchist women go in for free love then our foreign legionnaires and regular troops will show them what real men are, not like those poofter militiamen".'

'We've got to rid Spain of bandits.'

'As they say: fear guards the vineyard.'

It was almost in unison. The captain's aid, Corporal José Carrascosa Gil, a shy and extremely thin man, entered the private room with a black folder under his arm when the telephone rang on the bar of La Sacristía. The owner of the club answered it: the call was for Don Manuel Díaz Criado.

The corporal resisted sitting down even when the friends of the captain, Law and Order delegate in Seville, persistently invited him to. One of them insisted with his mouth full; he had fleshy lips shiny from fat.

'José, have something to drink. Don't be like that, man, on duty, my foot!'

The soles of Corporal Carrascosa's feet hurt. He had walked all the way to the La Sacristía.

'José, don't fuck things up for me and hurry up. Tonight I need the official car for other business.'

Withdrawn in his thinness the corporal squeezed the black folder against his chest and watched from out of the corner of his eye how the captain returned to the table rubbing his hands after having answered the phone call. His purposeful stride, his small hard eyes, Díaz Criado seemed to be in a hurry.

'Nothing, I haven't been able to go to the police station and Father Uriate has asked me for the list to hear their confessions. José, let's get down to business.'

Corporal Carrascosa sat down next to him. He opened the black folder, took out some papers and began to read out names.

'Secundino Cárdenas Millán.'

'Yes.'

'Mariano Antolín García.'

'No.'

'Fermín Hidalgo Castejón.'

'Yes, that one yes. Kill him, be sure to kill him.'

'Juan de Dios Ruiz Amaya.'

'Yes.'

'Celestino Alquézar Atienza.'

'And that one? Who's he?'

'The second-hand bookseller in Argüelles Square, señor, he who had hung the Republican flag in his shop window. He who we've got on the *Cabo Carvoeiro*. He was cleansed with castor oil, do you remember?'

'No, that one no. Maybe tomorrow.'

'Diego Orellana Maqueda.'

'Yes.'

The corporal continued reading to the end. When he finished he raised his hand to his peaked cap, stood to attention with a click of his heels and left taking quick steps with the folder under his arm. On the list of names there were forty-six crucifixes marked in pencil in the margin.

Only a slight clearing of throats and the murmur of amontillado being poured into glasses tore the silence that had thickened amongst Díaz Criado's companions. Someone dared sigh and mutter 'poor devils'. The captain scratched his receding hairline and thumped the table; a glass smashed onto the tiled floor. The women at the bar instinctively gathered up their skirts at their laps.

'Poor devils? Poor? Do you know what you're saying, do you perhaps know? We have to rid Spain of that vile rabble, to the point where they won't even dare breathe. You too have been tricked by Marxists, as I can see. Have you forgotten what they did in the Salesas church? And in Montesión? And in El Arahal? The Falangists they had locked up in jail were spayed with petrol and then set ablaze, alive! Those you call poor devils are nation-less, Godless hordes, and we mustn't loosen our grip. I know exactly what I'm doing and you have to agree that I'm right. We have to exterminate them at the roots. Without contemplation. Sys-te-ma-ti-ca-lly.'

'Let's have a peaceful party, Manuel. Don't get so riled, we're amongst friends. Let's toast. Paquito, bring us another bottle, boy, we're thirsty.'

Díaz Criado leaned back in his chair and breathed deeply. Alcohol tied his tongue. Once again he began to stroke the butt of his pistol with his fingers. He raised his hand and asked the waiter for a plate of fried baby birds. He looked at the clock: five to one. Aurora the Knife had not arrived yet.

'Aurora, you whore, you bitch... You want to ruin my life.'

The lorry driver who transported corpses and prisoners to the cemetery rolled a cigarette tip opposite the police station under the light of a gas street lamp.

Every night the prisoners who were to be shot were brought together out onto patio number three of the Jesús del Gran Poder police station. The Dog whistled to amuse himself while waiting and they used to say that even blindfolded he was able to drive to the very walls of the cemetery. He projected the route in his imagination with all the details he could muster: the ghostly silence of the curfew, the white sheets on

194

workers' balconies imploring clemency, the barking of dogs in the vegetable fields on the outskirts, the detour a few metres from the cemetery gate – the Dog mechanically crossed himself on sighting it – the lorry's headlights piercing the whitewashed wall like insomniac eyes.

The Dog covered his ears when the Moors got into the trailer and rifle butted the prisoners out. Like that he did not hear the firing either. The graves where the corpses were buried were dug at the back of the cemetery, next to the walls, and ended in the main path. The pits were three meters wide.

The Dog whistled, waited and cursed his luck. That night, after work, he should cover the cemetery path with fresh sand. Until there were no signs of blood.

'I crap on the devils. Now I've got to go get sand for hiding all this shit. And I'm ravenous; I haven't even eaten a piece of bread since this morning.'

14

More than the swelling breasts and buttocks hidden under blue smocks, Señor Aiguadé, manager of Casals' Cloth Manufacturers, has a predilection for the working girls' legs, from the playful fold at the back of their knees to their ankle cartilages, which he imagines tender, gelatinous, like stewed pig hooves. The manager plunges into the enjoyment of calves from May onwards, when the girls' skin, free at last of masculine socks, toasted at picnic areas on the outskirts and on the beaches of Badalona and San Adrián, shines in the torrid heat that isolates the factory in a cloud of vapour and suffocated sensuality. The workers call Señor Aiguadé 'Shitfly' because his trouser fly is stained with rub marks of machine oiling grease. He squeezes into his overalls, like the rest, and is the only employee whom the owner, Don Guillermo Casals Pallerols, allows to smoke on the factory premises. Despite the license seniority confers – Agustín Aiguadé started working at Casals' Cloth Manufacturers before the war, taken on as an apprentice reeler by the owner's deceased father – despite being the doyen of the employees he stubs out his Galician Farias cigar on the rubber sole of his boot each time the owner suddenly comes out of his wooden and emerald glassed cubicle where he is shut up for hours going over account books. When they argue or the atmosphere is ruffled because of a delay in meeting an order, Señor Aiguadé does not relight the stub. He bites on it, grunts and spits out bits of loose tobacco between the reels until it is time to go home. Señor Aiguadé keeps in the front pocket of his overalls a pair of thick-rimmed glasses with magnifying lenses which he only uses to see close up, when he is looking for defects, thick threads and ladders on the ends of fabric or when he takes out his watch to measure the time an employee takes in knotting the threads of the warp when they accidentally break on being lifted by the loom shuttle's threading wire. The speed and skill of a worker is recompensed with bonuses which the coldness of the chronometer determines, but Señor Aiguadé's impatience multiplies the victim's clumsiness and leads to paralysing him, in such a way that the manager ends up placing his glasses on the end of his nose and, with his Farias between his teeth, ties the broken thread himself.

'*Cagundéu*... – I shit on God... – It's clear you're not up to it. I'd like to know what your mind's been on.'

The Casals' Cloth Manufacturers company is located on industrial premises comprised of a rectangular building, lined with a double row of windows covered with metallic grilles. On the ground floor are to be found the looms and the warehouse for storing balls of wool, cotton reels and raw silk cords that in the midsummer heat give off an unmistakable pong of salted anchovies. When the sun sets, the rows of fluorescent lights on the ceiling silhouette the machines with a violet patina of unreality. Señor Aiguadé has a somewhat bad temper and employs a peculiar language for reprimanding the workers in which he combines phrases in Castilian with the odd insult and word in Catalan, in a shouted and confusing amalgamation that, at the same time, all the staff understands.

'*No t'amaguis* – Don't hide – poofter, I'm watching you.'

'Girls, that's enough *xerrameca* – gossiping.'

'Stop all this *merder* – shit – and will you please be up to the *feina* – job.'

When he is angry Señor Aiguadé's shouting climbs to the upper floor, connected to the looms by a slippery metal staircase. The upper floor remained unused until just five years ago, and only stored boxes of useless bits and bobs covered in dust, and the glassed department of accounts and of hiring lorries for distribution. But Don Guillermo Casals Pallerols, devoted to effort and the four pillars of bourgeois dogma – work, order, saving and family – with a diabolical intuition for perceiving where business is to be made, solved how to make the unproductive space profitable and installed a dressmaking workshop at the beginning of the nineteen fifties.

'Aiguadé, get it into your head. We got to be ahead of the times.'

Casals' Cloth Manufacturers now employs thirty women – cutters, darners, sewers, ironers, finishers – producing ready for sale garments. Don Guillermo Casals Pallerols even suggests experimenting with new synthetic fabrics and organising a night shift. The factory does not close, not even in August.

When the hot months arrive humidity inflames the factory's emissions and muffles the noise of the machines. The pungent and sexual sweat of the workmen, the gusts of Farias smoke, the genuine mentholated vigorous Floïd massage, the volcanic puffing of the industrial iron and the mineral smell of lubricant are sharpened and mixed together into bewilderment. The windows, fixed to their frames by chains, open for ventilation to an angle of forty-five degrees. But on sulphur-hot days, the owner allows a worker to momentarily abandon his task and with the help of a ladder take out the windows and leave them hanging from the frames like immense yawns, leaning against the wall's glazed tiles the colour of green mould. The roar of the looms thunders, but brain and habit grind the noise, converting it into a homogenous cadence, monochord, into a soporific hum, like a background sea breaking on the coastal headland.

Señora Anita Claverol is the person in charge of the upper floor. A widow, tireless and generous, Anita operates the industrial iron and supervises the dressmaking tasks and finishings of the female brigade, made up in its majority by Andalusian girls and some from the poorest parts of Castile. The toponyms of their home towns are repeated in a dull litany: Alcalá de los Panaderos, Osuna, Los Santos de Maimona, El Arahal, Marchena, Zafarraya, Alhama de Granada, Cañete la Real, Puente Genil, El Puerto de Santa María, La Carolina, Lucena, San Juan de Aznalfarache, Bollullos de la Mitación. Anita, with powerful arms and a sergeant's feet, hides a small handkerchief in the cup of her bra, her initials embroidered into one of its corners, with which she cleans the lenses of her glasses when they are soaked with the iron's animal breath. Anita Claverol unwillingly accepts – a question of the owner's insistence and it has always been like this – Señor Aiguadé meddling in the girls' work, lowering the transistor's volume when the serial is on when he is in a bad mood and keeping the metallic stairs covered in sawdust to prevent slipping when he goes up and down them at will with his cigar butt in his mouth and dragging his suede boots with their deformed heels. Anita knows the manager's lustful intentions but pretends not to notice because, after all, Agustín Aiguadé respects both her work and the limits of her territory. But when the manager returns down to the looms Anita curses him in a whisper, reprimands some of the girls with affection and does up the occasional imprudent button. One of the manager's favourites is the finisher Socorro Altuna, a mouthy woman from Malaga.

'Señor Aiguadé, I don't know why you insist we continue with this sleeve pattern. It's not worn these days. You'll see how in the end you'll have to say I'm right.'

Socorro Altuna is over thirty and has a not very attractive face, but she is flirtatious, funny and has generous breasts. She lets herself be looked at without embarrassment and even raises her skirt and smock above her knee when Señor Aiguadé comes to her table to check her work under the light of an adjustable table lamp. Her colleagues tend to provoke Socorro, one of the most veteran employees at Casals' Cloth Manufacturers, when, at seven in the morning, they see her enter the factory dressed to the nines, raised on stiletto heels, the seam of her stockings impeccably vertical and her flounced petticoat dress swaying to the rhythm her hips set.

'Where are you going Socorro, girl, to the Rigat Club?'

'Into your mother's cunt, that's where I'm off. Do you want me to come to the factory like you lot, disguised as mops? Not on your life would I think of doing it.'

Juana Merchán works as a finisher at Socorro Altuna's table. As a child, on lethargic afternoons in Puebla de Acebuche, she embroidered mantillas of finest tulle with silk thread for the landowning women of Seville, her fingers became elastic and well practised in the use of needles. However, Juana does not enjoy her work: she watches her colleagues, asks, unpicks seams, checks again and again the basket of finished garments in a stubborn desire to surpass herself, to learn, to not get behind, so that Señor Aiguadé does not tell her off and throw her out on the street. Four of her sisters have also found work at Casals' Cloth Manufacturers and Señor Aiguadé has no big complaints: while they do not rate among the most productive workers, the Merchán girls obey, are tidy in their work, they agree to do overtime when there are peaks in demand and, most of all, they are pretty. Isabel is a cutter; more purposeful than Juana, her hand does not shake when her scissors bite into the cloth; Elvira, on the darning machine; Consuelo, a sewer; and Luz, fourteen years old, an errand girl: ordering sandwiches for the loom boys at Marciala's bar, sweeping threads and fluff with the broom or refilling the earthenware drinking jug at the fountain.

'Girl, go to the tobacconist's and get me a Farias. And don't forget the *càntir* – drinking jug.'

In the morning, Luz, with sleep in her eyes and still too young to be vain, carries her sisters' lunch boxes in the trolley bus.

'Have you got all the *gracekellys*? Hurry up, Luz. Because of you we're always late.'

Once they have walked down the neighbourhood's hill, at the bus stop in the square, the Merchán girls no longer call the lunch boxes by their name, rather *gracekellys*, like the blonde princess, dazzling and with perfect teeth, in whose aluminium interior the breadcrumbed loin fried the night before has become soggy with time. Marciala reheats the cold meat for them in her bar for the price of having a lemonade, although most of the time there is not enough money and the Merchán sisters drink mouthfuls from the earthenware drinking jug and chew the cold and stale meat on brown

Manila paper placed with the delicacy of a white tablecloth on the corner of a sewing table.

Throughout the summer the days get longer, and the electric light is not switched on at the factory until after eight o'clock. The swallows scream and fly, making circles in the grids of the purple sky glimpsed through the other side of the metallic mesh covering the windows. Señor Aiguadé is busy concentrating on a broken machine and has not come up to the upper floor all afternoon. His swearing cuts the factory's purring with hatchet blows.

'You've broken the shuttle, you blockheads! *Aneu amb compte* – take care. I've already told you the Durán Cañameras is a very delicate loom. You got to handle it like your girlfriend's tits.'

Señora Anita Claverol operates the industrial iron with arms naked up to her armpits. She puffs and is quiet. Occasionally she wipes her forehead dry with the handkerchief she hides between her breasts. Behind the dense cloud of vapour the woman in charge of the upper floor looks like a blacksmith forging iron in a furnace.

'What a way to sweat! No one can put up with this.'

Juana reinforces strips of mother-of-pearl buttons, rocked by the metallic to-ing and fro-ing of the looms and by the snippets of conversation crawling from table to table.

'He walked me home and gave me a kiss in the doorway.'

'They say there's going to be an orchestra dance. And we girls go in for free.'

'I like it when they play that one by Antonio Machín... "Why shouldn't they know / that I love you, my darling; / why shouldn't I tell them / you join your soul / with my soul; / what does it matter if later / they see me crying one day".'

'I don't trust that boy. He's one of those who first kisses

you then leaves you.'

'Are you a fool, or what? Haven't you seen the Sanglas motorbike he's got?'

Socorro Altuna's voice shakes Juana out of being withdrawn within herself.

'And you, where will you go to party on the bank holiday? Juana, girl, what is it with you... Are you deaf or asleep?'

'Sorry, Socorro, my head was somewhere else.'

'You're always daydreaming, matey... I asked if you know what you'll do on the Feast of Saint John.'

'Well, to tell the truth, I don't know yet.'

Her colleagues' voices drift away, return, swirl around, grow, fly up to the still unlit fluorescent lights on the ceiling. She is always somewhere else, on the moon, with absent thoughts, like at school in the afternoon when the nasal voice of Doña Amalia struck up into the ceiling rafters.

'Girls, don't ever forget; knight, knot and knee are spelt with a K.'

Juana recalls what she did on the last bank holiday. She and her sister Isabel had arrived in Barcelona three months earlier and spent the midsummer night of Saint John's Day on Casa Antúnez beach.

A low evening sun. Its red light shrouds the figures moving along the landscape of greyness and salt. A group of kids pile up planks, rags and old furniture to burn on a bonfire when darkness engulfs the sea and the shadows. Juana is sitting next to her sister Isabel, both in borrowed swimsuits. Salt draws white lines over the wet skin of their legs. The bitter taste of beer and olives. Together with the girls, Manuel Merchán and two friends, the three dressed in scaffolding clothes, rest on their knees on the seashore pebbles. Merchán, the Cordovan Lucas Naranjo and Antonio, a monumental mason from the Malaga neighbourhood of El Perchel, wear red cardboard fezzes with silvery half moons over their heads, held to their chins with elastic bands. The sun's orange sphere sinks into the horizon and all the sadness of dusk is concentrated in the Chinese lanterns adorning the doors to the beach hut stalls. With his party fez on Manuel Merchán raises his hands to the sky as if imploring Allah. He smiles with white uniform teeth. Rachitic, small, his face sunburnt, his trouser legs irremediably short.

'Sing something, Merchán.'

'Lemon and cinnamon, / mixed with jasmine, / that's how your body smells to me when / you snuggle up to me.'

Juana thinks about Sunday mornings, mornings still new, about her father's feeble body, exhausted from the scaffold, from accumulating effort upon effort. His suntanned torso and his pallid calves on the little patio, behind the washing line dripping from the bed sheets and knickers made from cotton pinched from the factory, knickers that have blue coloured numbers stamped on them, reference numbers identifying the pieces at the end of the reels of cloth. Juana projects her compassion onto the two white legs of her father, thin and tired from walking along paths.

'*Girl, listen to me carefully. Life is as it is, as it has always been, and you have to play along with it as it comes. Always forward, girl, move on forward, even if you have to urge on your horse with paper spurs.*'

No; Juana has not decided where she will go to party on the Feast of Saint John, that magical night when fire devours

204

winter in a fog sharp from yellow gunpowder and pieces of ash raising up to the sky in anticipation of the carnal joy of summer. Juana knows, however, that her mind and her desire will be together with the man with eyes of rain, next to the echo of his voice caressing her eardrums with new words. Juana imagines the watchmaker on the shortest night of the year: alone in his flat on Baños Nuevos Street, with Proudhon the cat, the dining room crammed with books, his crutches leaning against the chest of drawers. Liberto Pech will curse the sweltering night, the noisy crowds and the thunder of firecrackers. He will soak the soft gizzard of his soul in Gandesa and silently invoke a five-letter name.

'Juana.'

Señor Aiguadé grips the end of the chain and rings the bell announcing the end of the shift. The tinny clanking loosens up the bodies and slows down the movements of the female workers. Yawns, stretches and all in a hurry.

'You Merchán girls, are you coming to the trolley bus stop?' Socorro Altuna folds her blue smock and puts it into her bag.

From amongst the flutter of women Juana tries to catch the eye of her sister Isabel. They understand each other without needing to speak.

'No, we'll walk home.'

A purple strip underlines the horizon when the Merchán sisters walk towards the slums on the edge of town with their lunch boxes empty and their eyes sore. Rarely do they talk on returning to the neighbourhood on foot to save on the price of trolley bus tickets. Juana squeezes the tips of her fingers against the flesh of her hand. On summer sunsets the walk home can even be pleasant in relaxing their bodies, as they breathe a little and alleviate their eyes, sore from dressmaking, by looking into the distance. The girls instinctively quicken their pace when the buildings become sparse and the scenery is transformed into one of naked bricks, weeds and rusted train tracks. In winter they cover the distance in less time, spurred on by the damp wind and the open space's dark desolation. Their shoes tread mud they cannot see. The ghostly clearness of the moon hardly lightens the way they take around industrial walls, iron gates and rachitic trees. Sometimes the cry of a little owl, its eyes hypnotic and yellow, can be heard among the poles carrying overhead electric cable.

When the girls climb the hill and reach home the Cordovan is already in bed. His wife, Sole, washes up the dinner plates in a earthenware bowl and Manuel Merchán, his back against the street door, hums and peels potatoes. Another working day. Juana already cherishes the moment to stretch out on her shared bed. Stretch and sleep. Resting is her only very own moment, one of privacy. Giving herself in to being tired and to sleep, sleep, sleep.

15

The only fair skinned man amongst all the prisoners on board the *Cabo Carvoeiro* was perhaps the Argüelles Square second-hand bookseller, with the exception of a schoolteacher and a myopic youth.

'That one's studying to become a civil servant or a lawyer's articled clerk, boy. I'll bet you half a ration of bread.'

The school teacher had arrived on the ship ill, and they injected morphine diluted with camphorated oil into him to silence his groaning and stimulate his heart beat. He was an elderly man and had hardly enough strength to stay standing, and a lot less for walking down the ship's gangway, cramming himself into the lorry and putting up with the horror of an intuited journey to the slaughterhouse. The soldiers guarding the prison ship, anchored to the coal wharf, did not know what to do with him. One night, while the prisoners toiled away in the useless attempt of trying to sleep, the bookseller heard a shuffling of quick boots. He quickly put out his wick lamp, hiding it under the straw mattress where his companion Manuel Merchán rested, and pretended to be asleep. Two guards walked down to the hold with carbide lamps, dragging stretcher poles. A short while after voices were heard coming from the deck, and the echo of a dull gunshot, at close range. The bookseller – his eyes wide open in the mournful bowels of the cargo ship – also thought he heard a melody whistled from below, on the dock, and imagined the Dog waiting for the lorry's load with his hands in the pockets of his overalls.

Celestino Alquézar had a smooth milky face, shielded from physical effort and the elements amongst shelves covered in dust, silent volumes and a rustling of turned pages in the liniment of quietness. He looked like a ghost – weightless, his skull and eyebrows shaved – in that rubbish heap full of rags and scraps arrested in the working-class neighbourhoods of Seville. The doctors, town councillors, professors, soldiers loyal to the Republic, the prisoners who had socks and hats to wear trembled in the Jáuregui cinema police station, in the basements of España Square or at the Variedades cabaret club.

While they remained together on the floating prison, Celestino and Manuel Merchán were inseparable. In the reduced mobility of the ship the young day labourer followed him everywhere, like a puppy frightened in the middle of a hail storm. To blow away their fears and shoulder the wheel of time in its arduous passing, the bookseller and Merchán kept themselves amused by guessing the jobs of the other prisoners given away by the tanned skin of their faces, strong hands, sailor tattoos, hard patches on shoulders or on the back of their necks sunburnt from harvesting. They played, chatted and confided in each other in the common destiny of death.

'Sing me something, boy.'

'Don't ask me to do that, Celestino. I've got my voice stuck in my throat.'

'Sing; so that you don't have to think. It's only to pass the time. Go on, sing me that one that smells clean; the one about lemon and cinnamon.'

The bookseller limited his wearing of glasses to indispensable tasks because he feared a knock, carelessness or an unfortunate slip and then being deprived of the semi-clandestine pleasure of reading. When on the twentieth of July they arrested him at the second-hand bookshop in Argüelles Square, Celestino Alquézar, without losing his nerve, as if he were expecting it, picked up an untouched copy of the Old Testament he wanted to take with him from next to a pile of disembowelled volumes. Puzzled, the Falangists could not say no. Then on the death ship his mistrust and fear of angering the guards persuaded him to unbind the book and keep its loose pages in his pockets, the straw mattress, his shoes and the hemp rope-soled sandals of his companion Merchán.

The bookseller also put on his glasses to delouse the day labourer Merchán's head. He combed the youth's hair matted with dust and dirt with an exquisite touch and when he came across a nit he crushed it between his thumb nails until he heard it snap.

'This one will now miss its baptism, boy.'

Both of them took turns sharing the mattress, and the toothbrush made from a pencil nicked from the guards and a shred of shirt, and they smoked the last of the tobacco the bookseller's mother had sent on a Wednesday delivery and lined up together for lunch.

'It's looking at me, boy! There's a worm in my bowl of lentils looking at me.'

Merchán accompanied the bookseller even when he went to urinate in the drum installed in the ship's bilge which the prisoners emptied at nightfall by pouring its contents over the side of the ship. Merchán the day labourer, orphaned of both mother and father, without brothers and sisters, with only the affection of a godmother who did not know where they had taken him after his arrest, grew fond of that quiet man with mild manners and voice, the man who searched for joy everywhere and tried to teach Merchán to read.

'I've already told you I'm very slow. Leave things as they are. In short, what's the use...'

'Don't sulk, you mule, and try it again. It's only to pass the time. Slowly. Listen and then you repeat after me. We're reading a verse from the Ecclesiastes; pay attention: "For the living know that they shall die, but the dead know not any thing, neither have they any more a reward for the memory of them is forgotten".'

Death. Its invisible and sticky presence blended in with the suffocating midsummer heat and the faint, hardly perceivable rocking of the ship anchored in the oily waters of the Guadalquivir. Minds, exhausted from tightening the cord of fear, incapable of resisting the pressure, stopped thinking about the certainty of death by chewing it over.

Merchán and the bookseller passed the time in clumsily reading, sharing cigarettes rolled with Bible paper and by overhearing the constant flow of rumours. Among the detainees on the prison ship there had spread the supposed news that Saturnino Barneto, the communist leader of the dockers, condemned to death earlier in May thirty-six, had managed to escape from the mutiny in Seville to Gijón, hidden in a cargo ship. The flow of gossip doing the rounds on board the *Cabo Carvoeiro* kept alive the hope that in the end their captivity was just some kind of misunderstanding, a passing nightmare, a lie. Endlessly repeated, the hearsay and the inventions acquired the emphatic weight of truth.

'They're going to free family men.'

'They're not going to shoot under twenty-year-olds.'

'They say Queipo and Captain Díaz Criado save the lives of those who voluntarily enlist in the Foreign Legion.'

The bookseller's lamp light burnt out as sleepless nights went by, interminable days of hunger and damp heat and the lists of names read out just before midnight with the sophistry of a transfer to another prison. His last few days Celestino shut himself into an armour-plated silence.

'Let's read a bit?'

'I don't feel like it today, boy. My rheumatism is killing me.'

'Oh yeah.'

'Tomorrow, perhaps.'

'Celestino... Perhaps we'll be lucky.'

'Things are turning sour, boy. We smell of death; as the Dog says when he's cleaning out the lorry trailer on the dock.'

16

A Monday in July approaching midday. The Angelus is read out on the commercial radio station after the news when Liberto Pech enters the glazed door of the Torne wine cellar, its shop window displaying bottles of liqueur clustered together and arranged by colour on the shelves. Light falls shredded into dust onto the street paving and the fern hanging from balconies.

'*Bon dia, mestre* – Good morning, master.'

The watchmaker responds to the greeting with a slight nod of his head. Tock, tock, tock. A hollow sound follows him on the concrete floor. The rubber tip ending his right crutch is a continuation of his very self, a coriaceous tentacle scenting the terrain before treading it and advancing ahead of his body in the damp interior of the wine cellar, between the two rows of barrels marked with chalk over scars of grime. Ten minutes earlier the watchmaker caught sight of a tiny object glittering between cobblestones on the Vía Layetana: a nut. His crutch, an insect's hard proboscis, sniffed the metal hexagon and knocked it into the road with a dry blow, almost out of repulsion.

'What, been out for a walk?'

Liberto Pech detests the ceremony the owner of the wine cellar traps him in, but he accepts the game that is repeated every Monday, every week, every month, for the last two years. Years of cork and silence. And Liberto Pech always surprises himself by perpetuating the ritual with accommodating words.

'I went to the market... Look at how lovely this mackerel is; it looks like it's just been fished.' In the newspaper wrapping the fish a photograph, pearly with scales, sticks out of the Minister of Work Girón de Velasco and the Caudillo, Franco, dressed as an admiral, shaking hands with a worker dressed in his Sunday best.

The owner of the wine cellar knows where the watchmaker has just come from and, despite this, asks questions, assumes and adorns the artful conversation. At the same time the watchmaker knows that the owner of the wine cellar knows. Both splash about in the pool of understanding, but neither dares break the glass parapet separating them. Both pretend. The wine seller, because he respects – a certain fear glows deep inside – the mutilated customer filling up with wine on Mondays around midday. Liberto Pech, because he senses – deep inside lies a mixture of anger and tiredness – that he is talking to a person without malice. Every Monday when he goes down the steep stairs of his building with studied movements of crutches and trunk, Liberto Pech leaves his demijohn at the wine cellar and picks it up full of Gandesa wine on returning.

'The heat's getting worse today... See you next Monday, Llibert.'

213

The watchmaker hooks three fingers of his right hand onto the demijohn's handle and clutches his thumb and index finger around the cross piece of his crutch. In six strides he plants himself in front of number five Baños Nuevos Street. Before placing the key into the front door lock he looks back down the street, overheated with urine, from where he has retraced his steps from the Vía Layetana police station.

Eight hundred and fifty-three steps taken slowly, with the sluggish rhythm of a cripple dragging a wooden leg with the help of two crutches placed under his armpits. The watchmaker has counted his steps an infinite number of times and his calculations do not always coincide. He has even broken down the route – every Monday he repeats it – into sections whose number of strides and minor details along the route – a piece of broken glass, the barber shop sign, a geranium on a balcony – he could remember with his eyes closed, automatically, even if he were sent to the last place on earth. For each stone on the itinerary there corresponds a determinate number of strides. From the fragment of Roman wall in Obispo Street to the centre of the soulless square measures one hundred and seventy steps. From the centre of the square to the crossroads of San Severo and Bajada de Santa Eulalia, fifty-three. From the narrow bend of these two streets to the gargoyle opening its jaws with claws to vomit its threats over the surrendered city, eighteen. The watchmaker adds up the steps he takes every Monday, the day he goes to the Vía Layetana police station to stamp his red mark as an undesirable on an official document. He collates the calculations for the simple pleasure of doing so, for no other reason. The resulting figure depends on the tiredness he feels on returning home, on his state of humour and most of all on the delivery men who can block the way with their handcarts. The watchmaker estimates the exact number of steps he takes from the Vía Layetana police station to his home on Baños Nuevos should be between eight hundred and fifty-three – the number most repeated – and nine hundred and thirteen – the maximum amount cropping up in his sums.

Numerical obsessions numb the brain. It is a mental gymnastic exercise beyond understanding. On Mondays Liberto Pech Solans, a master watchmaker by profession, escaped to the south of France in January of nineteen thirty-nine, captured in Madrid in July nineteen forty, moved to the Modelo prison in Barcelona, tried by a military court and condemned to twenty years and one day of prison for rebellion and hostility to the Regime, goes to the Vía Layetana police station to sign a paper that verifies his supervised liberty in blue ink. The humiliation of it now does not sting him, but the city air spreads ash forcing him to lower his eyes and look for nuts between gaps in the cobblestones.

The watchmaker keeps his weekly appointment, dragging his false leg, pleased about feeling different, about being marked out, a black bloodsucker, someone who stinks and who puts out the last embers of his suffering with Gandesa wine. The watchmaker likes to feed the image of himself as an enlightened and unsociable madman, as knowing his trade well – who charges the least for repairs in the neighbourhood – as a solitary man who on summer evenings smokes on his balcony with his elbows resting on the rusted rail with his cynical stump uncovered.

'Here you'll get gangrene spreading through all your leg. Do you understand, Liberto? Are you capable of understanding it?'

215

The shrapnel wound in the watchmaker's leg, reopened from the effort of crossing the Pyrenean passes from Figueras on foot with snow up to his groin, is infected. Pus draws spirals over his mauve flesh. Liberto Pech bursts his blisters and washes his ulcers with sea water. He bites his lip.

The shattered bone responds to the teeth of the saw with the obedience of wax. The knifing pain burns the centre of his marrow until the pain stops being pain and transforms itself into delirium.

'Perhaps it was an unnecessary amputation, I'm not arguing with you over it, but I had no other choice. What did you want me to do? The infection would have devoured it.'

Since the watchmaker was let out of prison, two years ago now, it is not necessary for him to open his mouth each time he goes to the police station. Liberto Pech knows which door to knock on. The policemen do not ask him anything; they do not even look him in the eye. A morbid and recurrent idea always crosses his mind when he walks down the stairs to the basement: running into the fierce look of the man who tortured him.

'Liberto? What kind of fucking name is that? Have you heard? They gave this big, crippled, piece of shit the name Liberto. And his surname, Pus. Pestilent pus like an old bag's warts. We're going to cut off your good leg so that you crawl like a slug, since that's what you are.'

When he completes the formality and signs the paper, Liberto Pech emerges into the saline light of Vía Layetana. Returning home he invariably follows the same route, taking the long way around the alleys of the Gothic quarter until number five Baños Nuevos Street because this habit of doing things calms his mind. He leaves the side of the cathedral behind him and turns into Montjuïc del Obispo. The narrow side street leads to San Felipe Neri Square, an air bubble of quietness in the heart of the medieval city. Twenty years after the defeat there is still rubble left up against the few walls still standing after the bombardment. Teeth marks of shrapnel have bitten the church's façade where a stone heart burns under the rose window and sculpture of the saint. The tumbledown walls surrounding the square still show traces of stuffed life: green paint on the third floor wall, the outline of a crucifix, remains of white tiling of what was once a humble kitchen. Except for some old female devotees of Saint Felipe Neri there are few people who adventure into the desolated cityscape. There are no bars, or shops, or houses, or voices in the square. Only the shadow of destruction lives there. Even so the spectacle of desolation does not make the watchmaker feel sad. Liberto Pech rests his back against the lamppost still standing straight in the centre of the site, which was a Jewish cemetery several centuries ago, and savours its calmness. There is something in contemplating the ruin that blends with his soul: broken, tired, with his leg cut off and the bitterness of disillusionment on his tongue, the watchmaker still manages to stand upright like the damaged walls resisting and sinking their roots over the dead.

It was on the last but one day of January nineteen thirty-eight. It had not yet struck eleven o'clock in the morning when the German Junker dropped its bomb on San Felipe Neri Square. On hearing the howl of the air-raid sirens people ran for cover inside the church. The shock wave tore the main door's hinges out by their roots, flinging them against the presbytery. A

217

terrible silence followed the explosion. Twenty children were buried under the collapsed houses and among the adults they found the white body of Emilia.

Emilia Saumell was a nurse and worked in the Military Hospital in Valldonzella Street. Liberto met her during the summer of thirty-six in one of those working-class restaurants where militiamen and women with vouchers given out by the CNT or other trade unions had lunch. Emilia and Liberto often saw each other in the queue outside the nationalised Atlantic Café where the menu was inevitably the same every day, although it was true that ingenuity strived to disguise the meal on the poster stuck to the window.

Monday: rice with lentils.

Tuesday: rice with black beans.

Wednesday: rice with scallops and red pimientos.

Thursday: house rice.

Friday: *barreja de llegums* – mixed legumes.

The watchmaker saw her sitting at the next table. He said aloud, so that she would hear through all the shouting:

'What joy, Quimet! Don't tell me today we're having legumes.'

And she smiled with all her teeth.

They informed him by sending a local kid who arrived at the warehouse of the Atarazanas barracks out of breath. He had hurt his shin on the bicycle pedals. Hot wounds do not cause pain.

'*L'Emília és morta! L'Emília és morta! Diuen que vagis al dipòsit* – Emilia is dead! Emilia is dead! They say for you to go to the morgue.'

Liberto Pech was desperately in love with that body so white, her snow-white flesh minced by shrapnel, her arms torn off, her red hair scorched cement grey, the loveliness of those teeth of hers broken by bad luck. There were to be other

218

awakenings, other beds, other aromas, but the watchmaker promised himself never to feel the agony of loss again.

If happiness exists, it is this summer's noon. Light penetrates slanting into the dining room through the open balcony. An aroma of fried garlic and parsley impregnates the living room. The sticky heat of July coats the watchmaker's movements with a varnish of slowness and separation, while the distant rhythm of a paso doble rises from the street up towards the roof gutters. The watchmaker savours the taste of mackerel, the sips of red wine and Proudhon the cat's purring as he licks the fishbone under the chair.

Happiness is the last sop of bread, soaked in an oil-shiny plate. Liberto Pech cleans his fingers and lips on the corner of the tablecloth and goes out to the balcony to smoke with a book, like his father taught him.

'*Kid, leisure is a thing for the rich.*'

The city falls asleep at this lazy hour between lunch and returning to work. Not a soul crosses the sunbathed street. The owner of the wine cellar leaves his shop door half opened just in case someone turns up late while he is eating in the backroom. Liberto places a newspaper over the pigeon excrement dirtying the balcony stool. When he is not expecting customers the watchmaker leaves his orthopaedic leg hanging from its leather harness from the bed's headboard.

'*This has got three legs, Juana, the same as me.*'

He makes his stump comfortable between the wrought iron bars, leans his head against the outside wall and closes his eyes. The watchmaker concentrates on finding a word to define that ductile pain located at the level of his chest, a tame pain, a tiny breakage between amazement and the plenitude of being alive, an orifice expanding and contracting with the bellows of his breathing. The hole is an old friend that has never had a name.

'Juana.'

The nameless heartache only eases when he watches the secure movement of the clouds, their fleeting loose threads ploughing the fragment of blue sky limited by roof eaves.

'Juana.'

Juana's dark profile and that of Emilia do not match in anything except in the naïve brightness sparkling in the corner of their eyes, in the tone of their skins, perhaps in their frightened femininity. After Emilia Saumell's death the watchmaker left for the Ebro front. A mortar destroyed his leg close to Fraga.

Nothing can now hurt the man with the severed leg reading on the balcony. There is no more room for salt on the raw flesh of his memory. Nothing could damage his soul. Neither the loneliness that surrounds it nor betrayal nor the most painful and humiliating illness. Liberto Pech is a little over forty years old and carries the weight of a granite skeleton.

'I don't believe in anything. I don't hope for anything.'

He does not hide even a piece of bitterness in his unbelief. Fifteen years ago, when torture turned his body into a quiver, and later while he was in the Modelo prison, he believed the most coherent thing to do would have been to shoot himself in the roof of his mouth. One single shot, boom, and abandon himself to darkness. But now there is no fury or anxiousness to run away in someone like him who does not hope for anything. The watchmaker is an exhausted being worshipping the shreds of his solitary life: the light of dawn from his bed, the Borne market with its pyramids of cabbage and red apples, the domestic yelling, the morning bustle of boxes and handcarts, the damp smell of books, the sawdust in the Barceloneta bars, the breeze through the banana trees on the Rambla, the devastated and silent sight of San Felipe Neri Square, the insomnias of concentration at his worktable.

And for the last few months he cannot get out of his thoughts Juana's pure gaze.

'Juana, I don't believe in anything. I'm disgusted with myself.'

He does not know how to say how the light of this girl interrupted his simple life, limited by Gandesa wine, the discipline of work, the silences of a stubborn cat and his visits to the police station. He does not know how to say how he began to wait for the girl who appeared one afternoon in his house with two gold ingots wrapped in sweet shop paper, when he felt vertigo for the first time at a gaze so crystal clear. Vertigo and fear.

The watchmaker loves and desires Juana in silence. Quiet, sweet, uncertainty in her big almond eyes. And her hands, most of all her hands. Small hands like Emilia's. Hands disproportionate to the rest of her body moved him. Refined hands, her thumb nail twisted and rebellious, hands with white nitric acid bites and with blood scabs on her knuckles.

The watchmaker is more than twenty years older than Juana.

The girl listens to him with devotion, as if she were discovering the world blindly with the worn out words of a heretic. The girl's black eyes see him clean, tall and pure because truth and beauty are in them. Her restrained gesture, absent, almost frightened, her green reed and fragile ankles, that aroma of impossible flowers, the smell of woman, the insolent curve of her breasts, the profound blackness of her

221

gaze, the harsh and yet at the same time soft feel to her hands. And that goodness in her that only listens, accepts and asks for nothing. Her still immaculate innocence.

'I don't believe in anything, Juana. Man is a despicable being.'

Man is rubbish who on nights of insomnia, when sight gives in to tiredness, lets the image of the girl strike the apex of desire with the insistence of a horsefly. The watchmaker cannot think of anything else and bites on the corner of his pillow, he squeezes it against his groin – between his intact thigh and his stump – he strokes his hurt animal's penis and hits his testicles until he hurts himself.

'Juana.'

He cannot get her out of his thoughts. He has no right to demand anything of her, he should remove her from his life, expel her, never see her again. And yet he pieces together and takes apart her profile, reconstructing her improbable smell, of yellow violets, imagining her naked body next to his.

He does not even dare brush against her.

'Juana, it's best we don't see each other again.'

When he thinks of her he succumbs to the devastation of tiredness. He is missing a leg, he is an oppressed undesirable, an impostor of his own life, a ghost who is still breathing. Moody, unsociable, misanthropic. Others want to see him like this.

'I'm just a coward, a loser.'

Juana will never know how much he loves her.

The Persian blinds at number five Baños Nuevos Street are drawn. The golden reflection of the afternoon does not enter the dining room because natural light disturbs Liberto Pech when he is working with his eyeshade on and the goldsmith's eyepiece is against his eye. The woman who gives him work and odd jobs of making her rings will never discover the watchmaker's secret. Salud Monterde could not know of his robberies because she does not understand the trade.

'Madame Monterde, it's a pleasure to work for a woman of such noble birth as you.'

Since he started to work for her after being let out of prison Liberto took gold dust off each piece he was working on, a tiny speck, imperceptible drops, hardly a breath, an iota, a shred of light. For the simple pleasure of robbing from a thief, in case one day he will need it to survive, only just in case. The watchmaker keeps the gold shavings in the first drawer of his worktable, inside a test tube, next to the strange gem he also pinched from her.

'This isn't worth anything, Salud. Crude corundum. But it'll be good for me for cutting; it's a very hard crystal.'

A mistake of nature. A gem with sparkles oscillating between orange, purple rose and yellow. A monstrous sapphire with the same colours as that of a setting sun. *Padparadscha.* A pure state of beauty.

'Juana.'

Suddenly the street doorbell rings.

'Who would that be? I don't even know what time it is.'

The watchmaker closes the drawer with a bang without worrying to protect the *padparadscha* with the piece of black velvet. He runs his fingers through his hair, stands up and, intrigued, pulls on the cord to open the street door. He leans over the stairwell as he tries to find a face among the shadows.

She had not yet reached the second floor and already he can smell her. He hears her puffing in her fatness propped up in high-heel shoes.

223

'Good gracious, it's the boss. Such a long time since you were last here!'

Three steps from the landing Salud Monterde stops. She catches her breath and concentrates on looking at the watchmaker with all the contempt of her pea-coloured eyes. Liberto invites her in with burlesque reverence.

'Have you closed the door properly?' Salud's eyes flash, looking from one side to the other.

The unexpected visitor makes herself comfortable on one of the dining room chairs and lights a Chesterfield. She looks round the room, its yellow walls bare of decoration, the newspapers piled up on the floor, the cracked mosaic. The watchmaker wipes the table top with circular movements of his shirt sleeve and passes her an ashtray. He looks out of the corner of his eye at his worktable in case he has left his drawer of secrets half-opened.

'How long has it been since we last saw each other, Salud? Three years, perhaps?'

'What does it matter; these days I only count deaths and bank notes... Oh, my varicose veins! I can't climb up two flights of stairs. We've turned into oldies.'

'Some more than others. Women like you age badly.'

'And this welcome? Where did you learn such compliments, in the slammer?'

Her loud laughter does not make him feel uncomfortable; if anything, it provokes disgust in him. But the watchmaker controls himself; he holds his tongue. It must be an important matter for Madame to come to Baños Nuevos Street.

'Do you want a glass of wine?'

'Well alright. If there's no brandy, pour me a wine.'

Sitting at the table face to face they scrutinise each other

224

distantly and with strangeness. They avoid each other's eyes, but both grope around for reproaches and traces of the past in the other's gestures, in the tone of voice, in a wrinkle.

The watchmaker recreates her, protected behind militiamen breaking the jeweller's plate glass windows with stones and rifle butts. It was she who shouted the loudest. Or she was heard more than the others.

'Up to the rooftop, up to the rooftop! Throw him off head first into the street.'

'What brings you here, Salud?'

'Have you closed the door properly?'

'Yes, woman. Can you tell me what's happened?'

'Lock it. Do me the favour of turning the key and bolting it shut.'

Salud Monterde unfolds her bag, unzips it and delicately places a pistol, a Llama Gabilondo & Co make, onto the table.

'Are you crazy? You've come up to my flat with that!'

'I always carry it. I always go out accompanied since the old days.'

The watchmaker leans back into his chair; he feels suddenly uncomfortable. Salud Monterde undoes the button holding in her skirt, introduces a hand into her waistband and, from inside her underwear and girdle, pulls out an object wrapped in a shiny cloth.

'Open it.'

Inside the piece of damask cloth Liberto Pech discovers a choker with a bow and three pendants set with rubies mounted on cast gold. The watchmaker swallows saliva. Still looking at the piece of jewellery he mutters:

'What's this?'

'Well you're looking at it.'

225

'Yes, I'm looking at it and I'm asking you in a clear and loud voice: do you think I'm a fence?'

'I don't care what you call yourself. How much can I get for it?' Salud Monterde takes a long sip of her drink. She blinks. 'I need the money, Pech.'

'It seems incredible that after so many years... It can't be placed on the market like it is, it's impossible. Anyway, it looks old. Do you want them to lock us all up?'

Salud Monterde puffs and stubs out the butt of her cigarette in the ashtray. A strand of black hair has come loose of the hairpins holding her bun over the crown of her head. She insists.

'How much?'

The watchmaker strokes his chin.

'It's impossible to sell it like this... Listen, tell me something: this wasn't in the booty, was it? This didn't come from the jeweller's.'

'You're right, comrade. The necklace didn't come from there.'

'Do you know what you're getting into, Salud? Are you aware of it?'

'Here we go, the priest in you is coming out... So much morality, so much faith! What use has it been to you?'

'We can't place it! Can't you see that? You were always careful, Salud. To take the smallest risk we'll have to assay the gold, break up the necklace, mount the stones onto rings, perhaps a bracelet or two, and sell it outside the neighbourhood, of course, outside the city even, and drop anchors in Valencia or Madrid, and even then... Also, working alone it'll take me months. And I'll tell you something more, I don't want anything to do with it; take the choker and go. Out. I'm not interested. I don't want anything to do with this.'

'Wow, wine doesn't go down well with you! Do you want me to tell you something, Pech? Do you? Well listen: you live off this shit the same as me. No, your situation is a lot worse. You depend on me; on me and on luck.'

'You're mistaken.'

'Don't make me laugh. You haven't got a place to drop dead in. What are you trying to prove with your fussiness? Take the piece apart and do what you have to. I need the money.'

'I wouldn't think of doing it.'

Salud Monterde bites on a thumb hangnail. She studies Proudhon's bewitched eyes, seemingly listening to the conversation from on top of the chest of drawers. She lights another cigarette.

'Look, Pech, I'm very tired and it's not easy for me either. What's up with you? What do you want? More money?'

'No.'

'Well?'

'You know I shouldn't run too many risks. The rest of you are clean...'

'Excuse me, but it's Merche and me who walk the streets, who show our faces. You never leave here.'

'Don't delude yourself! We'll all fall, one after the other, like dominoes: you, me, your daughters, the fucking pianist, the waiter, the baits... Don't you realise?'

'Take it apart. Do your job, Pech, and I'll do mine. Are you forcing me to tell you? Yes? If this is what you want, for me to tell you what will happen? Very well then: you'll continue working for me because you have no other choice. You've nothing else to do.'

Liberto Pech drinks up his glass of Gandesa and wipes his lips on the back of his hand. He scratches his severed knee

227

under his trouser leg. He breathes deeply and forces a smile. He says:

'Salud, can I ask you a question?'

'Damn it, today you're unbearable... Spit it out.'

'After raiding the jeweller's on the Rambla, where did you hide the loot? How did you manage to hide it for so many years?'

Salud Monterde reclines back into her chair. She strokes her belly as if her voice emerged from her stomach.

'It's been so long! Let's see, my husband and I moved it out of Barcelona the morning after the raid, we hid it in the false bottom of a suitcase, under the inner soles of our shoes and in the lining of my raincoat – I was up all night sewing it. We caught the first train to La Seo de Urgel and from there I alone crossed over into Andorra by coach. The stones and the ingots were kept in a security vault until the Stalinists bumped Andrés off.'

'Your man tricked us all like dimwits. He was looking for a spraying with bullets.'

'I waited for six months to pass and then I brought the loot back to Barcelona. In three journeys, just in case.'

'And how did you manage to cross the border? Three times, none the less. If I'm not mistaken, Lerida was occupied in the spring of thirty-eight.'

'Let's say it wasn't difficult for me to get safe conduct. One emerald, one paper: that's certain barter, and don't forget that Andrés had been a customs officer. They never suspected me. I went with my little girl, with Merche, who was five years old then, and you know what a posh actress I am. Once in Barcelona Feliu hid them for me in his mother's house. I couldn't touch them for fifteen years.'

'The pianist? That berk? And for fifteen years! Where?'
'In the fireplace draught.'

Salud Monterde has just left. The choker is lying on the worktable wrapped in a shroud of purple cloth. The watchmaker dares not touch it, not even look at it. Through the balcony window he looks at where so many times he has retraced the steps of his defeat. If only he knew how to cry. Liberto Pech rests his cheek on the cold glass and closes his eyes.

'Man is a despicable being.'

He cannot contain his rage, he hits the window with a fist and breaks it. He has hurt his hand with a piece of glass. He licks the earthy taste of blood. If only he knew how to cry.

'Juana.'

17

Back then, in that torrid summer of thirty-six, nobody called Chachachica, with her breasts still firm and defiant, an insignificant woman. She waited in line in front of the office of Captain Díaz Criado, recently named Law and Order delegate in Seville by General Gonzalo Queipo de Llano.

'You, the next. What's your name?'

'Juana Expósito.'

'And the member of your family? Give me his name.'

'Manuel Merchán Vázquez... He's my godson.'

'Profession?'

'Day labourer.'

'Date of birth?'

'On the fifteenth of September he'll be eighteen.'

'Woman, I asked you for his date of birth.'

'You work it out, please.'

'What prison is he in?'

'How should I know, señor. They came for him late at night and took him away in a lorry without telling me where.'

'Wait in the room with the other women; the captain hasn't arrived yet.'

'Yesterday I came and they sent me away; the day before, I waited and he didn't see me. At least tell me where they have taken him.'

'Woman, the captain has a lot to do and a pile this high of paperwork to go through. You should understand that the situation is very delicate these days and you should be grateful that he's so kind as to see you. Go wait there inside. And close the door behind you.'

The waiting room, drowned in the half-light of an atrocious summer kept out behind the shutters, smelt of oldness. Only a crucifix broke the room's nakedness, with no other furniture than various wooden benches randomly placed against the walls. Sleepy in the airless drowsiness of the room, another two women, both dressed in black, awaited the captain's arrival; they seemed to be mother and daughter. Despite the heat, the older woman wore a black scarf tied around her head and thick darned stockings. She leaned her head on the other woman's bony shoulder. The mother looked Chachachica up and down with tear-tired eyes. She fixed her gaze on her skinned knees, the wounds closed by then with scabs, and then looked her in the eye. Both women studied each other in the connivance of fear and desperation. Not one of the three women attempted the useless endeavour of opening their lips: everything was said inside those four walls. Footsteps behind the door, a creaking of a hinge, a rustling of papers, other people shouting – men, always old men resignedly retracing their stone-heavy steps – at those who

231

denied them access to the captain, even the possibility of enquiring about a missing family member, cushioned the wait in the drowsy, bland and confused hours of thoughts that scorched hungrily like burning wood.

'Your eyes are full of fright... What have you done? Where have you been? And the sack? What have you got in the sack?'

'Open it and take a look.'

'Holy Christ of Paño! What do we two want with a silver candelabra? Tell me, what for? What have you done? You're looking to get us into trouble, Manuel.'

The sliding door suddenly opened. A small man dressed in a corporal's uniform appeared, his thinness highlighting the hardness of his expression. He carried a piece of paper in his hand. He read:

'Teresa Martínez Picón.'

The girl with bony shoulders sat up with a start.

'That's me.'

The corporal tilted his head, indicating that the young woman should go into the office. The woman with the darned stockings stood up with the intention of following her. She limped.

'Where are you going?'

'I'm her mother.'

'Wait outside.' The man talked without looking at her.

'But...'

'I'm telling you to wait outside, in the street! Are you deaf? And you, the other one, go too. He won't be seeing anyone else.'

Manuel Díaz Criado turned up at his office at about five o'clock. He had quickly crossed streets that panic had kept deserted, threading his way under awning shades and acacias

232

to avoid the vertical light of August. He walked up the stairs with his head down, without taking notice of the uniforms standing to attention at his pass. His secretary, Corporal José Carrascosa Gil, immediately recognised the wearied expression in his face and, uncomfortable, he withdrew and crumbled up the sheet of paper on which he had noted down the incidents at the Law and Order office since first thing in the morning.

The captain calmly undid his uniform jacket, stroking the buttons, and hung it on the only clothes hanger inside the wardrobe. He tapped the butt of his pistol before placing its leather strap on the back of his chair. He wiped the back of his neck with the palm of his hand. He was sweating.

He closed the window blinds swollen with light, switched on the table lamp and was dazzled staring at its tungsten filament. He found it hard to concentrate; the centipede of his hangover blurred the lines of words. He moved the black folder with the dossiers and the list of corpses picked up in the last few hours to one side of the table. Díaz Criado had learnt to live with the pain of stabbing headaches that only lessened their rage two hours after he woke up and after his second drink. He pulled out the glass with grooves of grease stains and the bottle he hid in the bottom drawer. Acidic and nocturnal sick rose to his throat.

He drank down his first glass of brandy with half-closed eyelids. He looked down at the floor with his pupils saturated with light. The black and white tiled floor of his office multiplied itself onto the whitewashed wall, the colours inverted. The captain only stepped on white floor tiles when he was enjoying bed games with one of his girlfriends. He refilled his glass with brandy; the burning seemed to placate his nausea. He had a stiletto nailed into the nest of maggots

233

that was his brain: the fathers of the Heart of Mary had complained to General Gonzalo Queipo de Llano about the Law and Order delegate's repressive methods in Seville and about the murder of so many innocent people.

'Fools led up the garden path by Marxist scum! Idiots.... Put on a gangplank, it's all the same to me signing ten death sentences as three hundred.'

Díaz Criado crossed the room – black tile, black tile, black tile – cursing the monks' audacity, and his vision became clouded with hate. But it was another image – white tile, white tile, white tile – that weakened him: Aurora the Knife – her rosy and rebellious nipples, those hips of hers, the indelible smell of her vagina impregnated onto his fingers.

'Aurora, you whore, you bitch... You want to ruin my life.'

Díaz Criado pressed the buzzer with fury. His assistant stood to attention on entering the office even when he saw him with his back to him.

'At your command, captain.'

'How many people are waiting outside?'

'I only let four women come in, señor. Hem...'

The corporal's nervous little cough drove him mad. He bit the tip of his tongue to stop himself from shouting at him.

'What is it?'

'Hem... señor, let's see, it happens that one of them has been coming for several days. She asks after her stepson arrested a week ago. She walked here all the way from Puebla de Acebuche.'

'Walking?'

'That's what she says, señor. Her feet are ruined.'

'She's not family of yours, is she?'

'No, no, señor. I'm not...'

234

'My head is burning, José. It's like there's a crow pecking at my brain... Let her in, but in a while. In half an hour. I'm going to lie down.'

The anteroom was banned to men. Díaz Criado had a peep-hole put into the sliding door separating his office from the waiting room, but whenever he looked through the hole he could only pick out featureless bulks, diffused silhouettes in the semi-darkness. The alcohol weighed down on his eyelids.

His assistant slid the door open slowly and let Chachachica in.

Her legs shook as she advanced through the cotton air. When she entered the office she found the captain sprawled over a wooden armchair with his shirt tails over his khaki trousers. Díaz Criado looked into the void. Chachachica – her face burnt from gleaning on arable land, her eyes strangely sky-blue, her black hair collected in a bun – remained standing, alternating the weight of her body onto each leg. The back of her knees hurt. She stood bare-footed on the office floor tiles with her hands behind her back holding a pair of threadbare rope-soled sandals; she wanted to show her sore feet so that the captain would take pity on her. She did not dare breathe. The hare of her heart beat in her mouth.

Díaz Criado spoke when the evening melted into violet streaks and the squawking of sparrows quietened behind the wooden strips of the Persian blinds.

'What's your name, woman?'

'Juana Expósito, at your and God's service.'

'Are you married?'

'No. No, señor; I've never been.'

'Are you a virgin? I mean, have you ever been with a man?'

'Only one, may he rest in peace. He was the father of my stepson, señor.'

'Really, only one man... You wouldn't be one of those revolutionaries predicating free love, would you? Come here, woman, come closer. Bring me my tobacco pouch and the flint lighter; they're on the desk.'

The captain's black eyes, as hard as cockroach wing cases, looked her over with the cold resolve of a forensic scientist. Chachachica bent down and delicately placed her rope-soled sandals onto the floor. She feared pestering, making herself visible, even provoking an unpleasant noise. Díaz Criado picked at some tobacco shreds and spent some time separating out the hard bits in the palm of his hand.

'So your stepson is innocent and hasn't got blood on his hands.'

The office stank of the Moriles oloroso wine on his breath.

'Take your dress off and let me see your breasts. Don't be afraid; nobody enters without permission.'

Chachachica obeyed. She took off her slip and her percale housecoat and left them on the floor next to her rope-soled sandals. She could not look at the man, sitting on the chair, clicking his tongue each time he sipped brandy.

'Although you smell like a stable, you've got a lovely body. Yes, a healthy strong woman's body, one for being inseminated. And what did you say your stepson was called?'

'Manuel Merchán Vázquez, señor. He isn't even eighteen years old yet... He didn't do nothing, señor. He's just a poor wretch. Have mercy. Do what you want with me, but spare his life.'

'None of them did anything, sure... They never do anything. They are all innocent.'

Chachachica stared into the void. Naked in the austerity of that office, she did not feel shame at his gaze nuzzling at her flesh. Instead she felt shivers down her spine, a horror that she was only capable of putting her finger on when she saw out of the corner of her eye how his moving tongue wetted the rolling paper: disgust, from the tip of her damaged toes to the roots of her hair.

'Señor, what you're looking at is only the shell of an empty nut.'

His loud gaffing frightened her. The echo of her spoken words froze in her mouth, and she then believed that her strength was about to abandon her and that she would collapse on to the floor tiles.

'Look at what the little red whore is saying... An empty nut! What I've to listen to! Who taught you to speak like that, hey?'

The captain stood up, went to his desk and poured himself another glass of brandy. He laughed. He emptied it in one gulp.

'An empty nut... Do you want me to crack you open? You've never had pleasure from a man in your life. Come here, closer, you're going to learn all there is, all at once.'

Chachachica did not move off the white tile she stood barefoot on. Her body did not belong to her.

'I told you to come here! On your knees! Aren't I speaking clear enough?'

She obeyed. Panic prevented her from crying. Her feet and her skinned knees stopped burning. With great difficulty she went closer to the man with his trousers around his ankles and his backside resting on the edge of the desk.

'Put it in your mouth. Slowly.'

She stopped herself from retching and closed her eyes. She tried not to think of anything, she left her mind blank and submitted.

She would remember it for years: the captain's penis smelt

of liquorice and the watered down ammonia Gavilana had her clean the brothel floors with. She could not cry. She was dry.

The captain's thick fingers ran over her hairs on her neck, the skin of her cleavage, her shoulders, her breasts. The man insisted on pinching her nipples; hurting her.

'Don't you like it, bitch?'

His penis remained limp, dead, drunk, far from the lure of desire. The captain grabbed the woman by her hair and suddenly threw her aside.

'Get dressed.'

Díaz Criado tucked his shirt tails into his trousers. He refilled his glass with brandy and hid the bottle in the bottom drawer of his desk. He opened the office window. He pressed the buzzer. The corporal stood to attention again with a click of his heels; he did not dare look at the woman buttoning up her percale housecoat with her hair bun loose.

'Get her out of here, José. Find out where her stepson is and get them to free him. They're to give him the address of Uruguay Pavilion and he's to voluntarily enlist in the Foreign Legion. And get rid of everyone. I don't want to see anyone else today.'

18

RUBIO BOARDING HOUSE – BEDS

The sign – ochre background, red stencil painted lettering – is seen as soon as you turn the corner and enter Los Arcos Street; hanging from the mezzanine balcony, fixed to the rails with rust eaten grey-green chains. Liberto Pech advances slowly with the cushioning of his crutches deep in his armpits. His spotless shirt, his limp more pronounced than ever, his hand bandaged.

'What happened to you?'

'Nothing. The balcony door got stuck at home and on trying to open it, I broke the window and cut myself.'

'How clumsy... Sorry, I didn't mean to say that.'

Juana follows him two steps behind, shrunken, frightened; the heat stubbornly sticks her skirt to her thighs. Sweltering August heat in the city.

The main entrance to the boarding house is half-open. The

tip of his right crutch sniffs the semi-darkness of the lobby before the watchmaker's body enters it. On crossing the threshold Juana, with her head bowed, steels herself against the few faces walking down the street at this uncertain time on Sunday. Behind the counter there is a bald man, his flesh withered and softish, reading a novel about gunmen. The greying hair on his chest peeps sweating out at the top his shirt.

'Have you got any rooms?' The watchmaker's voice sounds weak.

The man behind the counter nods his head and, from above the frames of his glasses, scrutinises the odd couple. He, thin but well-built and with a wooden leg – mutilated in the war and a radical, he supposes, because he has no medals on his lapel. She seems shy. She is pretty and very young. There must be a big difference of years between them.

'Are you going to stay all night?'

'No, no. A few hours perhaps.' Liberto wets his dried lips with the tip of his tongue. He is thirsty.

'You should know that here guests pay on the nail.' The tone of his voice sounds intentionally vulgar. 'Hortensia, Hortensia! Come, there's work to do.'

Liberto searches in his wallet while the owner studies the girl accompanying him with her eyes fixed on the toes of her shoes. She is beautiful. The whiteness of her blouse is reproduced in the shine of her skin. Her tight flesh, her succulent mouth, her short unvarnished nails. She seems upset, and by the way she crosses her arms over the pit of her stomach the man behind the counter would swear she was not a streetwalker. She is young; she is certainly not yet twenty-one. The man behind the counter could not care less about the girl and the cripple placing creased peseta notes onto the top. Since the authorities closed down the brothels, the owner of the boarding house does not ask his guests for identification. He keeps his mouth shut, allows it and raises his prices.

The woman answering to the name of Hortensia appears from behind the glass door noisily flip-flopping and doing up the last fasteners of her cotton housecoat. Juana, with her eyes fixed on the floor, notices the cracked skin on the woman's heels. Her hair, flattened over the crown of her head, shows undyed roots. It seems that the woman has just got up after her siesta.

'Number six, Hortensia. They are only going to be two hours.' The man behind the counter holds out to her a key fixed to a piece of cardboard dirtied by its key ring.

Juana dislikes the elasticity of each minute and the gaze of the man behind the counter flying up from her calves without stockings to the roots of her hair, collected in a high ponytail. She wants to run out, but shame paralyses her. The watchmaker also seems uncomfortable. Since entering the boarding house Liberto has not even once looked at Juana.

The woman who answers to the name of Hortensia appears again, dragging her feet with a tangle of dirty bed sheets between her stomach and her fleshy arms. Juana imagines them still hot, stained with the bodily fluids of anonymous people.

'I've left you the bedspread folded on the chair because it's hot. Over its back there are a few clean towels. It's room number six, at the end of the corridor. The key doesn't work on the inside these days, the lock isn't too good. If you must, use the bolt.' The woman talks slowly; her eyes do not even suggest curiosity. The man behind the counter sits down again and begins reading from where he left off.

The room smells stuffy and of sour milk. A crucified Christ and an engraving of a shepherd girl – her body supported by a staff, her infantile bust on show in the middle of a herd of sheep – preside over the metallic headboard of the bed filling most of the room. The bed, covered in bleach-yellowed bed sheets, does not hide its function or its severity. A cigarette burn adorns the turnover: the innumerable times it has been washed still have not faded the singed trimming. A bedside table, a washbasin and mirror. The partition wall on the left connects the adjoining room, through which quiet panting can be heard, a woman's laughter and bed springs groaning. On the main wall to the right there is a tall window hidden behind a thick curtain that opens onto the inner patio. Grey-brown mezzanine light and moaning drainpipes.

Juana sits on the edge of the bed, her back to the watch-maker, with her burnt hands on her lap. Her feet do not touch the floor. She feels dirty and miserable, surrounded by tarnishing poverty. The accustomed patina of shortage.

Liberto Pech has sat on the only chair in the room. He has taken off his shoe. He lights a cigarette. He rests his head in the hollow of his hands with his elbows driven into his thighs and his eyes fixed on his big toe.

'Why have you brought me to a place like this?'

The phrase slashes the halo of silence. Juana does not get an answer. On the other side of the wall they hear voices and a murmur of water. The cigarette's glowing tip dyes the watchmaker's skin and the vertical wrinkles framing his mouth orange. The air runs out. The August heat sharpens desire.

'I'm sorry. If you want let's go right now. I didn't want to humiliate you, nothing further from my thoughts. But in Baños Nuevos...'

242

'The man at the counter looked at me as if I was a tart.'

'Juana, I didn't mean to make you feel awkward. You know that my house is always open, there I've got my workshop and the neighbours arrive unexpectedly with a watch, something for soldering, or some silly little thing.'

'On Sundays too?'

'Yes, sometimes they come on Sundays.' The watchmaker lowers his voice. The tone of it shows a slight sign of loss.

The hot afternoon smells of something rancid, of melancholy, of a gagged voice. A toilet is flushed down the inner patio drainpipes, behind the curtain.

'Juana, listen to me; I want to make myself understood. I wouldn't have been able to put up with the memory of your body at home, amongst my things. You are not for me, and I know you'll disappear from my life sooner or later. I don't deserve you.'

'When you speak to me like that I don't understand you. I don't know what's going on.'

'What can I offer you? Tell me. I haven't got anything. Nothing. Why did you leave your village in the south? Tell me. Why did you come to Barcelona? To change one miserable existence for an even worse one? It doesn't make sense, Juana. You know I live on a few odd jobs from Monterde and I can't hope to get a job because they won't give me one, Juana, they won't give me one. I'm an undesirable with a leg sliced off. It doesn't make sense, and also, child, I'm twenty years older than you.'

'If you truly loved me, you wouldn't speak to me like that.'

'How could you say that to me? Yes, true... It must be your age. In a few years time you'll understand. You're still too young.'

A swarm of words sting the stifling heat.

Liberto stands up with a moaning of wood. Tock, tock, tock. Juana, with her back to him, tenses her spine and tightens her jaws. The watchmaker's trembling touch – his finger tips unsure – strokes her temples. Juana cannot open her eyes. His elastic hands caress her face and he stretches them against her white blouse, at the height of her breasts. Juana breathes in the incense of tobacco and Floïd massage. He smells of vanilla, vermouth from the barrel and autumn sun. His shaking hands unbutton her white blouse. He does so slowly, insecurely.

The contour of their bodies dignifies the worn bed sheets. Juana has not opened her eyes yet; she cannot. With her eyelids sealed, so as not to see, Juana takes off her knickers made from a remnant pinched from the factory, with the reference number of the piece stamped onto the cotton cloth. She hides them in her fist. The August heat coagulates the blood on the palms of Christ's hands looking down on her in bed from above.

'Juana, go up to the pigeon loft and put a rag there below. And playing in the street with boys is over, you hear me?'

Juana squeezes her eyelids, causing phosphorescent spirals to come from her pupils. She wants to snatch at time, embalm it, detain it in the Sunday afternoon.

'Girls, it's a sin to look at a naked body. On Sundays when I wash for going to mass I don't cover my breasts in soap.'

His wooden leg hangs in its leather harness from a headboard bar. Liberto looks at the ceiling. His body is as stiff as a pole; he hardly dares to touch the young body he is hugging. The nameless hole expands with the bellows of his breathing.

244

'I have no right. I can't expect anything of you.'

The open hole in his solar plexus – that old friend of his – throbs. The girl lying next to him, stuck next to his skin, will never know how much he loves her.

'I'm just a coward, a loser.'

She could never understand him.

The girl curls into a ball against his mutilated body. Skin against skin. Desire has the fragile feel of a butterfly's wings. Neither of the two want to hurt their fingers on the broken glass of vertigo, the unrepeatable moment, that which is escaping from them, that which will never be again.

Juana's hands slowly go down the watchmaker's body, moving by instinct. Juana clings to his incomplete leg and hugs it against her naked breasts. Her tongue licks the scars of his stump hot. Her teeth bite its dark crimson flesh. Her tears comfort his severed knee.

Nobody ever rummaged in this intimacy. Nobody, only the teeth of a saw.

19

The waters of the Guadalquivir, dirty from night and tar, syncopatedly hit the ship's hull, anchored at the coal wharf, when the howl of a siren tore the suffocating heat in the bowels of the *Cabo Carvoeiro* with the sharpness of a bad omen. Startled, the second-hand bookseller from Argüelles Square – perhaps the only insomniac soul in the ship's hold – wetted the tips of his index finger and thumb, put out the wick of his oil lamp and put the page of the Old Testament he was reading into his pocket. He did not get as far as hiding the tin under the mat on which Merchán was sleeping naked. The last flicker of flame captured his companion's foreshortened body in his retina; hunger had thinned his backbones. Celestino drew his knees up to his chest: it was the first time the prisoners on board the floating gaol heard the whine of a siren.

Inside the ship's stomach whispers and a growing mumble of

agitated limbs were sparked off in the darkness. When their wrists were untied a voice in command bellowed through a loudhailer.

'On deck, all on deck! Quickly.'

The prisoners blindly tied on their rope-soled sandals. The prisoners slept naked to placate the sultry heat and, before lying down, they made a pillow with their rags in that unbreathable atmosphere of crowded bodies, filth and terror.

'Move your arses. Quickly.'

The guards went round the hold, the bilge, the engine room and every nook and cranny of the *Cabo Carvoeiro* illuminating their way with carbide light and armed with riding whips and truncheons – for hitting the ship's timber and laggings – to hurry along the prisoners. The thrashing was accompanied by the ill-fated racket of kettledrums. The sluggish prisoners received rifle butt blows on their ribs and buttocks.

'They're all up top now, señor. We've searched the hull from one end to the other.'

The prisoners crowded on the prison ship's deck head to nose. There were barefooted ones, bare-chested or in underpants and tattered vests. Celestino and young Merchán had taken shelter in the back rows, close to the port side bow, from where they could not distinguish the face of the voice slicing the air.

'All those whose names I call out step out of line and go down the gangway onto the wharf. And don't try to hide yourselves.'

The words split the suffocating night. A slight blink, a drop of sweat, a grinding of teeth, the unfolding of paper kept in the pocket of a uniform jacket, all the sounds crystallised in the wait. In a spark of inspiration, Celestino ripped off his wrist watch, threw it onto the floor and smashed its face with the heel of his shoe. He bent down and cunningly picked it up. The hands, stopped at half past four in the morning, pricked the palm of his hand.

The booming voice began to read:

'Hernández Luque, Francisco. Twenty-two years old. Docker.'

'Millán Cuesta, José. Thirty-seven years old. Accountant.'

'Martínez Prieto, Agustín. Forty years old. Day labourer.'

'Vega Carmona, Juan de Dios. Fifty-three years old. Day labourer.'

'Conteras Conteras, Antonio. Thirty-four years old. Miller.'

'Álvarez Durán, Aquilino. Twenty-five years old. Turner.'

The bodies advanced towards the rope gangway with pupils dilated from panic, some with their flies wetted with urine. Only the whispering rising amongst the multitude convinced them that the horror was true.

'Aguirre Mohedano, Luis. Thirty-nine years old. Day labourer.'

'Quero Alcántara, Andrés. Forty-two years old. Cork worker.'

'Alquézar Atienza, Celestino. Fifty-four years old. Bookseller.'

On hearing his name, Celestino grasped Merchán's hand and placed the broken watch into his palm.

'Give it to my mother; so she'll know that I'm dead. My father wore it. Try to find her. Remember: the second-hand bookshop in Argüelles Square, opposite the law courts. Ask in the neighbourhood for the bookseller's mother. Rosario, her name is Rosario; remember it. I wish you all the luck in the world. Goodbye, boy.'

'What's happening there at the back? Hurry up.'

Manuel Merchán will never forget the last look on the bookseller's face, frozen at half past four on an August morning.

'Úbeda Alcázar, Francisco. Forty-three years old. Sheep shearer.'

'Acedo Pedrosa, Damián. Fifty years old. Foundry worker.'
Meanwhile, below on the dock, the Dog covered the floor
of the trailer with a double layer of sawdust.

20

The Barcelona–Seville express did not move for almost two hours in Alcázar de San Juan as the wheel axles were adjusted to the different track gauge. The immense night on the other side of the window, silence, stillness in the wagon suspended in the middle of nowhere and profiles paled by a slaughter-house-violet light. Outside, scrubland and voices absorbed by open countryside and the mother-of-pearl beam of the one single spotlight. Alcázar de San Juan – Saint John's Moorish Fortress. Names of impossible stations.

'The end of the war caught me in Almadén, in the province of Ciudad Real.'

Her father repeated the liturgy of unknown toponyms to quieten little Juana's sobbing in the humid midday heat, while her mother dragged her belly and sprinkled water from an earthenware bowl to ease the burning heat cracking the patio floor tiles. The acidity of empty stomachs. Her father listed the stations passed in the withdrawal, one by one, from Almadén to the city of Seville. The psalm confused the pangs of hunger. From Almadén to Seville, all the stations passed in the withdrawal, one by one. Corners of an invented map. *'Try to sleep, my little one. Let's see, repeat after me: Almadenejos, Los Pedroches, Belalcázar, Cabeza de Buey, Almorchón junction, Zújar, La Granjuela.'*

A twenty-seven hour journey from Barcelona. The toilet door cast sour gusts from the end of the aisle. Coal dust soot on cheeks. Song and the buzzing of a bumblebee trapped in the casing of a transistor radio. The impassive firmness of the bench, mechanical snoring of open-mouthed men, bundles lying in the net rack, her money in a cloth pouch tied to the shoulder strap of her bra. Fragmentary and predictable conversation.

'Are you getting off in Seville? We are too. We're from Cazalla de la Sierra. We've come from visiting our eldest son who lives in Sabadell.'

The train entered the station an hour later than scheduled. Juana dragged her suitcase down, brushed her shirt straight and began walking down the platform, freeing herself of the wagon's stale air.

A wedge of cheese, wrapped in a shroud of brown paper, oozed inside her bag and had stained the telegram with large grease spots. The plain to the point telegram, a black head scarf for mourning, the cheese left over from the tiring journey, the knife her father sliced up meatballs with at the foot of the scaffolding, a crust of bread and two ounces of floury chocolate that stuck to the roof of her mouth. The cardboard suitcase – white coffee coloured with cinnamon-coloured reinforcements on its edgings – travels in the coach's luggage rack next to other bulks and a cage with an indigo and copper-coloured feathered cock. Inside her suitcase, a well-worn grey wool skirt, a crinkled white blouse, two changes of underwear, a cardigan and a bar of Maderas de Oriente soap as a present for Dolores Iruela. The carpenter's widow organised the funeral.

The telegram arrived the day after the tea lights had foreseen it with ill-fated spitting. The postman – Juana imagined him climbing the hill on the outskirts by peddle-power, out of breath, his trouser legs held by wooden bicycle clips – delivered it to the Cordovan's wife. There was nobody else at home. Soledad Naranjo signed for it with a cross in the counterfoil's lower margin. Sole wiped her hands on the corner of her apron – she was washing up the dinner plates when Juana and her sisters returned from the factory – and handed it over.

'The postman brought it this morning. It was early. You hadn't yet got to the trolley bus stop when the man knocked the door.'

Juana felt a cold whiplash across her back on seeing out of the corner of her eye the sender address: Puebla de Acebuche, Seville. The paper was marked with Sole's wet and soapy thumb.

'Chachachica died last night. Suddenly. Funeral tomorrow. Hugs. Lola Iruela.'

The tea lights foresaw it. Sole had placed the ceramic bowl – water, oil and five candles ready for All Souls' Day – on the window sill. One for grandfather Curro's soul, disembowelled with a pair of sheep shears; another for her mother, died giving birth to little José; and three for the Cordovan couple's dead ones. Five tea lights in the damp slum house. Juana was alone

252

in the kitchen, putting on her nightie in the dark, when the little candles began to crackle, spitting burning stearin sparks, quivering with bursting blue hearts, beginning a sizzling dance of lost souls tossing and turning on the other side of death. Juana understood. The telegram arrived the next day.

'Chacha, I'd like to be at your side to close your eyes. I want it to be me. Will you send me a signal?'

'I'll send you one.'

'And how will I know it's you?'

'You'll know, girl. You'll know.'

Time does not exist. The present stretches from the overheated seat on the coach back to that spring morning when Juana and her sister Isabel left the village with shrunken hearts, their innocence intact, and where they came from fitted in a suitcase with cinnamon-coloured edgings, the same one that is now travelling in the luggage rack tied with a strap. Time is elastic, and the moment of reuniting herself with her past is prolonged into the infinity of a straight stretching road. There is only a little way to go before reaching Puebla de Acebuche.

Juana rests her head against the window. Her sunglasses tint the landscape passing by her eyes with unreality. Femurs of fleshless land, dried thickets silhouetted by a halo of apathy, slight undulations of gleaned arable lands, the vastness of the open country, disheartened sunflowers. The distance and the engine's lethargic humming temper her tiredness and the memory of an aroma piercing her in time to the holes in the road: tobacco essence, Floïd lotion, leather and vanilla, the memory of an absolute smell stuck to her skin, obstinately permanent, an accusing fragrance accompanying her on the last trolley bus home to the edge of town, shrunken on a seat, like now, with the intrusive staring of the other passengers sniffing behind her ears, in the smell of a man studded to the back of her neck and on the palms of her hands.

After their furtive dates at the boarding house in Los Arcos Street, Juana walks up the hill on the edge of town with Sunday night over her. Isabel's eyes scrutinise her like glow-worms in the room's darkness.

'Just back from Montecarlo cinema, are you? Well the session was certainly very long. What film did you see?'

Her father's tired voice from his bed, from the other side of the curtain dividing the room:

'That's enough, that's enough... Can't we get some sleep in this house?'

Amongst the warm bodies of her sisters Juana becomes totally absorbed in herself and hugs the aroma of the man with eyes of rain so that it does not escape, so that nobody notices it. She gets up at dawn, before the Cordovan taps the windowpane with the top of his fountain pen – twice, always twice – and she removes the aroma with freezing water and a scouring pad in the patio bathtub. The woman at the boarding house rolls up the dirty bed sheets in a tangle she squeezes against her stomach. Bleach-yellowed sheets, the same colour as that toning the countryside. The tepid air entering the window caresses her limbs stiffened by the journey.

There is only a little way to go before reaching Puebla de Acebuche.

The coach stops on the outskirts of the village, on a bend in the road, next to a poster with the Falange's yoke and arrows and the timetable of mass. The November light smears the whitewashed cemetery walls in amber.

'My father says Merchán is a coward.'

254

'Well your father is going to die. Chachachica says the carpenter has got TB and that's why he spits blood into the chamber pot.'

The mallow buds become frayed inside their stomachs like the souls of the dead.

'They taste the same as a block of dried figs.'

'You've never tasted a block of dried figs in your life.'

Juana remains standing still on the bend in the road, with her suitcase at her feet, surrounded by a cloud of dust thrown up by the coach going off into the silvery winding road through the olive grove silently extending to the line of the horizon. Alone next to the cemetery wall, where Chacha's flesh – her masculine hands intertwined over her stomach – rots covered in a percale housecoat.

The church tower bells ring five o'clock. The prickly pear and pitahaya cactuses, embalmed by years of dust and sun glare, are silently still there in the same place she had left them. Juana walks on the limy soil of Alameda Avenue, still deserted, and concentrates her distress and the strength she has got left on the handle of her suitcase, whose bottom edge knocks against her calf as she presses on. She is met by the image of a peach stone buried in this same avenue, the memory of a girl digging at the ground with her nails and dreaming of a magnificent tree, a peach tree that would be secretly hers and would remain shy amongst the poplar trees to provide her with shade, shelter and fruit in the summer. Everything is still in its place, immobile and sedated.

The trampled ground scents the girl, scrapes her heels and repels her: feet and soil do not recognise one another. The landscape of her memory is at the same time intact and distant. Juana looks around at the remnants of a stagnant life

255

that does not belong to her now. The market closed until the next morning with wooden boxes piled up next to its brick wall. An old man wearing a wide brimmed hat contemplates the passing of the afternoon with a reptile's indifferent gaze. The air disseminates the silky perfume of lime flowers. The club's white awnings drawn until the six o'clock game. The water left at the bottom of olive presses impregnates corners, the congealed silence, the manor houses with their coats of arms rotted by abandonment.

Two women looking out from a balcony scrutinise the stranger with the arrogance of those who do have a place in this world. Juana thinks she hears whispering behind her.

'She looks like the eldest of the Merchán girls. Yes, woman, those who lived in the patio house on Alpechín Street. She must have come back to empty the house.'

Her stomach tightens on turning the corner. The wrought-iron gate is open, as always, as before. Juana leaves her suitcase on the floor. Everything is still the same and yet everything has changed: the dust accumulating on the patio's red flagstones, usually shining red ochre, the maidenhair sleeping planted in gutted pots, the well shed, the vine shading the wash house now felled, Matías Iruela's carpenter's workshop now converted into a grain store, sweaty bed sheets being aired from the upper balcony handrails, a black slip and darned socks on a wire, old and strange noises. The hammering coming from the cobbler's workshop stops. Setefo – his hands stained with shoe polish, his bovine head now bald – comes towards Juana dragging his leather apron. The same apron as before.

'Juana, girl, please accept my condolences.'

'Thank you.' The cobbler's kisses leave saliva marks on her cheeks. Juana does not dare wipe them clean.

'You've come alone? And your father?'

'He's there in Barcelona, on the coast, working on a building site. We weren't able to tell him. My sisters have let him know by now, I suppose. The factory only gave permission for me to leave. We've all got jobs at the same place. The manager said he was very sorry but he couldn't let all six of us go because, true, who was to get all the work done. They're very serious about work up there... And the vine, what a pity! Why have you cut it down?'

'It had plant lice and had to be sawn down.'

Dolores Iruela's tender hug smells of laurel. Juana closes her eyes at the sandstone hands stroking her cheeks.

'Don't cry girl, don't cry. The poor thing didn't know she was going to leave this world. She watered the patio pots and sat down over there with her face pale; she said she had an upset stomach. It seems she got up to go to the toilet. Strangely enough the next day I didn't hear her, as you know she was the first to get up, always the first. So I went into the house and found her lying on the bed, in her percale housecoat, sleeping like an angel. She didn't even have the time to get undressed.' The carpenter's widow wipes her tears away with the cuff of her housecoat. 'Girl, and your mop of lovely hair, have you had it cut? How you've changed! You don't look the same.'

'It's more comfortable like this. We leave for the factory before sunrise.'

'How you've changed, girl. If my Andrea could see you! With how you two did fight each other as children and how highly she thinks of you now. She always asks about you. Soon it will be a year since she left for Madrid, how time flies. She's getting married in May, you know? To a teacher; he seems a nice boy... Juana, this is for you. In short, why should they be buried with her? So you'll have a keepsake.'

The jet earrings shake in the nitric acid scarred hand receiving them. The earrings swung from Chachachica's elephantine ears when she moved her secure and decisive head.

'Girl, this life is as it is and you have to play along with it as it comes.'

'Juana. Don't cry any more, come on... And those hands of yours?'

'It's nothing, I burnt myself. It was just a momentary lapse.'

'Oh dear me... When you've rested and calmed yourself you'd better go into the house and take her clothes and the kitchen utensils. Have you thought about what you're going to do with the stuff? I say this because the day before yesterday the owner sent an errand boy, she's already got new people for the downstairs room and the pigeon loft. Let's see if we can let her know tonight.'

The house of her childhood welcomed her in silence, incapable of recognising the woman searching for herself in its corners, in the kitchen empty of voices and aromas. The bowl of lard is still on the table. The frying pans sleep behind the little curtain covering the pantry's lower shelves.

'Mother, I want a skirt. Blue and polka-dotted.'

The staircase that leads up to the pigeon loft still shines from scrubbing and sand. The straw mattress lies on the floor covered with sackcloth bed sheets, whose embrace scratched the skin of their legs. TRINITARIO FLORES, FRESH FISH AND SEAFOOD, PUNTA UMBRÍA, HUELVA.

Time is stuffed into the objects, in the pieces of papers guarding hidden desires in the cracks, into the chest of drawers with Chachachica's woollen tights and the menstruation rags. In the bottom drawer, the forgotten box: an unfired bullet, a military campaign record, a watch with its face crushed and its hands stopped at half past four. And various pages torn out of Ecclesiastes.

'You read, you don't stumble.'

'For the living know that they shall die, but the dead know not any thing, neither have they any more a reward for the memory of them is forgotten.'

Juana lies down on the straw mattress and studies the pigeon loft's slanting beams. She closes her eyes and presses them with the palms of her hands until she provokes yellow spirals. Tiredness stops her from sleeping.

'Chacha, where do the dead go?'

'They go nowhere, girl. They prowl around among us and they send us signals.

21

The morning smelt of ozone and damp wool. The drizzle
soaked the greyish light of dawn and polished the cement
ground on which the muddy boots of the soldiers slipped; some
of them tried to shelter under the railway halt's porch. The
mail train, which had withdrawn the volunteers of Seville's
First Company and Larache's Third Battalion of Moroccan
regular troops, waited in the station with its doors open.

The war was over.

Manuel Merchán jumped from the wagon with his knees
numb from not moving. He turned his face to the overcast
sky and the needles of water comforted his eyelids. He
breathed in a mouthful of clean air and began walking along
the platform with his kit bag on his shoulder, from one end
to the other, disorientated, letting himself become dulled with
that new sensation and the muffled purring of voices and hugs
in the tamed enthusiasm of victory.

The jolting and the landscape travelled were still buzzing in his head. To ease the tedium of the journey, from Almadén to Seville, Merchán distracted himself by memorising all the places the train stopped. Wandering aimlessly along the station, he repeated to himself the names that under some spell resumed inside his skull the monotonous rattle and shake on the tracks leaving behind through the window a trail of abandoned working fields and waste lands: the geography of desolation. Almadenejos, Los Pedroches, Belalcázar, Cabeza de Buey, Almorchón junction, Zújar, La Granjuela, Bélmez junction, Villanueva del Rey, Cerro Murriano, Cordoba, Palma del Río, Lora del Río, Los Rosales.

At the end of the platform, away from the other soldiers crooning and drinking Valdepeñas wine straight from the bottle, Merchán sat down on his kit bag and covered his head with his blanket to protect himself from the rain. The shadows under the soldier's blanket accentuated his ears and edged his cheekbones. He considered the coincidence that the war had begun and ended on a Saturday, as if time had remained frozen and life regained its pulse exactly there on the horizon, at the point of flight where the tracks met.

They said the war was over. In a white flash, his mouth filled with fish bones and he saw the frightened boy that he was – his tibias shaking in panic – on the dazzling streets in the centre of Seville with a piece of paper between his fingers with the address of the Uruguay Pavilion, where volunteers enlisted in the Foreign Legion. Merchán's wrists hurt from the bites of hemp cord used for tying up the prisoners on the *Cabo Carvoeiro*. They had let him go from the prison ship with mistrust throbbing in the back of his neck. On reaching the barracks he broke down and cried.

'Come on, come on, enough snivelling and stand up, what we need here are men. Get your head shaved at the barber's in case you've got lice. Then have a good wash and put your uniform on. Then when you're ready go to the kitchen and have something to eat.'

The clear memory of his uniform – everything was too big for Merchán – and the troops' leftovers: fried whiting biting their tail fins with blinded eyes. He chewed the fried salty flesh of the fish without breathing, concentrating on the compulsive task of gulping down. The bones scratched at the roof of his mouth. The fish heads crushed by the fury of his teeth had a bitter aftertaste. He swallowed and swallowed and swallowed fish and forgetfulness. Alone in the barracks' kitchen, sheltering behind pots and pans.

'I became a fascist for a plate of whiting.'

Astride his kit bag, Merchán cleaned fluff off a small bit of tobacco he had taken out of his pocket. He pulled out one of the last papers he had left from his uniform jacket – the ones Celestino had torn out of the Old Testament – for rolling the cigarette. He read with difficulty, stopping at every syllable.

'And thou shalt remember all the way which the Lord thy God led thee these forty years in the wilderness, to humble thee, and to prove thee, to know what was in thine heart.'

Thoughts of the bookseller returned covered in the ashes of the charred remains of his memory.

'Things are turning sour, boy.'

His last glance. Lucid in the hallucination, clean, with a scythe's shine.

'Try to find her, boy. Remember: the second-hand bookshop in Argüelles Square. You can't miss it, right opposite the law courts.'

262

Merchán placed his hand into his kit bag and tapped the smashed face of the watch that had accompanied him throughout the war.

'Remember, boy, she's called Rosario. Ask for her in the neighbourhood.'

He would never find the bookseller's mother. She died before Merchán could give her the watch with its hands smashed at half past four on that suffocating August morning.

The rain got worse. The quaking bog of the sky fell as mud over the soldiers' caps. Merchán breathed in the cigarette smoke and the drag made him suddenly feel old, defeated at twenty years old. Turning his head towards the railway halt, thinking of taking refuge under the cramped porch, he noticed Hamito the Moor looking at him with a toothless smile. He was resting his back against a column with thick rivets eaten away by rust and had his hands in the pockets of his chickpea-coloured baggy trousers. It seemed he had been staring at him for some time. Merchán shouted at him:

'Do you want to smoke, caliph?'

The Moor refused the invitation with a slight shake of his head.

Hamito. The echo of his voice. Outside Madrid, Cerro de los Ángeles, Villaverde Alto. Enemy artillery boomed in the box of his chest, as Hamito, his kit bag on his shoulder, repeated his all-enveloping merchandise song oblivious to the thunder of bombs.

'Cold cedar, silly water, girlfriend writing paper...'

Hamito. The Moors let out terrifying shrieks in hand to hand combat. On the outskirts of Monterrubio: the body of a militia woman, positioned in the bell tower with a machine gun, fell onto the flagstones as the regular troops roared. Her body, still breathing, stabbed with bayonets and her clothing ripped off. Her uncovered vagina agonising. Her breasts weak. Her eyes wide open and full of earth. The greedy fingers of the regular troops over her. The spasms of the woman's white legs. Hamito's toothless mouth.

Manuel Merchán closed his eyes. He took off the blanket covering his head and let the downpour drench his clothes.

The war was over.

22

The city seems muzzled by its sadness on Sunday mornings in January. The dead season grisaille of the extended after lunch period, at that time of day when ownerless dogs sniff around deserted squares and the breeze blowing from the wharfs steams up the reflection of light bulbs behind windows. Words resist, stuck in her throat like broken glass, and despite the anguish inflaming her chest, Juana would swear that an instant ago, when he left, leaving her alone in the park square, a deep blot of sorrow stained the watchmaker's eyes.

The very idea of not seeing him ever again destroys her. Never again: two pieces of broken glass. Juana has walked several times – she does not know how many – around the perimeter of Ciudadela Park, sleepwalking, blind, urged on by the inertia of her movements. If she were to stop walking, if she were to pause to recover her orientation, she would collapse weak onto the pavement.

Ría de Vigo bar. Juana pushes the glass door open and sits down at the only free table, the closest to the plate glass window looking out into the street adjacent to the Borne market, closed on Sundays. She has never entered a bar alone before: the live coals burning her throat steel her against her shyness.

'I've drawn an ace.'

'Again! We've certainly had it now.'

'It's that you're not up to the game, and you're chickens with your cards.'

'Shut it, you sour sop.'

The purring of voices distracts her for a moment from the root of her pain. At a table behind her four men play a game of cards with toothpick tips and grains of corn. Another customer watches the game standing up, elbow on the bar and with a glass of anisette in his hand. A Sunday of only men.

At the back table, the bar owner and his wife eat rice at an odd time. A sign ochre from smoke warns: SINGING AND SWEARING ARE NOT ALLOWED. On the shelf behind the bar receipts and a bottle of aspirins rest among greasy bottles. A leg of ham hangs from a hook stuck into the shelf.

'What would you like, young lady?' The bar owner, with the sleeves of his jersey rolled up to his elbows and a dirty apron hardly covering his thighs, chews rice at the end of his question, aims his chin forward and cleans the corner of his mouth with the back of his hand. The man stares with curiosity at the sore corners of Juana's eyes.

'A brandy, please.'

'Do you want me to add soda to it?'

Juana shakes her head. She surprises herself ordering a brandy. She, lowly, invisible, small, with guilt encrusted in

266

the nape of her neck, alone in a bar on a Sunday afternoon, a little before the dance halls open.

'Girl, pour me a brandy, from the mesh-covered bottle, and bring me a washbasin of warm water and salt; my feet are swollen like barrels.'

Salud Monterde returned from doing the rounds inclined in her white shoes, varicose veins snaking up her calves, the jewellery inside her shoulder bag worn across her chest and squeezed against her stomach.

'Don't hang about with the watchmaker. You should know that he hits the bottle and it's not even been two years since he left prison.'

Her recollections, even the brightest ones, are ambushed in the quagmire of memory and flower on the surface when she least expects them, conspiring, treacherously, fleeting like the flame of a match lit at number five Baños Nuevos Street.

'Wait, wait for me to get my matches out, don't go on in case you stumble. There's no light on the stairs and unless the sun comes out you can't see what's in front of your nose... Stay still, I don't want you to hurt yourself. I can climb up feeling my way against the wall, even blindfolded and, if I need be, without crutches.'

And, suddenly, a crack in the darkness and a phosphorescent shine illuminating the watchmaker's face, the blue shadow of his shaved beard smelling of a clean shirt, of cinnamon, of autumn sun. The breathing of the two blend in the intimacy of the landing lit by the match. This Sunday afternoon now gasps at its death throes in the mud.

The bar owner comes to her table with a bottle of Terry brandy and a glass held upside down. Again he scrutinises the customer, this time with a thread of compassion that

267

Juana appreciates with a shy lowering of her eyes. The thoughts of the man generously pouring the alcohol are transparent: whores wear high-heel shoes and seamed stockings, and never cry on Sunday. The girl in the white blouse is a *charnega* – a dirty southerner – recently arrived, stood up by her boyfriend at the cinema door or with a still warm dead one stuck on her back.

The alcohol soothes the firebrand burning her throat. The first sip of brandy reaffirms her in the world. Juana could finish off the glass to the lees without losing her balance or her senses because pain keeps her inert. Sitting on the foldable chair she looks out at the deserted cobblestone street with a cheek placed against the window.

The bar owner and his regulars, concentrating on the card game, have stopped paying attention to the girl who finds herself alone with her skinned suffering, still raw, with its ravenous horns locked inside her brain, blind in its insistence of going over, returning to the beginning and examining every gesture minutely, every minor tremble, to at least get close to the pure meaning of words, all the words scattered from the park's square to the day when Juana and the watchmaker first met. One, a hundred twists, forward, backwards, in concentric circles, zigzagging.

'The sardanas – *Catalan music and dance* – begin at exactly eleven o'clock. Can you make it for eleven? I'll wait for you opposite Francia Station, and then we'll go to Ciudadela Park. See you next Sunday, Juana.'

On Sunday the mornings in the slums on the edge of town smell of chickpea stew and disinfectant. Juana gets up first and listens to little José's calmed breathing next to her father's tattooed arms behind the old blanket dividing the room into two, separating the women from the men as they rest.

The water carried up from the fountain, at the foot of the ridge, is heated on the stove in pans got with Home Saving coupons – maroon-coloured enamel on the outside, sky-blue on the inside – exchanged for household goods in Muntaner Street. Naked, her feet in the zinc washing bowl in one corner of the patio, Juana soaps her skin stiff from cold and observes the dirty clouds over the edge of town and the wall that opens its mouth out onto the sky with teeth of broken bottles.

'I'm going out with Azucena to see the *sardanas* at Ciudadela Park. I won't be back for lunch.'

Downhill, the exact pencil line at the base of her eyelashes, spruced up in rags, the course seams of her knickers made from end pieces pinched from the factory, her intact twenty-year-old's beauty, urgently needing to see him and almost happy.

Juana and the watchmaker, sitting on a park bench, watch the dance. The dancers' white rope-soled sandals, spotlessly clean, ribbons tied around their knees. Overcoats and bags in the centre of human rings. The circles turn, widen, expand, throb and contract to the tenor's monotone rhythm. Juana and the watchmaker hardly speak. He seems nervous and preoccupied, perhaps ashamed; she concentrates on the *sardana* dancers' movements: their foreheads high and proud, their hands entwined with the remains of defeat and silence between their fingers. Their hearts pump one single blood, their feet draw and rub out mosaics of air over the sand. Juana watches the dancers with admiration and with the placid and somewhat melancholic certainty of one who will never enter the circle, who does not belong to any place at all, who is a stray soul, expelled, exiled from herself.

269

Juana finally dares to raise her hand. She orders another brandy to help her piece together the scene.

A winter sun in the park. Olives and two vermouths with soda. Married couples with children throwing lentils at the pigeons, soldiers on leave, old age pensioners, groups of servant girls in their Sunday bests, the *sardana* groups and a wall of silence between the two. The swans swimming the artificial lake's waters have scabs of mud on their plumage. Words sandpaper the walls of his throat.

'I don't know how to say this to you, Juana... Perhaps we shouldn't see each other again.'

Juana foresees the coming storm more from the tone of his voice than from his message. The watchmaker is hoarse; he does not look up and, with the tip of his right crutch, sketches a circle over the sandstone. His words cut like broken glass.

'Nobody will ever love you like I do. One day you'll understand.'

Words and stale caresses remain inside. All flows to the same place, to the drain, to the bottom, to the bowels of the Earth to feed mallow buds.

'I'm not the one for you; I have nothing to offer you. What do you want? More poverty on top of poverty? I couldn't present myself to your father and say to him: look, I've got a chopped-off leg, I'm twenty years older than your daughter, I was in prison and now survive on odd jobs I won't detail you with to avoid confusion... Juana, be aware of it. We both knew this would happen sooner or later.'

The bar owner goes to the glass door and looks out at the empty street with his hands crossed behind his back. The card players begin another hand and their voices, their comments around the table, delimit Juana's suffering.

'Close your hand, Miguel, close it.'

'Hey, shut up; onlookers should be made of stone and give you tobacco.'

Juana strokes her glass with both hands and stares at the bites nitric acid left in her skin. She thinks about the watchmaker, the memory of his eyes, between grey and blue. The same colour as rain and steel.

'Why are you crying? Don't cry, I beg you. You're breaking my heart.'

Images and pieces of conversation come in a flood. Juana empties herself in tears.

'This separation hurts me more than you.'

Savouring the last caresses in the kitchen at number five Baños Nuevos Street, the hiss of gas, the words and colours learnt from him, their walks from the Rambla to the sea. The sun on their faces.

'You are so clean, so much a woman, so pure... You deserve something better than me. I'm only a coward, a loser. Furthermore, Juana, he who lives off a thief, tell me, what can he expect?'

The breeze flaps the awnings in the Barceloneta. Laughter is its accomplice.

'I'm not for you, do you understand? You are wind, and the wind can't be tied down.'

The bar owner's wife sweeps the sawdust and the cigarette butts mounting up on the floor. She comes to Juana's table and Juana raises her kitten-heeled shoes so that the woman can pass the broom under her feet. They both look at each other; Juana looks away ashamed. The woman has a Galician accent.

'Do you feel alright?'

'Yes. It's nothing, don't worry.'

'You'll end up loathing me. I don't want you to see me as someone pathetic; I couldn't put up with it. You embittered and me looking at your breasts with a stupid smile, full of saliva. You're still so young!'

The watchmaker loves her because the possibility of deceiving her would hurt her even more. Juana stands by this certainty; it is the only thing she has left.

'I'm hurting you, and that's precisely the last thing I want in life.'

He will not cry for her – Juana has never seen the watchmaker cry – but perhaps his face will not shine again. Juana imagines him in the coming days, alone in the darkness of Baños Nuevos, and Proudhon purring at his feet. Liberto Pech will go out to smoke on the balcony on summer evenings. He will read. He will recite poems aloud. He will talk to himself. He will cut himself shaving again. He will scrub his clothes in the bath. He will hop with his crippled leg across the mosaic. He will refill a hundred demijohns and curse Salud Monterde. Sitting at his worktable, with his eyeshade and eyepiece, he will silently caress his memory of Juana. Concentrating, the Persian blinds drawn, he will contemplate the stone wrapped in velvet, a stone containing flames of fire inside.

'Look, Juana, here, under the lamp. You see it? This is beauty.'

In winter, late Sunday afternoons are a sham. Soon the streetlamp lighter will ignite the gas and Juana will start walking to the tramcar stop. Then the trolley bus and the open space. She has almost a two-hour journey. Juana breathes deeply. She asks herself if she has enough energy left to drag her pain up the hill on the outskirts.

'How much do I owe you, señor?'

272

'Three-quarters of a peseta. I'll only charge you for one brandy; the other one is on the house.'

23

It is raining. Water falls systematically over the city's shell from when Juana opens her eyelids to the bite of dawn cutting through the skylight. Every morning, when the Cordovan lights his first Bisonte – the beasts lie in wait stamping their hooves on the hill on the edge of town – and calls Merchán by tapping the window opening onto the patio, her father pulls back the old curtain dividing the room into two so that the webs of light start waking Juana and her sisters.

A new working day. Six girls the same, with the same nose, walk down the swamped slope in the drizzle soaking the dismasted ribs of their umbrellas. Isabel, raised in stiletto heels, sinks in the mud. Juana wipes the excess of mud stuck to the soles of her shoes off on the running board of the trolley bus; her sticking plaster went missing in the slum.

Rain is cyclical and returns from the past. That which is now falling onto the grey city is the same that floods her memory and dilutes it into a murky sap, justifying her existence. It is the same begged-for rain of her childhood, when the priest brought out the Virgin of the Abandoned for a procession so that she would take pity on the cracked dry plains of olive trees and slash the clouds with the spikes of her crown. It is the same storm that announced little José's birth, while Chachachica, next to the leaking windows, crossed herself at the flash of every streak of lightning. It is the same flood that overwhelmed the village terrace roofs on a March morning when the gloriously honoured Lieutenant General Don Gonzalo Queipo de Llano passed away, and Juana's father returned drunk to the patio house and fell collapsing in his vomit and onto the patio flower pots. The rain is always the same and brings with it the echo of a faceless voice, stripped now of the grey-blue steel in his eyes, of his vertical wrinkles marking the area of his mouth. It is the same rain soaking kisses sheltering in a doorway, the same rain now drenching an innermost pain that, hour after hour, day after day, checks strips of buttonholes.

The raindrops sketch trembling mercury veins on the factory windows and tap on the corrugated asbestos and cement roof with a dirty murmur of seaweed and swollen beams. The female workers strive to rip off their covering of drowsiness and complete the order before the end of the shift. It is pay day at Casals' Cloth Manufacturers.

'What's wrong, Juana? You've been a long time as if you were far away; you're not the same.'

'Nothing. It must be that I miss the village.'

'You can't fool me, love. You're acting strange.'

'I'm alright. It's just me.

'I'll tell you something to make you laugh. Do you know Socorro is going to stop being a spinster?'

'Socorro?'

'The very same. Why do you think she has asked for holiday leave? Well to bring her mother from Malaga to help her get her house ready and to organise the wedding... You'll never guess who her fiancé is.'

'I can't think of anyone.'

'Ready for it: the manager, Shitfly.'

Agustín Aiguadé – his hands in his overall pockets and the butt of a Farias cigar between his teeth – watches through the window how the downpour blurs the warehouse patio. The bell rings deafening over the racket of the looms, over the rows of steam, over the purple patina of the fluorescent lights, over the working women's voices, above the noise of dragged chairs and the table lamps lighting the checkers' thimbles.

On rainy nights the trolley bus regretfully returns to the slums. Slowly crossing the flooded landscape devouring the blurred city limits; it advances with a caterpillar's invertebrated laziness, crammed full of tiredness and cheap raincoats. Juana walks arm in arm with Isabel, unsteady on her vertical heels, behind them their younger sisters, now climbing the last few metres of the steep slope without street lighting to illuminate feet feeling their way through mud.

Manuel Merchán sits up on hearing the creaking door.

'Well you really have taken a long time! I was about to go to bed.'

The six sisters camouflage themselves in the constriction of the house shared with the Cordovan couple. One after the other they enter the room adjoining the kitchen, shred themselves of their bundles and raincoats and leave the envelopes with their wages – the six names written in pencil in Señor Aiguadé's clumsy calligraphy – in a shoe box placed on the top shelf of the doorless wardrobe. Little José, sitting on the kitchen table, lets out cat yawns with his cheek resting in the palm of his hand.

Manuel Merchán lights the stove. The hovel's dampness softens the heads of the rachitic matches. Juana's father wears his grey jacket over the vest he sleeps in, and the sleeves hardly cover his forearms. Merchán's clothes never fit him: too tight or too short; sometimes the cloth covers him with the awkwardness of a packet left behind at a station's left-luggage office. With plaster-splashed shoes, Juana's father looks for the middle of the zinc bowl to adjust it to the centre of the dripping coming through the kitchen ceiling.

The Cordovan finishes off a glass of wine and gets up from the table to leave room for the girls' dinner. His wife, Soledad Naranjo, unplugs the iron connected to the light bulb and clears away her things: the iron, the threadbare blanket, the still hot clothes and the bowl of water. Sole tries to catch Juana's eye: she has something important to tell her. They understand each other's looks above the narrowness.

'Do me a favour and help me take these clothes to my room.'

Juana notices urgency in Sole's tone of voice. With her finger tips she picks up the Cordovan's shirt, hanging from its armholes on the back of a chair. She imagines Sole wants to complain about one of little José's pranks or ask her to lend her some money to send to her son in Ifni or tell her that they should make even more room because a cousin of hers from Montilla is about to come and stay to look for work. Juana bites the dry skin of her lower lip ready to listen.

277

She only wants to stretch her back on her shared mattress.

'Lucas, leave the room, Juana and I have to talk for a moment... Women's things.'

The Cordovan pulls his trousers over his underpants with the obedience of a sad dog. He picks up his packet of Bisonte, which he had placed on a chair acting as a bedside table, with the intention of going out into the ravine's night dew. Manuel Merchán stirs the potatoes in the frying pan with a scarecrow's movements. The happy spitting oil confuses the night.

'You haven't gone to bed yet, mate?'

'It's nothing, I feel like having a smoke.'

Juana rests her backside on the edge of the bed where the Cordovan couple sleeps. The room smells of chicken broth and perverted bodies. Sole, with her back to the bed and squatting, searches inside her suitcase lying on the cement floor. She moves quickly. Everything makes sense in her hands.

'This morning a man came asking for you.' Soledad lowers her voice. 'I can't figure out how the poor man could climb the hill with that limp of his, dragging a pair of crutches, raining like it is and with the sludge that forms here. He was very tall and he had a leg missing, the poor man.'

'And what did he say?'

'He asked for you and I said that yes, it's true, you live here, but that you had gone to work and won't be back until night. Very polite, the man, very polite. I invited him in and wanted to prepare him something hot to drink because he arrived soaked through. But there was no way he would. He said he didn't want to put me out and didn't come in. He asked me to give you this when you returned, and he went drowned alive back down the hill. You tell me, how could he use an umbrella with a pair of crutches?'

278

Sole hands her an envelope and a tiny packet wrapped in tissue paper which Juana recognises from a distance: SWISS CONFECTIONER'S. A mixture of curiosity and compassion contracts her housemate's eyes. Juana looks down and shrinks inside herself. Blood rises to her cheeks.

'I'll wait outside. So you can be in peace. Take all the time you need. And don't worry, my Lucas won't enter.'

'Thank you.'

The bulb light covers the room with hospital gauze. Juana, shrunken, unwraps the packet. Red ants run along her tongue. Her hands shake as she tears open the envelope. A few lines emerge written on the back of an electric bill.

Dear Juana:

This should be a letter full of pain, but at the last moment I decided to change it for something shorter: I love you.

Inside the packet you'll find a gold ring I made for you. I kept specks of gold with the idea of giving your tiny hands a present. It is a modest ring, although I hope you like it. I want to imagine it on your girl's fingers, your princess's burnt fingers, saturated with your smell of yellow violets. I'm certain it's your size: I know your hands off by heart. I mounted in it the stone I kept in my worktable drawer, the one I nicked from Salud Monterde. The lotus flower, the *padparadscha,* do you remember? This orange sapphire is like you: beautiful, impossible, different, one of nature's whims, with all the colours under the sky locked inside it. Beauty in a pure state... Juana, be free. Be happy.

Yours always, Llibert

Insomnia seethes under her eyelids. The bed sheets try in vain to put out the embers of her brain burning in the poor intimacy of her bed. The heartbeat of the alarm clock melts into the darkness with a weakened slowness, identical to drops of molten wax. The chorus of breathing perforates the room's uneven silence. Isabel's warm breath on the nape of her neck. The silky skin of her breast caresses the ring, hidden in the cup of her bra, protected like the last breath of a loved one. Juana would like to lick the ring, chew it, swallow it and bury it deep in her stomach.

Her pain does not hurt now; it simply is.

Juana has never desired the break of dawn so much, so that objects recover their outlines, so that the neighbourhood covers her with its smells and household voices, so that life pushes her beyond the muddy skies of the slum. Yes, she will trot down the hill and clock on at the factory with her first pain burning in her breast.

It rains; it is still raining over the slums. And rain is the only certainty.

Acknowledgements

To Antonio Bahamonde and Sanchez de Castro (*Un año con Queipo*); Manuel Barrios (*El último virrey. Queipo de Llano*); Francisco Espinosa Maestre (*La justicia de Queipo*); Ronald Fraser (*Blood of Spain. An Oral History of the Spanish Civil War*); Ian Gibson (*Queipo de Llano: Sevilla, verano de 1936*); Nicolás Salas (*Morir en Sevilla*); and César Vidal (*Recuerdo mil novecientos y seis...*). To their rigorous investigative work, to their endeavours and hours spent in thought, because otherwise it would have been practically impossible for me to plot fiction around the real-life figure of Captain Manuel Díaz Criado (1898–1947) and the brutal repression that took place in the southern lands during the Civil War. To all of them, thank you.

Translator's Acknowledgements

To Gwen Davies in Aberystwyth and Richard Davies in Aberteifi for their confidence in me. And to Lucy Llewellyn for her careful copy-editing.

For their help and suggestions: Miguel Rodríguez Moreno and Marina del Mar in Almería, Lynda and Mike Wareing in London, Margaret Thomas in Chippenham, Manuel Pedregal Feito and Marieta Pedregal in Madrid and the *Hijos de Antofagasta* in Aberhonddu and Pennorth.

Diolch yn fawr iawn – muchísimas gracias.

PARTHIAN

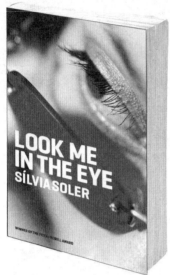

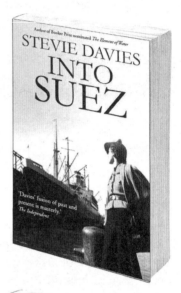

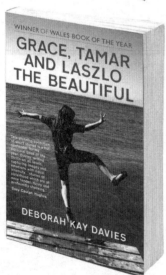

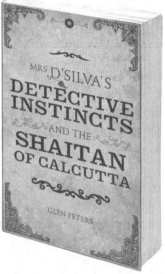

www.parthianbooks.co.uk